legacy

Montgomery Brothers ~ Book 1

laura pavlov

Legacy

Montgomery Brothers, Book 1
Copyright © 2020 by Laura Pavlov
All rights reserved.
No part of this book may be reproduced or transmitted in any form or by any means,
electronic or mechanical, including photocopying, recording, or by any information
storage and retrieval system without the written permission of the author, except for the
use of brief quotations in a book review.
This is a work of fiction. Names, characters, places, brands, media, and incidents are
either the product of the author's imagination or are used fictitiously. Any resemblance
to actual persons, living or dead, events, or locales is entirely coincidental.

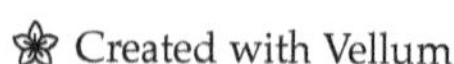 Created with Vellum

dedication

Greg, Chase & Hannah,
You are the inspiration for all that I do. I love you always.
XO

one

. . .

Ford

I DROPPED down in the chair to face my brothers. I wasn't in the mood for their shtick, but they were here, so I didn't have much of a choice. I'd given them the reins to rent out the space downstairs, and I was already regretting it. If I want something done right, I need to do it myself. That theory had always served me well. Harrison moved the box of donuts toward me and I shoved them to the end of the conference room table.

"Hey, those are the best donuts in town. You're welcome." Jack stood and reached over to grab another one. I knew it wasn't his first, because he had powdered sugar remnants all over his suit coat.

My brother in a nutshell.

"Yeah, if my day consisted of donuts and small talk, nobody would get paid around here." I sat back in the chair and folded my arms in front of me.

"Oh yes. The world would definitely come to an end if you indulged in processed foods." Harrison's head fell back in a chuckle.

"Well, I'll have you know—my body's a fucking temple, and that doesn't stop me from enjoying good pastries," Jack said, taking a bite of a giant maple bar.

I shook my head. What it must be like when your most important decision of the day is what donut you should eat. My brothers didn't have a clue what it took to run Montgomery Media, and today was not the day to push me. I was already irritated that they'd turned the simple task of leasing the open space downstairs into a ridiculous game. Our employees and offices took up every square foot of this high rise building with the exception of the main floor, lobby, and corner suite which my father had always leased out to small, local businesses.

"Listen, I appreciate you both coming in today, but I have the guys from Japan flying in for a meeting this afternoon, and I'd really just prefer to choose someone quickly to lease the space and call it done. I'm not sure why we've invested so much time into this."

"You could stop being a control freak and let us handle it," Harrison said before taking a long pull from his water bottle.

Jack cackled. "Yeah, that's not going to happen. That would mean letting us make an actual decision without his consent."

"You do realize that I'm actually sitting here, right? I can hear you." I tossed the file on top of the stack at Harrison. "And what is this crap? Why are there essays for each candidate?"

"Look, Ford, this is a great way for us to give back to the community. Eileen will run a story tomorrow after we select the winner." Harrison reached over and grabbed a donut, and I wanted to push the box in the garbage. Eileen was our senior editor and the best in the industry.

"A winner? This isn't a goddamn contest. The space goes to the most qualified business. This is prime real estate we're talking about." I leaned back and closed my eyes for a minute, taking in a long, slow breath. The best strategy I'd learned after five years of therapy— breathing. Thousands of dollars spent, when all I had to do the entire time was learn how to fucking breathe when I got pissed off.

I loved my brothers. But working with them was a challenge. Jack didn't have a serious bone in his body, and Harrison was so busy keeping the peace, he'd go along with whatever crazy shit Jack came up with. I was the CEO of Montgomery Media, a billion-dollar company and a lot of people depended on me. So, I didn't have the luxury of pondering over what flavor pastry I'd eat or coming up with gimmicks for the paper to run a story about.

"Dude. Chill. This is good business. We're going to get paid, but the money isn't the priority. God knows we don't need it. This is about giving someone a chance. A golden ticket, so to speak. It's a corner storefront on the busiest street downtown. We turned it into an opportunity for someone who otherwise wouldn't get the chance because they don't have the largest bank account or the resources to do the highest bidding. We nailed it down to these top seven contenders. They had the most compelling stories," Harrison said. Our middle brother had a gift for negotiation. He was the peacekeeper. Always trying to please everyone.

"And who doesn't love an underdog? I think it's brilliant." Jack raised one eyebrow at me in challenge.

He was the youngest of the three of us. Two years younger than Harrison and four years younger than me. In human years, that is. In maturity—the dude was a child. He lived for pranks, loved guys nights out, and existed on sweets and chicken fingers. He had the palette of a toddler and went through women faster than most people drank a cup of coffee. And everyone loved him. I swear he entered the world with a party horn in hand and a shit-eating grin. He was always down for a good time, and he didn't give a shit how many rules he broke doing so. Nothing bothered him. In life, there was no one I'd rather have beside me. At work—not so much.

I dragged a hand over my face. We owned the building, which happened to be the hottest real estate in the city. We didn't need contests or gimmicks. The location sold itself. The Coffee Cup had been leasing the space for the past decade, but the couple who owned it, William and Barb Wilson, had decided to relocate to Seattle. I wasn't happy about it. I wasn't a huge fan of change, and I liked my routine of grabbing a coffee on my way up to the office every morning. I was an early riser, got my workout in before most people woke up, and was always the first to arrive at the office. Now I'd have to find a new place to get my morning caffeine.

"You're joking? Because everyone wants to lease this space, you understand that, right? We could get top dollar. Why in the world did you turn this into a three-ring circus?"

"It's not a circus. It's an opportunity, Ford. It gives people something to get excited about. A mom and pop moving into the space, someone who maybe doesn't have the resources, but has a dream," Harrison used a napkin to dab his mouth.

I barked out a laugh. "You're serious? A dream? So, these people aren't even qualified? And you expect me to waste my time interviewing candidates who can't even afford the rent?"

"You don't need to be in on the interviews, we can handle it. And I didn't say they weren't qualified. They are. Maybe not in the traditional sense, but they all have something to offer, and all seven have a reason they want the space. And Jack and I spent the time reading every single one. We had over two hundred and thirty applicants." Harrison crossed his arms in front of his chest.

Did I mention he was a bleeding heart? The dude had been on more mission trips than I could count. He was all about giving back, and I'd always admired that about him. Until he came on at Montgomery Media and we saw our bottom-line drop.

I shook my head. "Not a chance in hell I'm letting you two run these interviews. I don't want to risk you choosing a pack of feral cats as our tenants. I think you've done enough damage at this point."

"Suit yourself, brother. Get ready to be dazzled. These are some amazing people you're about to meet," Jack said, clapping his hands back and forth while shaking the crumbs onto the floor. I pinched the bridge of my nose and closed my eyes.

"Well, keep in mind we're choosing tenants, not life partners. And we aren't going with anyone who doesn't have six-months overhead in the bank. I assume you asked them to bring their financials?"

"You know what happens when you assume." Harrison smirked.

There was a knock on the door, and my assistant, Sam, poked her head in. "The Right brothers are here for you. Shall I bring them back?"

I rolled my eyes. "You're joking. The Right brothers?"

Jack pushed to his feet and howled. He did that often for no particular reason. Just to keep everyone on their toes. "No joke, dude. The

Right brothers are a whole lot better than the Wrong brothers, *am I right?"*

Sam burst out in laughter. Like I said, everyone loved the guy, especially when he acted like a child.

————

I glanced down at my wrist because it appeared time was standing still. The interviews thus far had been a complete waste of time. We'd met with the Right brothers who had a meditation studio called: Make the Right Choice. This is who my brothers chose to rent out a floor-to-ceiling glass encased storefront on the busiest corner in the city. Did I mention they also had *no money?* Zero resources. But they offered trade. *Trade.* I'd have to meditate twenty-four hours a day, seven days a week, to break even. Not happening.

Our next meeting was with a girl named Lala. She didn't have a last name. She went by Lala. Her business was called Lala's. Shocker. And when I inquired about what she did for an actual living, she proceeded to tell me she paints. She paints walls and furniture. Pottery and canvases. Did she have a portfolio? No. A business plan? No. A bank account with any money in it? Of course not. She said she didn't like to put a number on art. Well, unfortunately for Lala, there was a number on the bill that would come every month, and she couldn't afford it.

The next couple interviews were better, but nothing overly impressive. A dry cleaner whose wife stared at me the entire time we spoke and slipped me her cell number on the way out the door. A jeweler who opened his trench coat and flashed me a bunch of sparkly shit and then patted his midsection to show me he was packing. Yes, he had a gun in his waistband and told me he couldn't wait to use it. And a florist who sneezed incessantly, because she was, "allergic to the outdoors." I stared at Jack and Harrison when she left, and they both smiled and said she was a top contender. I think my absolute favorite of the day was the magician. Because, hey, who isn't in need of a magician as they rush down a busy metropolitan street?

"Dude. You shouldn't judge. I mean, can you pull an egg out of your ass on demand? I don't think so," Jack said, reaching for the final folder.

Harrison laughed, but he tried to cover it with a cough. "Come on, they weren't that bad. The dry cleaner and the florist are good options."

"Ah yes. The dry cleaner whose wife stripped me naked with her eyes—in front of her husband. And a florist who happens to be allergic to flowers. How do you beat that?" I said, reaching for my coffee. Probably the last damn good cup of coffee I'd have for a while as today was the day the Wilsons would be packing up and shutting down.

"Well, the last one is my top choice anyway. She wrote the most passionate essay of all," Jack said, tossing me her file.

I didn't bother opening it. There was no need to. We'd run an ad tomorrow and find a practical tenant. I'd chalk this up to a morning off and a complete waste of time.

Sam opened the door for a young woman. She looked like a student dressed to meet friends at a coffee house, not a woman showing up to an interview. She wore a white T-shirt, a floral skirt that ended just above her knee, a jean jacket, yes... that would be a *denim jacket.* Apparently, this was her interview outfit. My eyes scanned down her toned, tanned legs and stopped at the white Converse. You've got to be shitting me. Did anyone take this seriously? If this was her idea of being dressed to impress, she may as well have stayed home. Her hair was pulled back in a messy bun of sorts. Otherwise known as, disheveled. She was pretty, no doubt about it. But good looks weren't going to be enough to seal the deal. Maybe that worked on my brothers, but I was unimpressed.

"Miss DeLuca, it's a pleasure. Please take a seat," Harrison said, pulling out the chair across from me for her to sit. "I'm Harrison, and these are my brothers, Jack and Ford." He used his hand to gesture to each of us.

She set a pink pastry box down on the table and took her seat, tucking the hair that fell from her bun behind her ear. "Thank you for meeting with me. And please, call me Harley."

I barked out a laugh. I couldn't help it. You had to be shitting me with this. "Harley? That's your name? Or that's what you drove to get here?" I raised a brow and shook my head.

"Ford," Jack snapped and flashed her an apologetic smile.

"It's okay. I mean, glass houses, *Ford*." Her voice was smooth and silky, but her combative attitude caught me off guard. "Is that what *you* drove to get here?"

"It's a family name. Ford Montgomery the fourth." I smirked.

"Mine is a family name as well. Harley DeLuca *the first*," she said the last two words slowly, making sure I got the message.

Both my brothers burst out in laughter. I folded my arms and leaned forward. "And do you drive a Harley, Harley?"

"How original. Did it take you long to come up with that?" She rolled her dark brown eyes and met my gaze head on. Her skin was tan, lips full and she dripped sarcasm. And this was an interview. I couldn't imagine what she was like when she wasn't supposed to be on her best behavior.

"I'm sorry, are you not here for an interview?" I tossed my pencil on the table and folded my arms across my chest.

"I'm sorry. I thought we were both here for an interview," she said, smiling at my brothers before stopping to glare at me.

"And what exactly am *I* interviewing for?" I asked, anger radiating from me.

"To be a partner in *my* business, of course. I've read all about you and I think we'd work well together," she said, pushing her pink box of crap toward me.

I chuckled. It was demeaning and childish, but she'd pushed my buttons, and this is what happened when you went there. "You think we'd work well together? I'm sorry Miss DeLuca, but if you'd really read about me, you'd know that I'm not interested in being a baker."

She laughed now. It was catty and condescending, and my brothers' heads ping-ponged back and forth between us. "Don't flatter yourself. I would never allow you to assist me in my craft. But I'm quite certain that you're in the business of making money. And that's what I'm here to offer."

Harrison reached over and grabbed the box. He untied the twine and flipped the lid open. I was able to see the name: DeLiciously

Yours. I assumed it was a play on the DeLuca name. Clever. But I had zero interest in owning a bakery.

My brothers were uncomfortable because they'd never met a stranger they didn't like, and things were off to a rocky start.

Buckle up, boys.

I was done playing games.

"We're not looking for a partnership, we're looking for a tenant. All I need to know is if you can afford the rent, and if you have your financials for us, we'd be happy to have our attorneys take a look." I watched her. Wanted to see her squirm, but it never came. She cocked her head to the side and squared her shoulders before pushing the box my way.

"This is the most important piece of my business plan. Please, try one." She raised a brow in challenge, and my brothers bit into their cupcakes and moaned like goddamn children.

"Wow, Harley. Best cupcake I've ever had," Harrison said.

"Mmmmmmm. Girl, you're the best damn baker I've ever met." Jack reached for another pastry as he spoke with a mouthful of cake.

Ridiculous.

"I don't eat refined sugar," I said, crossing my arms over my chest, though the smell coming from the box had my mouth watering.

She chuckled and rolled her eyes. "Why am I not surprised."

What the hell did that mean? She turned her attention to my brothers, and they made all sorts of over-the-top noises to let her know how impressed they were.

"So, do you only sell cupcakes?" I asked dryly.

"We offer coffee, tea, and a large selection of pastries. Here's my actual business plan. I'm offering you a percentage of the company, in exchange for the lease space, at least for the first year of business. We can renegotiate the terms the following year." She handed me a document with an extensive business plan. I highly doubted a baker came up with this.

"Who wrote this up?" I asked, studying the impressive business plan.

"I did. I have a degree in business," she said, one brow raised in challenge.

"From where? The Betty Crocker school of cupcakes?" I couldn't help myself, and Harrison shot me a look.

"From UC Berkley. I'm guessing you've heard of it?" She sat back in her chair and smirked.

"I wasn't aware that Berkley had a baking school?" I challenged.

"I graduated from Berkley with a degree in business and a minor in marketing. I then attended a prominent culinary and baking school, *Ecole Ducasse*, in Paris this past year, and voilà, here I am."

"Lucky us," I said, my voice dripped sarcasm as I flipped another page and tried to hide my surprise at her projection.

"Well, if you give me this shot, I do believe you'll be lucky. We'd all win."

"And why would I do that?" I asked.

"Well, for starters, you ran an ad looking for exactly what I've brought you—an opportunity. And, according to every article printed about you, you're a smart businessman, or at least people think you are," she said, and my brothers laughed. Traitors.

"You're correct, we are in the business of making money, and if your desserts have any say in the matter, I think you're going to make it big," Harrison gushed, a ridiculous attempt at flirtation.

Pathetic.

She batted her lashes and played right into him. "That just might be the best compliment I've ever received."

"Well this is definitely the best cupcake I've ever had." My baby brother shamelessly winked. Completely unprofessional. Jack had been the starting quarterback at USC all four years, and had offers to go pro, but chose to join us at the family business instead. The guy oozed charm and he had no problem using it to his favor.

"Jesus. You're a walking HR violation," I mumbled under my breath. "Well, thanks for taking the time to meet. We'll be in touch."

"Okay. Thank you," she said, pushing to her feet and hesitating like she wasn't quite done. "I just want to say, that I wouldn't take this opportunity lightly. I've dreamed of opening DeLiciously Yours for many years, and I promise if given this opportunity, I won't let you down."

Oh, please. This was going to play right into my brothers' hands. The girl was brilliant. She'd done her homework on all three of us.

"We will *definitely* be in touch," Harrison said.

"Let me walk you out." Jack rushed to help her with the door, and I rolled my eyes.

Harrison looked at me when they stepped out of the room. "I like her."

"No."

"Well, we'll have to see about that, Ford. We each get a vote, and Harley DeLuca gets mine."

I pushed back from the table and stormed out of the conference room. This day had gotten off to a terrible start.

And I wasn't in the mood to battle Thing One and Thing Two.

two

· · ·

Harley

I DROPPED to sit on the couch in my small studio apartment. My best friend, Molly, stopped by to celebrate.

"I can't believe you got it," she said. Her blonde hair rested on her shoulders, and she leaned forward to open the bottle of champagne she brought. "Champs for my champ."

I laughed. "Nice. Thanks. I'm actually shocked they chose me."

DeLiciously Yours would be opening in the hottest location in San Francisco, in the famed Montgomery Media building. Floor-to-ceiling windows, lots of natural light, and most importantly, endless foot traffic. It was more than I could have even dreamed up, and I'd been thinking about opening this bakery most of my life.

"I'm not. I mean, who better to take a shot on. And I doubt anyone else offered them a piece of the pie, so to speak," she said with a wink.

I'd taken out a small business loan, and my grandfather had co-signed, using his home as collateral. To say the stakes were high, was an understatement. Offering the Montgomerys a percentage of the company was much better than allowing the monthly rent to eat away at my budget. I'd offered them ten percent, and they'd countered back with fifteen percent, and we'd settled in the middle. I'd never expected to be in such a popular location, which would allow me to cater to the busy professionals downtown.

"Well, I'm excited. What did your dad say when you gave your notice? Was he upset?" I asked. Molly wanted to help me get the bakery off its feet, and she was tired of working for the family business while applying to law school during her gap year. Her parents, Dave and Caroline Lolly, owned over a dozen dry cleaners. They were the reason that I was able to move out of my grandfather's place in Oakland so I could be closer to the business. Being in the city would make my life much easier. The Lollys had a small studio apartment above one of their dry cleaners downtown that they rented out. The place had come available and they'd given me a great deal. It was small, but I was proud to call it home.

"Nope. He took it pretty well. He knows I hate it there. And working at the bakery will be a nice change." She glanced around the apartment. "Wow. You've been here for two weeks and you've already worked your magic."

"Yeah? Thanks. It's cozy, right?" I had a bed in the back corner, and I used floor-to-ceiling bookshelves to create a little wall to make it slightly more private. I purchased a small white slip-covered couch, a coffee table and a little dinette set which worked as a makeshift desk as well as a table to eat at.

"Only you could make this dump look like a cool, hipster pad. I see you brought your prized possessions," Molly said, glancing at the bookshelves. Books were something I'd collected since I was a little girl. Heidi had been the first hardcover book I'd read, and from there I'd collected hundreds more. I had dozens of baking books, but over the past few years, I'd collected all the classics and romance novels had become my kryptonite. There was nothing like fiction to help you escape your daily life.

And no one needed an escape more than me.

I laughed. "I think Gramps was sad to see them go, but he'll have more space now in the living room for his own things."

She filled two glasses and handed me one. "To my beautiful best friend who continues to chase her dreams."

"Ooh, that's sweet," I said after taking a sip and scrunching my face.

"Is that your polite way of saying it's cheap?" She fell back against the cushion and chuckled.

"No. You know I love a good deal," I teased.

"So, what's the update on your mom?"

Molly and I were roommates at Berkley, and she knew all the gory details of my relationship with my mother.

"Gramps said he hasn't heard from her since I got home from Paris." I'd been attending culinary school abroad and hadn't spoken to my mother in over a year. The last time I'd seen her, she and her pimp slash drug dealer had left me beaten in an alley. This was par for the course with her.

She'd been in and out of my life since the day I was born. My mom was a train wreck. A walking disaster. If you looked up hot mess in the dictionary, there would surely be a picture of her next to it.

I'd spent my entire life trying to be different, striving to make something of myself that was far removed from my mother.

My grandparents had always taken her back whenever she'd attempt to turn her life around. I hated to think about all the ways she'd taken advantage of them and preyed on their kindness. But after Grams passed away, and Mom didn't bother showing up at her funeral, something hardened in Gramps where she was concerned. The problem was, she always showed up when you least expected it. You could never really prepare for the storm.

Living in Paris this last year was my first real clean break from my mother. And yes, I worried about Gramps every day. But I actually felt like the weight on my shoulders had lifted off while I was gone. A weight I'd carried with me my entire life. I knew I needed to return home, because Gramps had always been there for me, and I couldn't leave him to deal with her on his own. Ever since Gram passed away, it's just been he and I against the world. Or at least he and I against my mother. Valentina DeLuca, aka the spawn of Satan.

"Maybe she'll just finally disappear into thin air. But no way are we letting bitchy V bring you down. There's too much to celebrate. Tell me about the Montgomery brothers," Molly said, making me laugh about the nickname she'd given my mother the first time she'd met her when my mom found me at the coffee shop Molly and I had worked at near campus our freshman year. The woman had no shame. She'd taken every penny I had to my name that day, and I'd given it to her willingly so she'd leave Gramps alone.

Molly opened my laptop and typed in the Montgomery brothers, just as hundreds of search bars opened up. They were the closest thing you got to royalty in San Francisco. People called them the Kennedys of the west coast. Beautiful, ridiculously wealthy, and photographed everywhere they went. I'd never paid much attention because let's face it—they weren't really my crowd. I wasn't big on Hollywood gossip or the tabloids. And now I'd be working with them. It didn't even sound real when I said it out loud.

"I don't think I can tell you anything you can't find online. I barely know them. I'm still in shock that they picked me, to be completely honest."

"Stop selling yourself short. Of course, they picked you. Just thinking about your pastries makes me hungry. God, they're so freaking hot though. Which one is this?"

I moved to sit beside her. "That's Ford. He's a complete asshole. He's the one who has come in *every single day* during renovations to give me his unwarranted opinion. Cocky, arrogant, and condescending. He may be pretty to look at, but that's as far as it goes."

She chuckled. "Nothing hotter than a good-looking asshole though, right? The other two are nicer?"

"From what I can tell. You know how I feel about rich, entitled men." I laughed. "That's Harrison and that one is Jack. They're all beautiful, but at least these two don't act like pretentious assholes."

"Come on, Harls. None of these guys make you want to come out of your dry spell? *No pun intended.* You know, I read an article last night that claims if you go too long without sex, your vagina can actually close," Molly whispered, like she was telling me some deep, dark secret.

I reached for a throw pillow and hit her over the head. "Shut up. You're lying. And it hasn't been that long."

"Dude. You were gone for almost a year, and you've been back for a few weeks. You haven't had sex since before you left for France."

"What are you, my therapist? Big deal. I'm not missing anything. Sex wasn't really all that exciting, if I'm being honest. And I went to France on a mission to learn, not to find a man," I said, shrugging her words off. Trust did not come easy for me, and to say I'd misread Todd Birmingham would be a massive understatement.

"Well, *Toad* is a psychopath. You know I never liked him from the beginning."

I chuckled. "It's Todd, but I won't fight you on calling him that anymore because you were right about him"

Todd and I had dated my junior and senior year at Berkley, and the last few months of our relationship had gone from bad to worse. It was like a light switch had gone off with him. He became jealous and possessive overnight. He'd wait for me outside my classes and accuse me of cheating with every guy that spoke to me. I didn't recognize him anymore. His behavior was the motivation I needed to study in France this past year, I was eager to get as far away from him as I could. The last few weeks he'd become verbally abusive and after a lifetime of training as Valentina DeLuca's daughter, I'd learned early on that words could be used as a weapon, and I wanted nothing to do with it. But breaking up with Todd had been a challenge. He was persistent, angry, and refused to accept that we were done. I'd blocked him on all social media as well as on my phone, and I'd moved to France for a year. I remember the distinct feeling of a weight lifting from my shoulders the day I'd arrived in my new home. Todd had gone radio silent, and hopefully he'd moved on.

"He's a manipulative prick. You were always way too good for him. I called that shit right out the gate. And he best hope he never runs into me in a dark alley, if you know what I mean."

I tried to cover my smile. Molly always had my back, and I'd always have hers. She hadn't trusted Todd from day one, and I should have listened.

"Are you traveling down a lot of dark alleys these days?"

"I'm just saying he better watch himself. Nothing Todd does surprises me. He just hid who he was well in the beginning. But that blows your whole rich boy/poor boy theory," she said, refilling our champagne flutes.

"It sure does. I guess it just means all boys suck." I'd always had this theory that rich guys were entitled narcissists. I can thank my rich, non-existent father for that one. And I'd been proven wrong because Todd had no money—so apparently, they were all assholes.

"Well, except for Oscar."

"Except for Oscar. The one wealthy, kind, devoted boyfriend on the planet," I said, lifting my glass to hers. "Cheers to you finding the only good one out there."

She clinked her glass to mine and we both laughed. "Here's to new beginnings. To you, opening DeLiciously Yours, and to me, working for you while I wait to be rejected by law schools."

Molly had just taken the LSAT and would be sending out applications over the next few months. She'd give me a year at the bakery, and I couldn't ask for anyone better to have beside me while I launched my new business.

"They are going to be lining up to have you attend their school. You know that, right?"

"I know no such thing. Let's get back to discussing the fact that your vagina is closing as we speak," she said, and we both fell back against the couch cushions and cackled.

My sex life was the least of my concerns.

———

I stood in the center of the dining area of the bakery and moved slowly in a circle as I took it all in. The contractor had finished the build-out on time and actually stayed right on budget. The black and white tiles resembled the flooring in my grandparents' home when I was growing up. I loved it. Everything was vintage and in great contrast to the modern building where I was currently setting up shop—but it worked. When you stepped inside DeLiciously Yours, you entered a special little world.

The floor-to-ceiling windows would allow for a ton of natural light, but right now it was just a little past six o'clock in the morning, and the sun hadn't come out to grace us with its presence just yet.

The walls were pale pink, the tables and chairs were painted in an antique white, and three vintage chandeliers hung above the dining area. I'd been collecting things for this day for as long as I could remember. I'd stored everything in Gramps' garage and was thrilled that it was finally all being put to use. The glass-encased pastry display sat beside the counter with the register. I'd baked a whole lot of options for opening day over the weekend, ranging from cupcakes, donuts, and brownies to macarons, chocolate ganache tarts, and crème brûlée. I would feel out my customers and adjust what I offered on the menu around requests and seasonal treats. Molly was in the back, in the kitchen, getting the coffee and tea started. I just needed a minute to myself to appreciate the fact that this was really happening.

Today was opening day.

A knock on the door startled me. There were two doors in the bakery. One that opened to the street, and one that opened to the lobby of the building. The knocking came from the lobby door. I didn't think Montgomery Media opened the doors until seven a.m., but when I turned to see Ford Montgomery through the glass, standing there on the other side, looking like the annoyed asshole he was, I wasn't surprised. Of course, he'd be up early. He'd probably come by to tell me once again that he didn't care for my design choices. He'd turned his nose up last week when he took in the flooring and told me that it looked "dated."

Yeah, that's the point, genius. It's called vintage décor.

I unlocked the door and opened it to him. He was after all, a partner in this business. "What can I do for you?"

"What time are you opening the doors?" he asked, his gaze made a slow perusal of me from head to toe, stopping at my feet and huffing. "Do you own anything aside from tennis shoes?"

I rolled my eyes. "We open at seven, which is when you open, correct?"

"That's when the building opens. I get here by six-thirty, and the Wilsons always had a cup of coffee ready to go for me," the smug bastard said, looking around and taking in all the details. "This actually looks—nice."

I laughed. "Thanks, I guess."

"So, I haven't found another place that makes coffee like they did. I was hoping you make a decent cup and I could stop here on my way up in the morning and grab it."

"Well, I won't be staring out the window waiting for your arrival, but you're welcome to stop by, and we'll pour you a cup to go, your highness."

"That's fine. As long as you can actually make coffee that's tolerable." He smirked. Ford wore a black suit, and a white dress shirt, tailored to fit his broad, chiseled body just so. His brown hair was a bit longer on top and styled to perfection.

"I can't wait to hear how high maintenance your order is. I mean, this ain't Starbucks, bud."

He rolled his eyes. "I take my coffee black."

My head fell back, and I barked out a laugh. "Black? And you're being dramatic about it? How hard is it to make a cup of black coffee?"

"It's all about the beans." He crossed his arms in front of his chest and raised a brow at me. Smug bastard.

"You know, this is why rich men get a bad name. You're ridiculous," I said before shouting out to my bestie in the back. "Molly, can you grab me a cup of black coffee to go. Use the *real swanky beans*, okay?"

He chuckled. Ford freaking Montgomery the forty thousandth actually laughed. I was surprised to see he had an actual sense of humor under his arrogant, annoying demeanor.

"Uh, we've just got the one pot of brew," Molly said, coming around the counter and halting when she saw who was standing there. "Ohhhh... *we've got business.*"

I rolled my eyes and mumbled, "If you want to call it that."

He smirked. "I'm not a customer. I'm actually her business partner."

"Don't get excited. It's a very small percentage and we can renegotiate those terms next year."

"I'm counting on it," he said, taking the cup from Molly and offering his hand. "I'm Ford."

"Oh, I know who you are. I've done my research." She winked, and I shook my head with disapproval. The last thing this guy needed was to have his ego stroked. "I'm Molly. Assistant baker and best friend of the owner."

"Nice to meet you." He took a sip of coffee and his lips turned up just a little in the corners. Most people wouldn't have noticed it, but I'd been studying the man's resting bitch face for the last ten minutes and the slightest sign of a human beneath the exterior was noted. "Wow. This is—decent."

I sucked in a long breath. He was offensive without trying to be. Like he was shocked that we could make an actual cup of coffee. I'd knock this guy down a few notches from his high horse if he wasn't currently my landlord and my business partner.

"Oh, you haven't seen anything yet. You need to try a pumpkin donut. Harls makes the best pastries around, and these donuts are *to die for*." Molly hurried around the counter and grabbed a bag.

"He doesn't eat refined sugar," I said, using my hand to cover my mouth to keep from laughing. I mean, really? Pull the stick out of your ass and live a little, dude.

His sapphire-blue gaze locked with mine and he raised a brow. "It's not necessary for you to speak for me. I'm quite capable, *Harls*," he hissed. "And I occasionally break the rules when I feel like it, and a pumpkin donut sounds like it's worth a try."

He sauntered up to the counter acting all charming and genuine when he turned to Molly. "Thank you for offering. That's very kind."

"Of course. This will definitely be worth it. I put a few extra treats in there in case you'd like to let your staff try them," Molly said, handing him the large bag. Traitor.

"We need to watch our bottom line, so let's not give it all away for free," I snarled. Not that it wasn't the right thing to do. I mean, we wanted these people to become steady customers, but the man annoyed the hell out of me. Coming in thinking everything is free because he's a partner.

Jackass.

"Let me worry about the bottom line. It's sort of my thing," he said before winking at me and waltzing to the door.

"I hope you don't get a cavity on your way to your office. You know how fast those sugar bugs travel." I held the door open for him, anxious to see him get the hell out of my bakery. He was ruining my mojo.

He studied me and his tongue darted out to wet his bottom lip. I couldn't help but stare. Annoying, yes. Beautiful, also yes.

"You're worried about me? That's sweet. Maybe you should put that energy into finding suitable footwear," he said with a chuckle as he walked out the door.

I pulled the door shut and turned to find my best friend watching me, her eyes danced with amusement.

"What?" I huffed, running a hand over my hair which was pulled back in a long ponytail.

"Nothing. You're just all flushed and flustered. I sort of love it."

"You're joking. I'm far from flushed or flustered. I'm irritated and annoyed. And don't go giving everything away for free. Mr. Moneybags can pay for his food like everyone else." I stormed behind the counter.

"Oh, he did. Look what he dropped in the tip jar." Molly held up a hundred-dollar bill and danced around like a fool.

I rolled my eyes. "Good. He's an asshole, so he should pay for coming in here and putting me in a funk."

"I think you're in a funk because your vagina is closing and it's sad and lonely," she said before we both burst out in laughter. "And now you have a hot man that's going to be stopping by every morning for coffee."

"Me and my vagina are just fine, and the last thing we're interested in is Ford Montgomery."

And that was the truth.

At least that's what I was telling myself.

three

. . .

Ford

I DROPPED the bag of pastries on my assistant's desk and patted my stomach after downing two donuts in the elevator.

Okay, they were damn good donuts. Maybe this wasn't such a bad investment. The girl could bake, I'd give her that. But she sure was a snarky little thing, as I'd experienced these last two weeks any time I made a comment about her renovation choices. I had a hunch her bite was as big as her bark, too. Today she'd worn a long floral dress that hugged her in all the right places, and she'd paired it with some white tennis shoes. She was cute, there was no doubt about it. Not my type, but I'm sure she garnered a lot of attention, gym shoes and all. Her hair was pulled back in a tie, and I was surprised to see that it ran all the way down her back in long, dark waves. I shook my head. Why the hell did I care what she wore or how long her hair was. I didn't.

Focus.

I looked at my calendar and responded to a few emails before I heard the chatter in the hallway as people trickled in. My door flew open and Jack walked in with a mouthful of food and powdered sugar all over his shirt.

"Dude, best decision we ever made. Her brownies are *un-fucking-believable.*" He dropped a box full of pastries on my desk.

Interesting. She gave him a box, and me a bag? She obviously liked him better. And why did I care? I avoided sugar most days, and I couldn't care less if she liked Jack. Everyone liked him. He probably went in there singing her praises, and she couldn't help herself. I didn't care.

I didn't.

"Do you actually behave like this around women? I mean, finish chewing for God's sake." I reached for a napkin and brushed the crumbs off my desk and into the garbage can.

"Let me tell you something, brother. Women love a man who's passionate. And I, my friend, am a passionate dude."

"About pastries?" I rolled my eyes.

"About life. You should try it. Live a little. Find the joy."

"Find the fucking joy? You're serious. Not all of us have that luxury," I snarled, annoyed that I was wasting time on this conversation. "And why the hell are you here so early? You never come in before ten."

"It's the grand opening of the bakery. I wouldn't miss it. I promised Harls I'd be there. Harrison is down there now with a few photographers. We're going to promote the hell out of this. You know—local girl out there living the dream."

I rolled my eyes when he called her Harls. He'd known her, what? Five minutes? Now they were the best of friends?

"Don't go overboard. She's not a gimmick or toy to flaunt around. I'd put her business plan up against any I've seen. She's smart. She's worked hard to get this up and running in the time frame mapped out in her budget, and she stuck to it because she micromanaged the hell out of her contractor. Don't sell her short or make a joke of it," I said, walking over to the bar area to grab a water.

Jack waved his hands in the air. "Whoa, settle down there, brother. Who's selling her short or making a joke of her? We're promoting the hell out of her bakery. She's passionate, and she's been working for a long time toward this dream. We're just—celebrating it."

"All I'm saying is don't steal her thunder. Don't make this about us. It's her thing. We ran the story that she was chosen for the space, it's enough. Every time you bring it up, it takes away from her."

Jack studied me and a big smile spread across his stupid face. "Who are you and what have you done with my brother?"

"Are we done? I have a busy day." I closed my laptop and pushed to my feet. I had an eight a.m. meeting and I was running behind.

"I have a busy day as well. If you need me, I'll be downstairs in the bakery." He wriggled his brows, and I opened the door, encouraging him to leave.

"I thought you were helping Mom today at the winery?"

"I am. I'm kidding. Harrison and I are taking the helicopter back. We leave in thirty minutes. Call me later."

"You got it. Tell Mom I can't come out this weekend, but I'll be there next weekend," I said.

The Montgomery winery was in Napa, where we'd grown up. The winery was really Harrison's baby, but Mom ran the marketing side of things, and Jack—well, he was PR for all the family businesses. We'd yet to meet anyone he couldn't schmooze, unfortunately, he spent most of his time schmoozing and very little time working.

My day blew by in typical fashion, and I ate lunch at my desk while I responded to emails. My phone buzzed and I saw the text from Blaire, one of my many booty calls. I had no time or interest in an actual relationship, and there were plenty of women that were completely content with a nice dinner and sex. No strings attached. I had a healthy sex drive, but zero tolerance for bullshit. So, this worked well for me.

Blaire ~ I'd like to see you tonight.

Blaire was a woman who didn't require or even want to share a meal. She wanted to get down to business. That was an offer I couldn't refuse.

Me ~ I'll be done at the office around 9 p.m. I'll meet you at your apartment at 9:30?

I had one rule when it came to sex. They didn't come to my place. Ever. We weren't dating, and there was no reason to stay after. I found it far more difficult to ask someone to leave versus leaving myself. Which I always did. Sure, I'd hang around for a little small talk. I wasn't a complete asshole. But there was no sleeping, no cuddling, and no gray areas. It's the way I lived my life both in and out of the bedroom.

Blaire ~ I'm looking forward to it.

My phone screen lit up with my mother's name.

"Hey, Mom," I said. My mom and I were very close. She was one of the few people that didn't annoy me.

"Hey there. Jack said you're going to come out next weekend. How about I make us lunch and we can have a nice catch-up."

"I'd like that. How are you? What's going on at the winery?" I asked.

"You know, it's crazy busy like always. Hanky stopped by today. He said you're having dinner with Chanel next week?" I could hear the dishes clanking around in the background. The woman was very much like me. She never stopped. She was always going.

"Yep. It'll be nice to catch up."

My godfather, Hanky, had been my dad's best friend. He'd stepped up when my father passed away five years ago, and we'd always been close. He'd been in the car with my father when he had gotten into the accident that took his life, so he'd been devastated by the tragedy as well. His daughter, Chanel, was more like a sister to me. We were the same age, and we'd grown up together, attending all the same schools up until college.

"I still think you two would make a nice couple," Mom said with a chuckle. Always the matchmaker. Chanel and I had never dated, nor considered it. We were more like siblings, so that was never going to happen, but it didn't stop my mother and Chanel's mother, Marie, from trying.

"Not happening." I shuffled through some files on my desk and found the one I was looking for.

"Well, you can't blame me for trying. You know Claire's daughter, Romy, is single again. She and her fiancé called things off. She always liked you in high school, didn't she?"

I pinched the bridge of my nose. "Mom. Stop. If I wanted a girlfriend, I'd have one."

"I know. But you haven't dated anyone since Madison, and I worry about you. I don't want you to be lonely."

I barked out a laugh. "You don't need to worry about me being lonely. I have plenty of company. I just don't care for repeat visitors all that much."

She gasped, and I could imagine her rolling her eyes at my words. "I don't need the gory details about that. I'd just like to see you happy."

"I am happy, Mom. I promise. I've got a two o'clock, so I need to run. I'll talk to you tomorrow. Love you," I said, slipping my suit coat back in place.

"Love you, sweetie. Looking forward to seeing you next weekend."

I ended the call just as Sam knocked on the door to let me know my next appointment was waiting in the conference room.

I thought about what my mother said as I made my way down the hall. Madison Carlyle and I had dated all through college. I'm sure we'd had good times together, but all I could remember now was the way that it ended. I'd found her in bed with my best friend. It was the ultimate betrayal from two people that I'd trusted. I'd cut them both off and decided to change course.

I just didn't realize how many lives that simple act was going to affect.

———

I finished up a little past nine and took the elevator downstairs. I was often the first to arrive in the morning and the last to leave in the evening, aside from the security guards. I think my father would be proud of my work ethic. At least I hoped he would.

"Goodnight, Mr. Montgomery," the deep voice of the night shift security guard called out.

"See you tomorrow, Leo."

I paused before pushing through the lobby doors when I noticed the light coming from the bakery. Was she here this late? The light went out just then, and she must have exited from the door to the street, because she didn't come through the lobby. I stepped out to find my driver waiting at the curb and gave him the address to Blaire's apartment. He pulled out onto the road and I spotted Harley DeLuca walking up ahead.

"Pull over, let me offer her a ride. She shouldn't be walking alone at night."

He pulled to the curb, and I put my window down. "Would you like a ride?"

She clutched her purse as my voice obviously startled her. She squinted to see who it was and rolled her eyes. "Jesus, you scared me."

"That's why you shouldn't be walking alone at night."

She squared her shoulders and rolled her eyes. "I've survived just fine for a long time on my own. I don't need tips from you on how to go to and from work, Montgomery."

"Are you walking to your car?"

"No. I'm not wasting money on parking when I live less than a mile away," she said, glancing over her shoulder as a couple walked by. "I'm fine."

"I happen to be going that way, so just get in the car and I'll drop you off."

"How do you know you're going my way? You don't know where I live," she said, arms crossed in front of her chest. I heard my driver, Jerome, chuckle, and I glared at the back of his head.

"Good Christ. You're walking the same direction I'm driving. Just get in the damn car."

"You're not the boss of me, *ol' mighty one*. I said I was fine. I'm walking," she hissed before turning on her heel and storming off.

"I guess it's a good thing you wore tennis shoes to work then," I shouted after her before sitting back against my seat and sucking in a slow breath. People didn't usually argue with me.

Ever.

"Just stay behind her a bit so she doesn't know you're following her. I need to make sure she gets home safely," I instructed Jerome.

I was an asshole, there was no question. But I wasn't immune to human decency. I mean, Jesus, my parents were strict as fuck when it came to manners. They didn't raise a complete dick. And she shouldn't be walking home alone at night.

I sent a text to Blaire to let her know I was running a little late to our booty call.

Like I said, I wasn't a complete dick.

"She's turning, shall I follow?" Jerome asked.

"Yes." I glanced out the window and spotted the bar I visited once a year just as we turned the corner. The neighborhood was quickly changing for the worse the further she walked. What the hell was she thinking? I couldn't figure this girl out. I'd stopped by the bakery almost daily during construction to check on the progress, and every single time she'd given me attitude. She was all laughs and good times with my brothers, but she obviously despised me.

She paused in front of a dry cleaners to speak to a man who was hunched down against a shopping cart and she started a conversation with him, before handing him a bag. What the hell was this? I saw the man reach in the bag, and I strained to see the cupcake he pulled out, and I rolled my eyes. She was feeding the fucking homeless while walking alone on darkened streets. Not the wisest choice.

Jerome pulled the car over a safe distance from her, and he had his lights turned off as I watched. She turned around to face us before flipping me off and jogging into the door beside the dry cleaner.

I laughed, which didn't happen often.

"Sorry, Mr. Montgomery. I guess she spotted us."

"It's fine. We can head over to the address I gave you now," I said, glancing out the window as we drove by and a light turned on upstairs.

At least she was home. I'd done my part. She wasn't my concern.

But something unfamiliar tugged at my chest.

I pushed it away.

Just like I always did.

four

. . .

Harley

MY BACK ACHED when I sat up in bed. I'd put in long days this week, and I wanted to get to the bakery early today to prep for another big crowd. The last few days had far exceeded my expectations, and I was hoping it would continue. But I needed the Montgomery brothers to quit trying to sell my fairy tale story to the entire city.

We got it.

Financially strapped girl strikes it big with hot location for new bakery.

Let's move on.

They had no idea that there were people I was trying to avoid. And I had a ton of missed calls from unknown numbers. I knew better. Unknown callers to most people were just an annoyance. A telemarketer. A political sales pitch. I'd wish for such an irritation.

Unknown callers for me were something else completely.

I had blocked my mother on my phone since returning from France, and Todd had been blocked for even longer. I didn't want either to know where I was. That was one of the benefits of moving out of Gramps' place. But my picture in front of the bakery had been splashed everywhere, so the unknown caller was most likely enemy number one or enemy number two trying to reach me. My mother would see this as a financial windfall, because I owned the place, which meant there was cash on hand. Todd would see this as an opening. It was neither. I had washed my hands of both of them—but keeping them at bay was the challenge now. I'd spoken to Gramps last night, and he said he hadn't seen or heard from Mom in several months, and I could only hope that would continue. I'd promised to come by this weekend and do the grocery shopping for him, and we'd have a visit.

I pulled my hair into two buns on top of my head, channeling my inner Princess Leia, and slipped on a navy and pink floral skirt that stopped just above my knee. I paired it with a white T-shirt and a denim jacket. It was still chilly in the morning. I sat down to slip on my Chucks and laughed as I tied them and thought about Ford's comment when he'd followed me home a few nights ago. Pompous ass. I'd known he and his driver were behind me, and I hadn't really minded. Not that I was scared. It took a lot to scare me. I'd visited much worse neighborhoods than the one I was currently residing in. And, well, growing up with Valentina DeLuca for a mother—I'd had my fair share of terrifying experiences over my lifetime. This neighborhood was swanky to me. But Mr. Moneybags probably thought it was dangerous because my building didn't come with a doorman or offer valet.

Fuck him.

I'd seen him every morning since, and he didn't bring it up. Instead he usually just snarled about the coffee not being ready or made a snarky comment about my sneakers. I usually had a witty comeback for him, which seemed to entertain him. Witty banter was my specialty, and Ford Montgomery could hold his own with me.

I walked to work and quickly made a few batches of butter cookies and pumpkin donuts as both had been big sellers this week. I told Molly she didn't need to come in until eight today, as the rush didn't start until then and she was exhausted.

There was a knock on the door, and I'd already put on the coffee because I knew Mr. Moody would be stopping by, but I was elbow deep in dough. I called out, "It's open."

The bell chimed on the door to let me know he had entered, but he didn't say anything, which was rare for him. Usually he greeted me with an attitude.

"I'm in the back. Coffee's on."

"Hey, Harls." Todd stood in front of me, leaning against the doorframe to the kitchen.

All the wind left my lungs. I hadn't seen him in almost a year, and I'd hoped he'd stay away.

"What are you doing here? And don't call me that," I snapped.

"You won't take my calls. You've blocked me on social media and your grandfather won't tell me where you're staying. What option did I have? You're all over the press with this bakery gig, so I took a shot. You know I'm not a morning person, but here I am." Todd was just under six feet tall, and his blonde wavy hair was longer than it used to be, he wore blue joggers and a gray T-shirt. He looked good, I suppose, but he disgusted me, which sort of canceled out his surfer boy, good looks.

"Yeah, and I made it clear that I didn't want to see you. We've already talked about it. It's done. There's nothing left to say," I said, reaching for a towel to clean the flour off my hands.

He moved closer and I tried to step away. My back hit the refrigerator, and I raised my hands up to put some distance between us, but he pushed forward, crowding me.

"There *is* something left to say. I love you, Harls. I've changed. And now that you're back, and you're finally opening the bakery, I mean, why not give us another chance?"

I laughed, an evil chuckle I'd mastered over the years dealing with my mother and shoved at his chest. "I don't do second chances, Todd. Not after you freaking showed me your true colors and then stalked me for several weeks. We're done. Please leave. I won't ask nicely the next time you show up, so I suggest you stay away."

He gripped my shoulder hard and used his other hand to wrap around the back of my neck before his mouth crashed into mine. My heart raced and I tried to push away, but his weight was too much. I bit down hard on his lip, but he pressed his mouth against mine even more.

He pulled back, or I thought he did. It took me a minute to realize what was happening. Ford Montgomery was there, throwing my ex-boyfriend against a wall. Ford's hair was a bit disheveled, which looked even sexier than usual. His tie was tilted to the side, and he had two fistfuls of Todd's T-shirt in his hands. The veins on his neck bulged as he pressed Todd up against the wall.

"She told you to leave. I suggest you get the fuck out of here before I call the cops," Ford shouted. There was no sign of the uptight, arrogant prick I was so familiar with right now. He was manly and sexy, and if I weren't seeing this with my own eyes, I wouldn't believe it.

"Who the fuck is this, Harls?" Todd shouted, shaking and twisting and trying to break free of Ford's hold. Ford stood a few inches taller than Todd and was clearly stronger.

He pressed his forearm up against Todd's throat, and I walked over to stand beside him. "Ford fucking Montgomery… *the fourth*. I suggest you do as he says and get the fuck out of here."

Ford let up on his hold and dragged Todd toward the door, but not the door that went out to the street, he opened the door to the lobby and called out for security.

"He's not allowed in this building again. Get him the hell out of here." Ford shoved my ex-boyfriend out the door as two security guards grabbed him.

He turned back to face me as I yanked off my apron, patted my Princess Leia buns in place and pulled myself together.

"Who the hell was that, Harley? And why would you let him in?" he shouted.

Yes, he actually shouted at me. I believe I'm the victim here, and he's full-on blaming me for what just happened? This dude was part arrogant prick and part sexy hero—but the arrogant prick always seemed to win out.

"Don't raise your voice at me, you jackass. I left the door open because *you* insist on having your coffee ready when you get here. Some of us have actual work to do, and can't stand by the door waiting for you," I said, poking my finger into his rock-hard chest.

And wow. Ford Montgomery had some serious muscle under his swanky suits.

He wrapped his hand around my finger and held it there as he stared down at me. The contact sent all sorts of chill bumps down my arms.

"I have a key. Next time I'll let myself in, so keep the door locked. You don't know this guy? He acted like he knew you." His sapphire blues locked with mine, and his warm breath tickled my cheek.

"He's my ex-boyfriend."

He continued to hold my finger in his hand and his thumb stroked the inside of my palm. I couldn't move, and as weird as it was, I didn't want him to let go or lose contact.

"You've obviously got shit taste in men," he said.

I yanked my hand away at his words. "You're an asshole."

"Well, let me remind you—I'm the asshole that just saved your ass."

"I don't need saving, Montgomery. I can take care of myself," I said, turning toward the kitchen. The man ruined everything. I had appreciated him stepping in, but I would have been fine if he hadn't. I'd have kneed Todd in the groin or bit him even harder. I didn't back down from fights, and I was no damsel in distress. I'd survived much worse than Todd over the years.

"You could have fooled me. Looked like he had you in a pretty vulnerable position from where I was standing." He followed me into the kitchen and crossed his arms over his chest before leaning against the refrigerator. I reached for a to-go cup and poured him his stupid cup of coffee.

"Well, you're wrong. I can handle Todd just fine." I handed him the drink and moved over to the island to clean up the flour mess I'd left when my asshole ex-boyfriend interrupted me.

"Are you always this stubborn. It's quite annoying," he said, raising a brow at me.

Cocky bastard.

Before I could stop myself, I flicked at the pile of flour and shot it at Ford Montgomery. It was quite comical to see the white powder scatter all over his pristine black suit. A little flour landed on his cheeks and nose, and I raised a brow in challenge. "Get used to it."

He didn't move at first, but then he set his coffee down and I thought he'd swipe at his fancy clothing and face—but instead he reached for the flour and grabbed a fistful in his hand before chucking it in my face.

I gasped and tried to clear the flour from my eyes as a white cloud formed around me. Ford's laughter filled the space, and I coughed and laughed at the same time. I couldn't help it. I hadn't expected him to do it. I thought he'd get mad and storm off.

"Next time just say thank you. No need to flick flour at your hero," he said with a smirk.

I shook the powder off the best I could and walked to the little mirror I'd hung in the kitchen to clean myself up. Good lord, I was a mess. My buns were covered, so I tipped my head over and tried to shake them out.

"You're delusional, Montgomery." I swiped the final remnants off my face, and aside from the little bit stuck to my scalp, I looked presentable.

Ford brushed away the flour from his suit, but he still had some on his cheek, and I wasn't about to tell him. "Thanks for the coffee."

And just like that, he was gone. In the last ten minutes, he'd come in and ripped Todd away from me, held my finger in his hand, insulted me and we'd had a flour fight. The man was a storm, even on the sunniest of days.

Had he rescued me? Maybe. I mean, as creepy as Todd had been, he'd never been physical before, and I'd like to think that I would have been able to shove him away. He certainly wasn't the first guy to push himself on me. But at the same time, my heart was racing, and I'd been nervous, and Ford Montgomery had come to my rescue.

I just wouldn't tell him that.

———

The weekend had come and gone, and another week had flown by. I hadn't heard from Todd again. I was thankful for that one reprieve. Ford and I had gone back to being snippy with one another, and I swore someone followed me home the last few nights, but I looked back a several times and didn't see a car. Maybe I'd imagined it. It was Friday, and I'd be lying if I didn't admit that I was looking forward to the weekend. I was beyond exhausted. Physically and mentally.

"So, what are your plans this weekend? You want to go out tomorrow night? Oscar has this friend that's super cute. I thought you might want to meet him. You know, a double date, so there'd be no risk of being stuck with him, because you'd have me," Molly said, jumping up on the counter to sit as she took a bite of her brownie.

"No. I'm not looking to meet anyone. But thanks." I wiped down the last table, as we'd just closed.

"Come on, Harls. We haven't been out since you got back from Paris. It doesn't have to be a date. Just a night out with friends. He's a really cool guy, and at the very least he can just be a friend, right?"

I shrugged. I never could say no to her. "Fine. But not this weekend, I need to spend time with Gramps."

"Yes." She fist-bumped the sky and jumped down from the counter. "So, it seems like Mr. Sexy scared the bajeezus out of psycho Toad, huh?"

I moaned. I'd filled her in on what had happened last week with Todd and Ford. We were both happy he'd given up after his one lame attempt. "Apparently, yes. At least for now."

"Damn. I wish I could have seen Ford with flour on his face. The man is deliciously sexy. I can't even picture him throwing flour at you." Molly burst out in laughter, and I couldn't help but join her. I wouldn't have believed it if I weren't there either. He was so formal all the time, and he had been ever since.

"Well, trust me when I tell you I flicked a little bit at him. He threw a fistful in my face. The man plays dirty. Don't be fooled by the Armani suit."

I pulled out some dough to throw in a few more batches of cookies that I could freeze for next week.

"Ooh, a dirty, sexy man in Armani sounds dreamy," she said, her head falling back with a chuckle. "Are you really going to stay and bake? Do you want me to help you?"

I knew she had plans with Oscar and I could use the quiet time to process these first few weeks as a business owner. I'd sold a hell of a lot more than I'd expected, but I'd also worked harder than I'd ever worked in my life.

"No. It won't take me long. Get out of here. It's Friday night. I'll text you when I get home."

"Okay. Love you, Harls," she said, leaning over to hug me.

"Love you."

I rolled out the dough for the butter cookies, put on some music, and enjoyed the quiet and the calm. I owned this place. This was my bakery. I thought of Gram and how much she would have enjoyed this. I'd started baking with my grandmother before I could even walk. There are pictures of me sitting in my high chair with a ball of dough and some flour. The woman was the best baker I'd ever known, and I aspired to be half as good as her. I called Gramps after I put the cookie sheets in the oven.

"Hey, sweetheart. Two weeks down. How do you feel?" he asked, his voice was warm and comforting. Just what I needed after another crazy week.

"I feel really good. Sales were so much better than we expected so I'm hoping to get that loan paid off faster than I'd planned to." I hated that my grandfather had put his home up for collateral when he cosigned my loan.

"My girl, you worry too much. Take your time. I can't take it with me. Seeing you live your dream, well, it's my greatest accomplishment. So proud of you, darlin'."

A tear ran down my cheek. The man had sacrificed so much for me. My mother had been a shit mom from the day I was born. She'd made it known that I was a mistake, and Gramps and Gram had stepped up and treated me like I was something special.

"Thank you. I'll be out tomorrow to visit, okay?" I said.

"Looking forward to it. I wanted to let you know that your mother called today. She asked if I knew about the bakery and where you got the money for it. I told her I wasn't discussing your business with her, and she hung up." His voice shook a bit when he spoke.

A sick feeling settled in my stomach. The woman's intentions were never good. Always paved with darkness and deceit. But I'd been living with this my entire life. It wasn't new.

"I'm sorry. I'm sure this puts you in a bad position."

"Not at all, honey."

"Love you, Gramps," I said.

"Love you, sweetness."

I disconnected the call and pulled the cookies out of the oven when a knock at the door startled me. It came from the lobby entrance, and I took off my apron and walked over to see who it was. Ford stood on the other side with a gorgeous blonde woman beside him. They looked like freaking royalty together.

"Hey. I was just closing up," I said, anxious for them to leave. For some reason, I didn't want to see him on a date with a beautiful woman. I mean, we had nothing in common, and it shouldn't bother me, but it did.

"Don't be mad at Ford. I'm the one who insisted on knocking. I've been hearing about this bakery for the last two weeks. I work two buildings down, and it's all anyone has talked about. I've been wanting to get over here, but I haven't been able to get away yet," the woman said. She looked to be a few years older than me, with blonde hair and brown eyes. She was about my height but stood taller in her high heels. She dripped elegance and sophistication.

"Oh, thank you. I'm just baking a few batches for next week. Would you like something?" I asked, moving around the counter as they stepped inside.

"We're on our way to dinner." Ford cleared his throat, appearing uncomfortable, which wasn't really abnormal for the man. "You can get dessert there."

"Will you stop being such a wet blanket. It's a pastry. She offered. By the way, I'm Chanel." She smiled as she took in all the cookies still in the display case.

"I'm Harley. Nice to meet you. I have the refrigerated items in the back, if you're interested in more than the cookies?"

"Nope. A coworker came back with a few butter cookies this morning and I've been craving them ever since," she said. Her hair was curled, and in a deep side part with a clip pinning back one side. She wore a cream dress and jacket, and I suddenly felt very self-conscious. I could feel Ford's eyes on me. I tightened my ponytail and forced a smile when I turned to look at him. His sapphire blues were intense as they studied me.

I placed four butter cookies in the white waxed bag and handed it to her.

"Thanks, Harley. I'll definitely stop by again next week." She opened her purse, and Ford shooed her hand away and reached for his wallet.

"Oh, no worries. I've already closed out the register. You are a partner, after all," I said with a forced smile.

He dropped something in the tip jar, and I didn't acknowledge it. It felt like pity money. He was on a date with a hot chick, and I was standing here in my tennis shoes and probably had icing on my face.

"Thank you. Have a great night." Chanel turned on her heels and made her way to the door.

"Sorry about coming in so late," Ford said, reaching over the counter and using his thumb to wipe something off my cheek. It was sweet but it made me even more self-conscious and I didn't like that.

I pushed his hand away and wiped at my cheek. "No problem. Have a nice weekend, Montgomery."

He nodded before walking out the door.

I made my way back to the kitchen and cleaned up before putting everything away. It was late and I was tired. When I finally locked up and made my way outside, the black car Ford had been in last week sat in front of the shop. A man stepped out.

"Miss DeLuca," he said.

I looked behind me, though I was pretty certain I was the only Miss DeLuca in sight. "Yeah?"

"Mr. Montgomery asked me to come back and offer you a ride home," he said.

"That's really not necessary but thank you."

"Listen. I'm going to have to follow you home, so it would make it a lot easier for both of us if you just let me give you a ride," he said.

I sighed. "Fine. He can win this one."

The man laughed before opening the door for me. "He usually does."

I rolled my eyes and slipped inside.

"So, how long have you worked for Ford?" I asked.

"About five years."

"Is he a prick of a boss?"

He barked out a laugh. "Not even a little. By far the best guy I've ever worked for."

"Really?" I asked, unable to hide the surprise in my voice.

"Dead serious. He's a good guy. I mean, look, he sent me back to offer you a ride. Not really typical prick behavior, is it?"

"Touché," I mumbled before sitting back against the seat and pondering the unexpected information.

five

. . .

Ford

"ISN'T THIS LOVELY. It's good for you to slow down and take a minute to have a chat," my mother said, as we sat on the patio at the winery enjoying a delicious lunch and a glass of chardonnay.

"It's great, Mom."

"How was Chanel?" she asked with a smirk.

"She's great. Kicking ass at the firm. She said Hanky's been having a hard time lately. I'm guessing that has to do with the anniversary of Dad's death coming up," I said, taking a bite of my sandwich.

She closed her eyes for a minute and shook her head. "Yes, I think this happens to him every year. I mean, I hate the month of June as well. But I think with him being in that car with your father, it just brings up a lot of dark memories for him. I try to focus on the positive ones. We had so many, right?" Mom said. Her blue eyes were watery with nostalgia and my chest tightened.

"Of course. Dad was the best," I said over the large lump forming in my throat.

"Are you still seeing your therapist regularly? Hanky's not the only one who carries the weight from that night."

"I'm still going. Not as often as I should," I admitted. "She's helped, I'm not denying that. But the truth is, she can't change what happened the night of the accident. No one can, trust me. So, it's something I have to live with."

Mom reached across the table and grabbed my hand. "Oh, my boy, I wish I could make you understand that none of this was your fault. Your father would hate that you're carrying this weight. He loved you so much, and he was endlessly proud of you."

I stared out at the grape fields. So serene and beautiful, all while a thunderstorm brewed inside me. Twisted and tortured. The guilt so heavy at times I thought it might suffocate me.

"Do you really think he was proud that last day? Be honest, we both know the answer."

"Ford," she said as her small hand squeezed mine. "He was proud of you *every day of his life*. People argue and have disagreements. That doesn't change the way they feel about you. You were hurting and you acted on it. You weren't wrong for doing so."

"It was a stupid thing to do. I was so fucking angry about my own stupid bullshit, and I lashed out. My whole life was about this legacy he was leaving me. How we'd work together and take this company even further—the two of us. We shared the same goddamned name, for Christ's sake. You know, Harrison and Dad shared their mission trips, and Jack and Dad shared sports. But Dad and I, it was all about me taking over the reins of Montgomery Media. The legacy he'd pass to me and I'd pass to my kids. That's the crazy shit we talked about. Hell, I remember wearing that ridiculous little suit you got me when I was five years old and going to the office with him on the weekends. I could see it, you know. He and I working side by side. And I pissed it all away in one stupid, weak moment. I crushed him because I was hurting. And I fucking hate myself for it, Mom."

"Sweetheart, you've always been so hard on yourself. You're so much like him, you know that, right? You're both stubborn and strong, with hearts of gold under those broody exteriors. Your father loved you. None of that mattered. He knew you'd work it out. You'd just found your girlfriend and your best friend in a, er, compromising position. Of course, you were upset. So, you wanted to escape. No one could fault you that, Ford."

"Dad did though. He was furious when I left for Europe. You can't deny it," I said.

"He was a stubborn man, I'll admit that. And you weren't doing what he wanted, which never sat well with him. You know I'll love him with everything I have until I take my last breath, but I didn't always agree with him. And there were times I thought he pushed you too hard, but it was always out of love, I knew that. So, I let it go. You wanted to fill those shoes so badly, and he loved it. I get that, I really do. But life happens, I for one, can vouch for that. And sometimes life throws you curveballs and you have to change course. It happens. We do the best we can, and that's what you've always done. You have to forgive yourself, Ford. He would want you to. He'd be so proud of the way you stepped up and did what was needed for this family. We all are. You're the glue that holds us all together, son. You're the only one who doesn't see it."

"Thanks, Mom. I guess it's better late than never. Just wish he could be here, and we were doing it together."

I'd leave out the facts she wanted to pretend weren't there. That if he hadn't been angry, he wouldn't have gone to the city. He wouldn't have been behind the wheel. Dad was the best driver out of all of us. The man never sped. He'd insisted on driving Hanky's car because my godfather had had a few cocktails. Dad didn't drink. But he also didn't drive recklessly. Hell, the man was the most solid, dependable person I'd ever known. But I'd pushed him that night. Devastated him. And in the end—I was the reason he wasn't here today.

"You know he's with us now. I feel him with me every day," she said. Mom's dark hair was pulled back in a bun at the nape of her neck. We shared the same blue eyes, but otherwise, I was the spitting image of my father. Jack and Mom were spirit animals. Both so full of life. Spontaneous and fun. I'd always been the mini-me to my father, and I'd loved it. I'd aspired to be just like him. And Harrison fell somewhere in the middle of all that. Kind and caring, dependable and strong. My family was rocked by the death of my father, but we'd all rallied, and no one had ever blamed me for what happened.

Aside from myself.

"I feel him with me as well."

She let my hand go and reached for her glass of wine. "So, tell me about this new bakery. The boys have been raving about it. Jack brought me a bunch of pastries and they were the best I've ever had. I'm thinking of placing some orders with her for the winery. Do you think she'd be open to that? I'm sure she's swamped right now. How many employees does she have?"

My mother's curiosity always made me laugh.

"Yeah, she's talented. She only has one employee. She works a lot. She's young and driven, so I'm sure she wouldn't turn away business," I said. I thought back to last night when I'd walked in with Chanel. She'd had icing on her cheek, and her hair was a mess, but she was fucking gorgeous.

I looked forward to seeing her every morning, even when I barked at her and she gave me attitude. It was the highlight of my day. I was anxious for the weekend to end.

How fucked up is that?

"Ah, that's probably the best compliment I've heard you pay a woman," Mom said with a laugh. "How old is she? Is she attractive? Single?"

"Good Christ, woman. I'm not looking for a girlfriend. She's twenty-three. I think she's single, but Harley DeLuca is definitely not my type." I sat back in my seat and reached for my glass. She wasn't. Didn't mean I wasn't attracted to her.

"Well, maybe Jack could date her. They're the same age, and he keeps talking about her bakery and how talented she is," Mom said. I stretched my neck to the left and to the right. I was agitated by the conversation and I had no idea why.

"No. Jack's a fucking playboy. She doesn't need that. She's a no-bullshit type of girl."

"Watch your language, please. How about Harrison then? He's as solid as it gets," she said, studying me as she spoke.

"Jesus, Mom. Leave the girl alone. Why does she need to date one of us? Let her be. She's a nice girl. She works hard." I set my wine down and picked at my sandwich.

"Someone sure is testy about this. Interesting." Her head fell back with a chuckle.

"I'm not testy. I just don't know why you're always trying to fix me up with someone. I promise you I have plenty of female company, if that's what you're worried about."

She rolled her eyes and held up her hand. "I don't want to hear about that nonsense. You're twenty-seven, Sweetheart. I just think it's time to start thinking about settling down. Your father and I were married, had you and I was pregnant with Har-bear by the time I was twenty-seven."

"Times have changed. People aren't starting families so young anymore. And I don't think that's something I see in my future, if I'm being honest."

"Bullshit."

My jaw hit the ground. My mom never cursed. "What? Didn't you just tell me to watch my language?"

She shrugged. "There's a time and a place for it. And, I call bullshit. You'd be an amazing husband and father. You're just afraid of getting hurt."

"We can agree to disagree on that one." I barked out a laugh.

"So, I won't try to fix anyone up with the baker, seeing as you're so protective of this girl." She smirked. "But I'd like to speak to her about placing some orders. Should I plan to come out next week, or do you think she'd like to come out and see the winery?"

Was I protective of Harley? Hell, for some odd reason I didn't like her walking home alone. Jerome had followed her all week, and he'd managed to stay far enough away to keep from being spotted. Last night after he'd dropped Chanel and I at dinner, I asked him to go back and offer her a ride. I was surprised to hear that she'd actually taken it. Obviously, she didn't seem to mind as long as I wasn't in the car.

"I'm not protective of her. I barely know her. I'll ask her about placing an order and see what she thinks. We can go from there."

"Sounds great, honey."

"Well, well, well, this is even better than I expected. It's a two for one Montgomery treat," Hanky said, walking our way.

The poor man had taken on the nickname when we were kids. He always wore a suit and carried a handkerchief. I'd donned him Hanky at a young age, and the name had stuck, and now the whole family called him by the ridiculous name.

"What a nice surprise. I wasn't expecting you today," my mother said, pushing to her feet to give him a hug.

"I wanted to drop by and see how you were doing. I know we've got a tough week coming up. Always makes me feel better to check on you guys, make sure you're okay. This saves me a trip. I was going to head to the city to see you this week," he said, pulling me in for a hug.

"Thanks. I'm doing fine. We were just reminiscing about Dad," I said.

"It never gets easier, does it?" he said.

"Time does heal our hearts, but it doesn't make me miss him any less." My mom pushed to her feet and walked over to the bar area to grab a wine glass for him.

He pulled up a chair and sat down at our table. "I miss him every single day."

"I know you do, Hanky," Mom said, taking the seat beside him and reaching for his hand.

"I heard you took my girl to dinner last night. She's still as bossy as ever, I presume?" Hanky said with a chuckle.

"Yes. Chanel never changes. She insisted on stopping at the new bakery downstairs and buying some cookies before dinner. She ate all of them in the car on the drive to the restaurant and then wondered why she had no appetite." I laughed.

"Sounds about right. I didn't realize the coffee place closed?" he asked.

"Yeah. And Harrison and Jack ran some ridiculous contest to rent out the space and we went with the bakery. But she actually seems to be killing it and we partnered with her to help get her business off the ground. I'm surprised you haven't seen it in the media. Jack and Harrison have promoted the shit out of it." I rolled my eyes.

"Eh, I've been slacking lately. You know, retirement has a way of keeping you out of the loop."

Mom chuckled and sipped her wine. "It's well deserved. You've worked hard your entire life. Slowing down is good for the soul."

Hanky was a bit older than my parents, and his son, Baron, had taken over his commercial real estate empire.

"Yeah, I think Marie is happy to have me home most of the time. But she was the one who encouraged me to come to the winery to see how you were doing, so I think she could use an occasional break from me."

We all shared a laugh. Marie was a calm and sweet woman, and Hanky was full of life. He had a big personality and an even bigger heart. But I'd never want to cross him. He was famous for his shrewd business tactics, and my father always joked that he wouldn't want to be on the receiving end of Hanky's anger. My father had always been the more even-keeled, down-to-earth one in the relationship. But they'd been friends since they were kids, and they'd remained thick as thieves until the day my father died.

"Well, you'll have to try out these pastries. I'm hoping to place an order for the winery, so you can just stop by anytime your sweet tooth kicks in," Mom said.

"That sounds good to me. So, Ford, you handling everything okay? You want me to come to the city and we can do dinner on Tuesday? I know it's a tough day for you," Hanky asked. The man was like a second father to me. He'd been the one I leaned on most after we lost Dad.

"Thanks, but I'm okay. I'll be submerged in work and get through the day like I always do."

I'd leave out the part about going to the hole in the wall bar and drinking myself sick, like I did every year. I purposely chose a bar that my brothers would never think to look for me. For some reason it was the way I'd handled it the last four years, and this year would be no different. It was my day to grieve, and the next day I'd be hungover as hell, and then I'd get back on track.

"All right, but you call me if you need me," Hanky said.

"Will do."

"You'll be okay?" I asked my mother. She'd always been so stoic about it, but I knew it was a tough day for her.

"Oh yes. Harrison is going to take me to dinner." My mother

reached over again and grabbed my hand. Her eyes wet with emotion. "We'll all get through it."

"Absolutely," I said, pushing to my feet. I didn't want to think about this any longer. "I'm going to go find Jack. I'll come say goodbye before I head back to the city." I kissed Mom's cheek.

"Sounds good, sweetie. Love you."

"I'll give you a call this week," Hanky said, pushing to stand and pulling me in for a hug.

The winery sat on a striking property, spanning hundreds of acres. The grounds were gorgeous, and people came for wine tours and hosted events here. There was an indoor/outdoor dining area, and a gift shop. I made my way inside the main lobby, as Jack's office was just down the hallway.

"Ford?" The hair on the back of my neck stood on end when I heard her voice.

I turned to see Madison standing there, beaming at me as if we were old friends. Not ex-lovers who'd had a horrific breakup and ended on a bad note. It had been five years, so I was most definitely over it; however, I'd never cared to be around her again. And, considering the anniversary of my father's death was approaching, it only agitated me more to see her today. Hell, she'd cost me my best friend and contributed to my father's accident in a roundabout way. Was it a rational thought process? No. But I didn't give a fuck. I despised her. And the few times I'd run into her had been awkward and uncomfortable.

"Hey," I said, squaring my shoulders. "What are you doing here?"

"Did Jack not tell you? My baby sister is getting married. She wants to have the wedding here at the winery. So weird, right? All the times we'd talked about having our wedding here someday, and now she's actually doing it." Madison had long blonde hair that trailed down her back. She was tall and lean, fair skinned, and attractive by most standards. But she was a haughty bitch most of the time, and I honestly don't know why for the life of me I'd stayed with her for as long as I had. Add in the fact that she'd fucked my best friend in the bed I shared with her—not so attractive.

"No, he didn't mention it," I said, unable to hide my irritation. Of course, he didn't. Jack hated confrontation and I wouldn't have liked this. I doubted my mother knew about it either, because she was not a fan of Madison Carlyle, and this would mean having her around more.

"Hey Ford," Francesca said as she approached, and leaned in for a hug. I'd always liked Madison's little sister. They were nothing alike. She was kind and caring and had actually reached out when my father passed away, unlike her older sister who'd wisely chosen to stay away. I'd have a hard time turning Francesca's request to marry at the winery down. I'd just stay away for a while to avoid the awkward confrontations.

"Hi, Francesca. You're looking well. I hear congratulations are in order."

"Thank you. Yes. We're doing final tours, so we haven't met with your mom yet, but I definitely want to have the ceremony here if the dates work."

I nodded. "I'm sure we'll do everything we can to accommodate you."

"So, how are you?" Madison asked, shooting her sister a look to leave us alone. Francesca waved and walked away, dropping down to sit on the bench near the gift shop.

"I'm fine, Madison."

"I know this is a tough time of year for you. You don't need to be so stoic. How about we grab dinner this week?" She tipped her head down and batted her lashes at me. We were so far past this shit having any effect on me. I was embarrassed she was still trying. Sure, she'd tried to patch things up at first, but there was no moving past what she'd done.

"That's a hard no," I said, crossing my arms in front of me.

"Come on, Ford. It's been years. I'm still single, you're still single. Doesn't that tell you something?"

"Nope. It's still telling me that you fucked my best friend. Take care, Madison." I turned to walk away, aggravated that I even had to deal with this bullshit at my family winery.

She reached for my arm. "Can't we get past this?"

I turned around. "Madison. I'm past it. It's old news. You need to move on. I have."

"But have you really? You're not seeing anyone."

"How the hell do you know what I'm doing. Trust me when I tell you—this is done. Has been for five years."

"I miss you. I know you must feel something toward me." Her voice was desperate, and we were standing in the middle of the lobby with her mother and sister a mere twenty feet away. Awkward didn't begin to describe the situation. I hadn't spoken to this woman in years, so this was coming out of left field. Knowing Madison, she'd had a recent breakup and was desperate to find someone new. She never could be alone. Apparently, not even for a weekend which is how long it took her to jump in the sack with Garrett.

"Madison," I said, keeping my voice low in an effort not to embarrass her. "I'm good. I wish you the best. Truly. It's in the past. I don't think about it, nor do I have any desire to revisit it."

It was the truth. I never thought about Madison. I occasionally thought about Garrett because he'd been more like a brother to me than a friend, so that wound ran deeper. But the truth was—my father was killed shortly after I'd walked in on them, and the loss of my father had been devastating. Madison and Garrett's betrayal paled in comparison to the pain of losing Dad. I resented them for the role they'd played in the last conversation I'd had with my father. But in the big scheme of things, I thought about them very little.

"You know, this is the reason I strayed. You're not emotionally available, Ford. You never were."

"You're probably right. But you're about five years late to this conversation. Take care," I said just as Jack strolled around the corner.

"Oh, hey. I was just coming to find you, Ford. I didn't know you were coming with Francesca today," Jack said, looking incredibly uncomfortable as he spoke to my ex.

"Well, why wouldn't I? She's my sister," she huffed and stalked away.

"You didn't think a heads-up would have been nice?"

"Today was just a tour, so we don't even know if she's choosing this as her venue. I didn't want to bother you with it unless it was actually happening. And I had no idea Madison would be coming with her," Jack said, running a hand through his overgrown dark hair.

"Whatever. I'm not even here all that much, so it's fine. And I actually like Francesca, so if she wants to have it here, she should. I'm heading back to the city. I'll see you later."

"Hey." He grabbed my shoulder to stop me. "You want to grab dinner Tuesday night?"

"I've got plans, but you should do dinner with Mom and Harrison."

"Okay. I'm here for you if you need me. You know that, right?" he said.

"Of course. Love you, brother." I gave him a half-hug before walking out the door.

Everyone always got a little more emotional right before the anniversary of my father's death. It was par for the course.

And I hated it.

six

. . .

Harley

THIS WEEK WAS off to a crazy start. I knew what to expect now, was prepared for the early rush, and had found my rhythm at DeLiciously Yours. Monday had been crazy busy, and I knew today would be no different. I flipped on the lights, put the coffee on, and pulled out a few samples of pastries to display in the glass case. I laughed when I thought about how many people asked for a coffee and said they didn't want anything else, only to change their minds and add in a few pastries while I rang them up. Amazing how quickly one could change their mind when they came eye to eye with a cupcake.

The door chimed letting me know someone had entered and I called out, "Is that you, Montgomery?"

It was either Ford or Molly, and my best friend was a lot of things, but an early bird was not one of them.

"Yep." He stopped and leaned against the doorframe leading into the kitchen.

I looked up because he usually said something snarky or rude, and this wasn't the norm. I'd come to look forward to our morning banter.

"Everything okay? Did your penthouse catch on fire? Your driver run out of gas and force you to take an Uber like us common folk?" I teased.

He didn't laugh or even smile. He pushed away from the door-frame and moved into the kitchen to pour his coffee. Yesterday I'd informed him that it wouldn't pour itself, so he should feel free to jump on in and help himself. Mornings were for me to prepare for my actual customers, not wait on my landlord slash partner. He was more than capable of pouring a cup of coffee, after all. But yesterday he'd joked back. Today he was closed off and, what? I couldn't put my finger on it. Not irritated. Vulnerable, maybe?

"Hey, I was kidding. Are you okay?" I asked, wiping my flour-covered hands on a towel and walking toward him.

"I'm fine." He struggled to get the lid to fasten to the cup. The man ran one of the most successful media companies on the planet and pouring a cup of coffee appeared to fluster him.

"You don't seem fine," I said, yanking the lid out of his hand and popping it in place before handing him the cup.

"I'm a busy man, Harley. I don't have time for games." He turned on his heels and stormed out the door.

Well, okay then.

The guy was impossible to read. I never knew which Ford I would get. Sometimes he was moody as shit, other days he was actually funny. Typical rich kid. He probably had to wait two seconds for his posh car to pull up this morning and he'd been inconvenienced.

Well, he wasn't the only one with a life. I was a busy woman as well. And I didn't have time to decipher his many personalities.

The door chimed again, and Molly walked in. I tried to push away thoughts of the pompous ass who'd snapped at me for no reason at all.

Molly and I hustled through the rush, and things were just starting to slow down when Harrison and Jack walked through the door.

The more tolerable Montgomery brothers.

"Hey, Harls," Jack purred. He really was adorable. Tall and lean with dark hair and dark eyes.

"Hi there. Let me guess, you want to frost some cupcakes again. I told you, it's addicting."

"Come on. I'm about to do a few batches now," Molly called out, and he followed her back to the kitchen.

"Only if I get to eat a few while I work," he said.

"Deal," I yelled out to him as I continued to wipe down the tables. Two people sat at the back table, but the place had cleared out for now, at least until the lunch rush. I glanced over at Harrison, who stood near the display case, but appeared distracted. "Are you okay?"

"What? Yeah, of course. Just an off day." He was also tall and lean. The Montgomery boys all had that in common. They'd all been blessed with a god-like physique, along with their natural good looks. Harrison seemed to be the most kind-hearted of the three, and definitely more soft spoken than his brothers.

"Yeah? Your brother seemed a little off this morning as well."

"Ford?"

"Yep. He was moodier than usual," I said with a chuckle.

Harrison walked over to a table and pulled out a chair, dropping to sit. "I'm not surprised."

I sat in the chair across from him. "Everything okay?"

"Yes and no. I mean, it's a tough day for our family. We all handle it differently. Jack acts like nothing happened, Ford acts like the world has ended and he won't talk to anyone, and I sort of go through the motions. I guess that's grief for you, huh?"

I didn't know what we were talking about and I didn't want to pry. I leaned closer, I wanted him to know he could talk to me. I had my own experience with grief, and I knew it was tough to navigate. Gramps and I had done the best we could, and time had a way of healing some of those wounds, but I felt the loss of my grandmother every day.

"I don't think there's a right or wrong way to grieve. I think you just have to let yourself feel it, and go through those emotions, you know?"

"Yeah. It's five years today that we lost Dad. It was just so unexpected. That one loss changed all of our lives so much. Ford came home from Europe and immediately started running the company. Jack decided he didn't want to pursue the NFL any longer and finished out his time at USC playing ball, and then came to work for the family business. And I, well, I left school and came home to finish up and be near my mother. I walked away from a lot of things that were good in my life because I didn't want to feel happy at that time, if that makes sense. Anyway, I don't mean to dump this on you. This day just always takes me back to a different time."

I nodded. "It makes perfect sense. I think that's all normal, but I also think it's okay to feel happy again. I'm sure your father would want that for all of you."

He chuckled. "You're right about that. He'd be pissed that we all changed course, but he'd be happy that we rallied as a family. That was the most important thing in the world to him."

My heart ached for all three of them. I couldn't shake the way that Ford looked this morning now that I knew the reason. He was grieving. I'd misread him.

"Check out this one." Jack came around the counter holding a cupcake with twice as much icing as we usually put on them. He pulled out a chair and took a huge bite.

I laughed. "Wow. You want some cupcake to go with your icing?"

I smiled at Harrison and he nodded. I was glad he'd opened up to me. And I'd be a bit kinder to his moody older brother the next time I saw him.

"The frosting is the best part," he said around a mouthful of cake.

"Glad you enjoyed it." I laughed.

"Did you tell her about Dad?" Jack asked, looking between Harrison and me.

"Yep."

"I could tell. You've got that sappy look on your face, Harls."

I shook my head and smiled. "I don't do sappy. But I am sorry to hear about your dad."

"Yeah. It sucks. We're heading out to Napa to have dinner with Mom tonight."

"What about Ford?" I asked before I could stop myself.

"No. He likes to do his own thing. He doesn't like thinking about it or talking about it," Harrison said, pushing to his feet.

"Oh, trust me, I just went up there to check on him and he ripped my head off," Jack said. "But on the bright side, there's a hot new intern working in the media room, so at least something good came out of me going up there."

Harrison and I both laughed, and I shook my head at him. "I thought you told me you liked the girl you met over the weekend?"

"Harls, Harls, Harls… it's all about the options, babe. Sort of like when I come in here. Some days I want a cupcake, and other days I want a donut or a brownie. Why limit yourself?"

I rolled my eyes. "You didn't just compare women to baked goods, did you?"

"He did," Harrison said with disgust.

"Jack, get your lazy ass back here and help me clean up the mess you made. There's pink icing everywhere," Molly shouted from the kitchen.

"That one scares me," Jack whispered about my best friend before walking to the back to do as he was told.

"Like I said, everyone deals with this day differently," Harrison said with a smile.

Just then a few women stepped inside, gushing about how cute the interior was. Harrison called out for Jack and said they needed to get to the winery as their mother had just sent him a text. I gave them each a quick hug before turning my attention back to my customers.

The rest of the day was a blur. To say we were slammed was an understatement. Molly had left an hour ago, and I was just getting things prepped for tomorrow. It was late. Later than I usually left, and I was happy to see that Ford's car wasn't sitting out front when I stepped outside. I was looking forward to the walk and the fresh air after having been cooped up all day.

It was a warm summer evening, the sky had darkened, but between the moon and the streetlights, the sidewalk was easy to follow. There were a few people out, and I loved the sounds of the city after dusk. Cars drove past, horns honked, and laughter and chatter faded in the distance, but it was relatively calm. DeLiciously Yours had had its best day as far as sales go, and I allowed myself to daydream about all the things I'd hoped for when I started this business. I dreamed of paying off Gramps' home for him. He'd phoned me to let me know my mother had called again looking for me. She was obviously aware that I'd opened a bakery, and of course she wondered how it would benefit her.

As I approached the corner where I'd turn for home, I heard a scuffle and moved to the outside of the sidewalk as not to get caught up in it.

"You've had enough, buddy," I heard a man say as he dragged another man out the door of the bar.

"Fuck you. I'll tell you when I've had enough," another man shouted, and my spine went stick straight at the sound of his voice. He leaned against the building and slid down the wall to sit on the ground. The bouncer turned around to walk back inside.

I stopped and turned to study him. "Montgomery?"

"Why do you insist on walking alone at night?" His words were slurred, and he lifted his head to look at me.

"Um. Wow. You've just been thrown out of a dive bar, you're sitting on the ground in your high buck suit, and you're judging me?" My head fell back in laughter.

"The baker lady, the baker lady, she always likes to throw me shady." His words were barely audible and completely ridiculous, and I tried to cover my smile. Not that the man could see straight at the moment anyway. I was getting a front-row seat to how Ford Montgomery dealt with grief.

"I believe you mean, throw you shade?" I squatted down to get eye level to him. And holy crap, the dude reeked of liquor.

"No. I mean *shady*. Shady lady." He chuckled before leaning forward and vomiting. All over my favorite Chucks. I pushed to stand and gasped. Are you freaking kidding me?

"Um, you need to get off the street. Where's your driver?" I asked, shaking the puke off my feet, and reaching for his hand to help him up.

"No. Don't call Jerome. I sent him home. I don't want my brothers to know where I am."

I got him up on his feet and wrapped an arm around his waist to try to help stabilize him. Jesus, what was I supposed to do with him now?

"Okay. Well, you can't stay here. I live right around the corner. Why don't we go get you cleaned up, I can make you a cup of coffee, and then we'll call you an Uber."

"My dad died five years ago today." He was leaning all his weight on me, and Ford Montgomery was not a small man. I was trying to stay on my puke-covered feet while balancing this jackass against me and walking another hundred yards to my door, and my chest squeezed at his words.

"I'm sorry," I said, looking up at the flight of stairs I'd need to lug his drunk ass up. Thankfully this building only had two stories, and my apartment was on the second floor. Also known as the penthouse.

"You don't even know the worst of it." He slumped forward, causing me to fall as well. We were both sprawled out on the steps, and the smell of booze and vomit surrounded me.

"Oh my god," I said as I dry heaved and was unable to stop. I covered my mouth and nose with my hand and shoved him to the side. "Stop talking. We need to focus. You're going to have to help me."

"Leave me here. Just leave me here."

I pushed to stand, and he rolled on his back, making zero effort to get up. His arms flailed around him.

"Montgomery. Pull your shit together. Get up," I shouted, yanking his arm hard. Surprisingly, he did as he was told, and I was able to pull him to his feet.

"It's all my fault you know. You probably wouldn't be helping me if you knew I'd killed my own father," he slurred.

I reached for my key and propped him against the wall beside the door as I pushed it open. "Yeah, well, I'm sure you had your reasons. We've all got our baggage. Good to know your rich ass isn't immune to it."

He leaned against me and I helped him to the couch before kicking off my vomit-covered tennis shoes. I ran to get the wastepaper basket from my bathroom and set it next to him. "Do not puke on this couch. It's the first piece of furniture I've ever bought." I chuckled and walked to the kitchen to get him a cup of coffee.

"Where am I? You brought me to a goddamn *youth hostel*?"

Oh, no he didn't just insult my home. Was he serious? Like Ford Montgomery had ever spent the night in a youth hostel.

I walked back and set the mug on the coffee table and pulled him upright so he wouldn't tip over. "I assure you this is not a youth hostel. This is my home, you pompous ass."

"Your home? It's one room."

"It's called a studio, genius," I hissed before handing him the coffee. "Drink. I'll call you an Uber once you sober up a bit."

"You like my brothers more than me, don't you? Why is that?"

Well, that came out of left field.

"No. I don't like them more than you." I laughed. They were nicer to me, but of course I favored the broody asshole. But I wouldn't tell him that.

"Good. I just need to sleep it off. I hate this day. I miss my fucking father," he slurred before leaning forward and setting the cup on the table. He tipped back and rested his head on the arm of the couch. His feet still on the floor. It looked very uncomfortable, but the man was loaded and probably too far gone to notice.

Shit. I felt bad for him. He appeared to be truly broken up over the loss of his father. I pushed to my feet and paced in front of the couch.

I reached for my phone and dialed Molly.

"Tell me you aren't just getting home, Harls," she said, her voice sounded groggy from sleep.

"Well, I have a little situation."

"Why are you whispering? You live alone. Ohhhh, a situation," she said. "Oh my god. Did you finally bring a man back with you? It isn't that asshole, Toad, is it?"

I moved to the bathroom. It's not like my guest was even conscious, but I didn't want him to hear my conversation.

"Different asshole. I was walking home, and I ran into Ford Montgomery—"

"He's so hot. I knew he was into you," she interrupted.

"I can hear you." I heard her boyfriend Oscar grumble in the background and she shushed him.

"No. It's nothing like that. I found him slumped against the wall outside that bar around the corner from here. He got kicked out. He was super drunk and can barely stand. He puked all over my shoes." I didn't hide my irritation.

"Not the new Chucks," she said with a laugh.

"Yes. I'm sure they're ruined now. Anyway, he didn't have his driver. He's all worked up about it being the day his dad died, and he just told me he *killed his father*," I whisper-hissed.

She laughed. "You sure can pick 'em, kid."

"I didn't pick him. I said I'd get him some coffee and sober him up a bit and then call an Uber. But he's passed out sitting up on my couch. What do I do?"

I held the phone away from my ear as she continued to laugh uncontrollably.

"A hot billionaire that may have killed his father is still a step up from Toad," she said. "Come on, Harls, the guy is harmless. Pretentious? Sure. A murderer? No freaking way. He'd get his Oxford loafers dirty. Rich people hire others to do their dirty work. I think you should let him sleep it off. He can barely stand. He's not going to hurt you."

"I'm not worried about him hurting me. I just, I don't know. I don't know him that well. He's my landlord slash kind of business partner. It seems very inappropriate," I said, peeking my head out to see if he was still in the same position.

He was.

"Whatever. I think you're just nervous about a hot man sleeping in your apartment. It's been a while."

I rolled my eyes. "Please. That's not it. I mean, we're friends, I guess. Kind of. I don't have much of a choice, right? I can't just drag him out on the street. I thought about calling his brothers, but he was so adamant about not letting them know where he was, that I feel like I shouldn't." Jack and Harrison had both given me their numbers. The only one who hadn't exchanged information with me was the one currently passed out on my sofa.

"Exactly. Just let him sleep it off. He'll probably be embarrassed in the morning. Especially after confessing to murder."

I covered my mouth to muffle my laughter. "Fine. I'll see you in the morning. I'm going to bed."

"Love you, Harls. I'm excited that you have a man on your couch. A hot, sexy man. Even if he's passed out, it's progress."

"Goodbye." I rolled my eyes before ending the call.

I walked over and reached for the mug that remained full of coffee and took it to the sink. I grabbed a pillow and blanket from the closet and did my best to help the oversized man on my couch lie down. I took his shoes off, because no way in hell was I going to let him put his filthy loafers on my new sofa. I looked down at him. He really was a beautiful specimen. His dark hair still looked styled to perfection. His chiseled jaw, dark brows and the peppered scruff covering his chin were so sexy. I bit the inside of my cheek as I took a minute to just take him in. I usually avoided staring at him very long because, well, he usually irritated me too quickly. The man was perfection. Until he opened his mouth and spoke, that is.

His hand came up and wrapped around my knee, and I nearly fell back onto the coffee table. I pulled his arm away and tucked it beside him on the couch.

"You're beautiful, Harley," he slurred.

What the hell? He was dreaming. But those weren't words I'd ever imagined coming from his mouth. Hell, he was rarely even friendly.

"Goodnight, Montgomery," I said before walking to the bathroom to wash my face and put on my jammies.

"I'm sorry, Dad." I heard him say from the bathroom, and my heart squeezed. And that never happened. Only when Gramps and I were missing Gram.

I turned out the lights and climbed into bed. I was dreading the awkward encounter in the morning.

seven

. . .

Ford

BANGING AND CLANKING STARTLED ME. My feet were hanging off an unusually small sofa. Sunlight flooded my vision, making it impossible to open my eyes and focus.

More banging and rattling.

My head spun.

My mouth was dry. I was in desperate need of water.

I pushed to sit up. Where the fuck was I? I forced my eyes open and saw two gorgeous tanned legs in the distance. I moved my gaze up to find boy shorts and long dark hair trailing down her back. I turned to look around the place. It was a one-room apartment? There was a bed, a kitchen and a couch—all in one room.

Where the fuck was I?

"Drink," her voice said as she handed me a cup of coffee. "We need to leave in fifteen minutes."

Harley DeLuca.

Holy shit. Did I sleep with the baker? Jesus. I couldn't remember a thing.

I took a sip of coffee. The girl made damn good coffee.

"How'd I get here?" My voice was hoarse and gruff.

She tucked her hair behind her ear. I'd never seen it down. It was long. Much longer than I'd thought. Her face was bare of makeup and gorgeous. No doubt about it, Harley DeLuca was stunning. But she had a mouth on her. And she hated me most of the time. There was no way she'd have taken me home willingly.

"Well, I found you on my way home. You were slumped against the building after being thrown out of the bar." She watched me, and she wasn't as harsh as she normally was. Jesus. What had I said to her? She was giving me pity eyes—huge pet peeve of mine. I hated it when people felt sorry for me.

I cleared my throat. "I'm sorry to ask this, but, uh, we didn't sleep together, did we?"

Her dark eyes doubled in size and she gasped. "You're such an asshole. No. We didn't sleep together, you pig."

My head continued to pound, and the banging started again. "Jesus, what is that banging?"

She stormed to the bathroom, which was a mere five feet from the living room and slammed the door.

"I'm above a dry cleaner. Those are the machines," she yelled from the other side of the door.

I pushed to my feet and took another swig of coffee, walking closer to the bathroom. Which literally meant taking three short steps. "Hey, Harley."

"What?" she hissed through the door.

"I didn't mean to offend you. I don't remember anything from last night. I just wanted to make sure I hadn't acted, er, inappropriately." The girl was hot as hell. Not my type, obviously, but she was gorgeous. And how the hell do I know what I'd do when I was three sheets to the wind. I was attracted to her, no denying it.

She walked out of the bathroom. Her hair was in a bun piled on top of her head, she'd put on a little bit of makeup, but she didn't wear much. She didn't need any. She had a black cotton dress on that ended at her knees and a pair of booties.

"It's fine. Are you ready? I don't want to be late for work."

"You're the owner." I glanced down at my phone to see the time. "It's not even six in the morning. How early do you go in?"

"I like to get there at six, and you've made me late, because we have to walk. Not to mention I didn't get much sleep with your drunk ass on my couch," she said, raising one brow at me. She was so fucking pretty she nearly took my breath away. Jesus, how much did I have to drink last night? I was off.

I sat down and slipped my shoes on. "I see you aren't wearing your tennis shoes."

"You noticed that, did you?"

Why the hell was she suddenly so angry. I just asked if we'd slept together. It's not that farfetched. People do it all the time. "I just know you like them, that's all."

"Well, they're soaking in the sink because someone vomited all over them."

I scrubbed a hand down my face. "Jesus. I'm sorry. I'll get you a new pair."

She rolled her eyes as I pushed to stand. "I don't want a new pair. I had a perfectly good pair. You think you can just throw your money at everything and fix it?"

"Whoa. Don't go making assumptions. I puked on your shoes and I'm offering to replace them."

She led me to the door, and we made our way out to the street. "I'm not making assumptions. I actually know a hell of a lot more about you than I want to. You also confessed to murdering your father."

I came to a stop. The sun was barely out, thank god, because I didn't have my sunglasses with me. "Are you fucking kidding me right now?"

"Nope. You told me you killed him. And I still let you sleep it off even though my life was basically at risk. *You're welcome.* You puked on my favorite shoes, and then you woke up and asked if I slept with you? Sorry to tell you, Montgomery, I'm slightly more memorable than that." She turned on her heels and started walking. I was tempted to call Jerome for a ride, but I figured this conversation needed to happen and the girl was hell-bent on walking.

I moved beside her with my suit coat slung over my arm. "I'm sorry. Thank you for helping me last night."

She came to a stop again. "I accept your apology."

We started walking again. I clearly needed to explain what I'd meant, because I didn't want her to think I was a cold-blooded murderer. But at the same time, it angered me that she'd let me spend the night after I'd confessed to killing someone. Not the wisest move for a woman who lives alone. But it seemed like a bad time to bring this up.

"My father was killed in a car accident five years ago."

"And you were the driver?" she asked, glancing over at me as her heel booties clicked against the cement.

"No. I wasn't in the car with him."

"You were in the car that hit him?"

"No. I wasn't fucking there," I snapped because I hated talking about it.

"Don't bark at me. You're the one who confessed to a crime you weren't even at."

"You're right. I'm sorry. I just don't like talking about it," I said.

"You know, Montgomery, if you were a superhero, I'd call you *The Apologizer.*"

I rolled my eyes. "And why is that?"

"Because you're a complete dick most of the time, and then you throw out a few apologies and you think that makes everything better. If you really feel bad, then stop being a dick. And, no offense, but you confessed to a crime you weren't even at, so you're clearly a shitty criminal as well."

I barked out a laugh. She was a straight shooter. I didn't have a lot of those in my life. "All right, I'll think before I apologize next time."

"That's a start."

We walked in silence for a little bit before I finally spoke. "My father and I had a fight the night of his accident. I was angry about something and I acted like an asshole."

"Surprise, surprise," she mumbled.

"Anyway. I'd really pissed him off. He went to the city to have dinner with Hanky," I said, pausing when I realized she wouldn't know who that was. "He's my godfather. My dad's best friend."

"All families fight," she said, coming to a stop once again and studying me.

"Well, he died in a car accident that night. The car hit a tree and he and Hanky were both ejected. Hanky ended up being okay, but my father didn't make it. So, my last conversation with him was an argument. One that sent him out angry."

"And you think the accident was your fault?" Her empathetic gaze locked with mine. I had never talked about this with anyone outside of my family and my therapist. And Hanky of course.

"Well, obviously he wouldn't have been there if we hadn't fought."

"You don't know that for sure, and either way, that didn't cause the accident," she said as she reached out and squeezed my forearm.

"I do know that for certain. Hanky said they were arguing about it in the car when my dad lost control. He was upset about our disagreement and Hanky was trying to calm him down."

"I didn't know your father, but I can promise you that he would not want you to feel responsible for the accident. I mean, people drive upset all the time. Hell, I'm pissed off every time I'm behind the wheel dealing with shitty drivers. It was an accident, which by the very definition means it was an unexpected and unintentional event resulting in damage or injury."

I barked out a laugh. "Thank you, Merriam-Webster."

"It's quite the party trick. I have all sorts of definitions in my head ever since studying for my SATs. But that's a conversation for another time. You're being irrational, Montgomery. And trust me, if I thought you killed your father, I'd be the first one to tell you so."

I studied her. The sidewalk was pretty desolate at the moment, and traffic was sparse. The city was still asleep as Harley and I made our way to Montgomery Media. "Why is that?"

"Because you puked on my favorite Chucks." She raised a brow in challenge.

"Fair enough," I said as we continued walking.

"I'm guessing you don't talk about it much because if you did, I don't think you'd be blaming yourself five years later. You know it's not good to keep all that stuff bottled up."

I rolled my eyes. "You're an expert, huh?"

"Sure. I'm the queen of bottled up emotions." I glanced over at her, but her expression gave nothing away.

"Is that so?"

"It is. So, all I'm saying is now that the cat's sort of out of the bag—feel free to come to me if you need someone to vent to," she said, looking over at me with those dark brown eyes and an empathetic smile.

"I actually have a therapist, but thanks."

"Well, it's been five years and you don't seem to have made much progress seeing as I found your drunken, hot mess, ass out in the street last night. And here you are today doing the walk of shame."

My head fell back in laughter, and damn if it didn't feel good. "A hot mess, huh? So, you think I'm hot, do you? This is good to know. Although I don't fraternize with employees. And this is far from a walk of shame because I'm completely fine."

She came to an abrupt halt. "First of all, I'm not your employee. I'm your business partner. Secondly, sure you're a good-looking cat—I'm not blind. But I'm also not interested. You're not my type. *At all.* And as far as walk of shames go—this is top notch, Montgomery. You're wearing yesterday's suit. You've got puke on your collar and on your shoes. Your hair is a mess and probably reeks of vomit. And you're walking to work after waking up and not knowing where you were. This is a walk of shame at its finest! Welcome to the shit show, Mr. Perfect."

I tried to cover my smile. I didn't want her to know how fascinating I found her. "How do you know I'm not your type?"

She laughed now. "That's what you took from what I just said? And I know because I know my type. And you aren't it. I don't date uptight, pompous, demanding rich boys. *'Oh, I need my coffee ready and waiting for me when I arrive.'* Not my thing. No offense."

I studied her. "I'm not pompous."

"Just demanding, uptight, and rich?"

"I mean, yeah. I guess. And I don't apologize for it."

"Nor should you. And it's great because it puts you in the friend zone. Which is why you can feel free to talk to me whenever you want to. You'd never have to worry about me catching feelings, because that's not happening," she said, and a wide grin spread across her face.

I hadn't had a conversation that was so open and honest with a woman before. Hell, I hadn't had an actual deep conversation with a human being in a long time. My mom and my therapist, but even then, they never put me in my place quite like Harley DeLuca did. And I didn't mind it.

"Okay, then. If we're friends now, tell me what your type is. I'm guessing it's broody assholes who show up at your place of work and pin you to the wall and force you to kiss them. Very classy, by the way."

"Yeah. I'm the first to admit I have shit taste in men. That's why I don't date often. Todd was okay the first year we dated, I mean, there were probably signs that I missed. But the last few months he just got really possessive, and when I broke up with him—he really upped his stalker game. So I left for France, blocked him on everything, and I thought he'd given up. But with my picture in the paper, it just gave him the in he needed. Hopefully he stays away now."

"What a fucking creep."

"Yeah. How about you? You don't strike me as a stalker. A player—probably. Possibly a cheater, but it doesn't seem like your style."

"Hell, no. I'm a lot of things, but a cheater is not one of them," I said, and my gaze locked with hers when I glanced her way.

"Yeah, for some reason I'm not surprised to hear that. And thanks for intervening that day with Todd. I never did get to thank you properly for that."

"Don't give it a thought. I should have kicked his ass, too," I admitted.

She laughed. "I think we're going to be good friends, Ford Montgomery."

I rolled my eyes. "Yeah, I don't really do friends, but we can give it a try."

"What a shocker."

So salty. I didn't mind it. Usually people annoyed me in much less time.

But Harley DeLuca was full of surprises.

eight

. . .

Harley

ANOTHER WEEK MOVED by in a blur. We were swamped every day from opening to close. My new friendship with Ford Montgomery had surprised me. The man was such a moody asshole most of the time, but now that I was getting to know him, he could actually be fairly nice. Funny, even. He'd come in every morning for his coffee and chat for a bit. It was usually the highlight of my day because the man was very entertaining. But then he'd look at his watch and hiss at me about wasting too much time gabbing, and head upstairs. I'm sure today would be no different—and I couldn't wait for him to get here.

"Hello," Ford called out when he entered the bakery.

"I'm in the back."

He waltzed into the kitchen like he owned the place, which I guess he did, and made his way to the coffee machine.

"Good morning. Hey, there's something I've been meaning to talk to you about," he said. He was ridiculously good looking, with his chiseled jaw and full lips. I had to remind myself not to stare.

Focus.

I continued rolling the dough for the butter cookies and looked up to meet his gaze. "Go ahead, then."

He chuckled. "My mom is interested in ordering pastries from you for the winery. Do you think you could handle a side job like that?"

"You have a winery?" I asked curiously.

"Yes. Montgomery Wines. It's in Napa, which is where I grew up. That's where Jack and Harrison spend most of their time. Mom still lives there. She's nagging me every day to ask you about it. Of course, Jack can't stop raving about your pastries because the dude has the palette of a five-year-old."

I rolled my eyes. "I'd call it fabulous taste. You have the palette of a ninety-year-old man. Live a little, Montgomery. Eat the cookie. Walk in the rain. Loosen up."

"White sugar is the devil."

"White sugar is my profession, you jackass."

He laughed. "Fine. Your pastries are good, no doubt about it. So, what do you think?"

"Um, sure. I can always bake more. How much does she need? Would it be a weekly order?"

"I have no idea. You two can discuss it. She'd like to meet you. Are you free tomorrow?" he asked, fastening the lid to his cup.

His broad shoulders and lean physique caught my attention again. His brown hair was longer on the top and shorter in the back, and his piercing blue eyes were easy to get lost in. I found it hard not to ogle him when he wasn't looking. But that was acceptable for friends. Molly was my best friend, and I thought she was beautiful. It's completely normal to find your friends attractive, right?

It didn't mean I was actually *attracted to* Ford Montgomery.

Nothing could be farther from the truth. He wasn't my type.

It wasn't like I thought about kissing him. Or touching him.

I didn't.

Hardly ever.

"Tomorrow is Saturday," I said when he finally turned to face me, and I shook myself out of the daze I was currently in.

"Thanks for the update. I'm aware. Are you free?"

"I guess so. She wants to meet here at the bakery?"

"No. I said I'd bring you out to Napa so you can see the winery and meet her. Does that sound okay?" he asked, studying me with his usual intensity.

"Napa? I don't know if the Bug could make it that far." I drove a vintage convertible Bug that I absolutely loved. It wasn't the most reliable car, but I'd worked hard for it, so it was special to me.

He rolled his eyes. "What the hell is a bug?"

"A convertible VW Bug, you know, *the car*," I said, my tone oozing sarcasm.

"Oh, okay then. No, we'd take the helicopter. We can be there and back in no time. How does ten in the morning sound? Jerome and I can grab you on the way, and we'll take off from here?"

"Helicopter? I don't know if I'm comfortable with that."

"Of course, you are. You drive a death trap for an automobile. And it's a convertible. Even more dangerous. My form of transportation is much safer. Trust me," he said, sipping his coffee and heading for the door.

"Are you always this bossy?" I hissed as I wiped my hands on a towel.

"Always. Get used to it."

And just like that, he was gone. And I was equal parts annoyed at him and disappointed to see him go.

I walked out to see the line forming outside the door just as Molly entered.

"I see your new bestie was here again," she said, wriggling her brows.

"Stop. We're friends."

"Sure, you are."

We opened the door and let the craziness start.

"I can't believe I'm on a helicopter. This is not normal," I said, checking again to make sure my seat belt was fastened.

I'd been awake for hours, as I was anxious about my trip to Napa. I didn't know what I should even wear to such an occasion. Was it a job interview? A partnership? Just a chat? I went with my floral maxi dress and my newly-washed Chucks. My dress was fitted at the top and flowy at the bottom. It screamed 'winery'. I decided to wear my hair down and straight, as I wouldn't be baking today.

"It's completely normal. You worry too much. Especially for someone who drives a tin can as their form of transportation."

"Hey, I love that car. Don't hate on the Bug."

He chuckled. And when Ford Montgomery laughed, it did something to me.

"I like your hair down," he said, completely surprising me with the compliment.

"Oh, thanks. I always wear it up to bake, but since I'm just chatting today, I thought it was fine to have it down."

"Yeah, definitely."

"So, tell me about your mom. What's she like?"

"She's great. You're going to love her. She's a lot like Jack. She has an infectious smile and a wicked sense of humor." His whole face lit up when he spoke of his mother, and my chest squeezed a bit. I wondered what it was like to have a parent that you felt that kind of love for. I envied it.

"That's nice that you guys are so close. How about you and your brothers? You all seem like you're pretty tight." I was very curious as they all three seemed so different. Jack came into the bakery daily, and he was the life of the party. Hilarious and fun. Harrison stopped by a few times a week, and he was a bit more serious, but had a good sense of humor and always complimented the pastries he'd order. They'd both been quicker to open up to me, but I was most drawn to Ford and his broodiness. I wondered what the three of them were like outside of work.

"Very. They would probably say I don't spend enough time with the family. They're out in Napa every day. I'm in the city during the week and try to go see my mom every other weekend. My brothers don't always understand how much time Montgomery Media takes from me. They don't have a clue what it takes to keep the company running," he said, and I saw something in his expression as he spoke. Disappointment? Hurt?

"So why don't you just tell them?"

"Tell them what?" he asked.

"Tell them how much time it takes. Lay out all the facts. Maybe it'll help them understand," I said.

"Well, they've never asked."

"That doesn't mean you shouldn't tell them. It might give them a better grasp on what exactly you do and how much time is required," I said over the sudden noise from the propeller as we started to move.

"I'll think about it."

I grasped the side of the seat. I probably should have mentioned that I was terrified of heights. Or, as Molly explained to me, I was afraid of falling, not actually of being up in the air. Either way, I was terrified. When I flew to Paris, the doctor gave me something to help settle my nerves. I wish I had that now.

"Are you okay? Your face is pretty white." He studied me as we left the ground, and I forced my eyes shut.

"I don't think so," I said, digging my fingernails into the seat, when a hand covered mine.

"Relax, Harley. We have the best pilot out there. I wouldn't do anything to put you in danger. I mean, you're my only friend, right?"

I laughed and peeked one eye open. "Good to know."

He leaned in closer to me and intertwined our fingers. Ford Montgomery was sweeter than I would have guessed. "Look out the window. It's stunning."

I forced myself to open up both eyes and check out the scenery, but I quickly squeezed them closed again. "I'll just have to take your word for it."

"It's a quick up, then down. I promise, we'll be there before you even have time to get too nervous."

"Um, I'd say I'm already well past nervous," I mumbled as I squeezed his hand harder.

He leaned closer and whispered against my ear, "We're already landing. You did it."

Chill bumps covered my arms as his lips tickled against my skin. Once we were on the ground and the pilot informed us we could unbuckle, I let go of his hand, and quickly got the hell off that thing. I'd take my little Bug any day of the week over this.

We walked toward Ford's car. Apparently, they went back and forth from Napa to the city often, so they had cars ready to go wherever they went. It was a lot to wrap your head around.

It was a short trip to the winery, and I put my window down and let the breeze blow my hair all around. It smelled like flowers and sunshine. I'd never been to Napa, but I could already tell I'd like it here.

"Sorry about the helicopter ride. If you aren't comfortable flying back, we can just take one of the cars and I can drive us back," he said, surprising me with his thoughtfulness. I wouldn't have guessed him to be an empathetic person, but he was proving me wrong.

"No. I can muscle through it. I'm a big believer in overcoming your fears." I followed him up the walkway to the gorgeous winery. Lavender shrubs lined the path and overgrown trees offered shade over the entrance. "Wow. This place is stunning. Is your home far from here?"

"Just up the road. Mom walks back and forth most days, or just takes the golf cart."

When we stepped inside the lobby, there was a little gift shop and a café. Floor-to-ceiling glass walls that offered views of the grape fields. It was really something to see. I could only imagine the creativity a place like this would stir. The peaceful, serene setting would be hard to beat.

"There they are," a woman said, walking our way.

"Mom, hello. This is Harley DeLuca, owner of DeLiciously Yours. Harley, this is my mother, Monica Montgomery."

"It's so nice to meet you," we said in unison and both chuckled before she pulled me in for a hug.

"I have a nice table for us out on the patio. It's private out there, so we can chat. I ordered some wine and a few appetizers just in case you're hungry."

"Sounds great," I said.

Ford's mom was stunning. She wore jeans, a white blouse, and a cute sun hat. Her dark hair was pulled back in a chignon at the nape of her neck.

The waiter came over and poured us each a glass of chardonnay and set down a veggie platter, and some cheese and crackers. We sat in the midst of a picturesque winery. It was lush and green, and lavender wafted in the air. The sun was out, but the patio offered shade.

"So, Jack has brought me several of your pastries, and I have to say, yours are the best I've ever had," she said.

"Oh, wow. Thank you. I'm flattered."

"Were you just born with the gift? Or did it take years to perfect?" There was a genuineness about Monica Montgomery that I was drawn to. She appeared truly interested.

"Well, my grandmother taught me everything she knew when I was young, and it just grew from there. I'd dreamed of opening a bakery since I was a little girl, so honestly, this has been a long time coming. I've worked really hard to get here, so I'd say it was a combo of having a great teacher, combined with hard work to keep perfecting my craft."

"That's quite impressive. Well, it shows in your work. Obviously, you're quite passionate about baking, and it's refreshing to see someone chase their dreams in that way. Tell me about your family. Were you raised in the city?"

I shifted in my seat, and when I looked up my gaze locked with Ford's sapphire blues. "Jesus, Mom. I thought you were placing some orders, not grilling her."

"Oh, I'm so sorry. I just wanted to get to know you," Monica said.

"It's completely okay. I'm an open book." I fidgeted with my hands under the table. "I was basically raised by my grandparents on and off. My mom has a lot of, um, issues. I've never met my father, and my grandparents took full custody of me when I was in middle school. I was raised in Oakland and attended Berkley for undergrad. I spent a year in Paris working with some of the best pastry chefs in the world this past year. So, that's me in a nutshell," I said, holding my arms out. I had nothing to hide. People could take me or leave me. I certainly wasn't going to try to make myself into something I wasn't at this point in my life. I'm proud of where I am and how I got here. But talking too much about my mother was a different story. I didn't like to go there. That was the only chapter in my life that I'd closed. I'd been judged for her actions enough for one lifetime.

"Well, your grandparents must be incredibly proud of you now. Your hard work has paid off. I'm so impressed," Monica said, clasping her hands together and dabbing at her watery eyes. I would never have guessed my life story would bring out so much emotion, but she was warm and kind, so it didn't completely surprise me.

"My gram passed away a few years ago. She had breast cancer. It was really hard on Gramps and I, but it helped that I was close to home while attending Berkley. But yes, Gramps is very proud. Ridiculously proud, really."

"Yes, I can imagine that was tough on him. I lost my husband five years ago, just when Ford was graduating from college and both Harrison and Jack were away at school. Ford was going to attend grad school in Europe, but he immediately came home. Harrison did the same. I don't know if I would have survived that first year without them," she said, shaking her head.

My gaze locked once again with Ford's. He had a bigger heart than I would have guessed, and I didn't miss the way he looked at his mother. Like the sun set there. He reached over and squeezed her hand before pulling away. "Okay, so how about we place some orders. You've gotten her life story, let's move on."

Monica rolled her eyes and patted his cheek. "My stoic boy. He hates the mushy stuff."

I chuckled. "It's nice that you all rallied and supported one another."

"Always," she said. "So, how would you feel about just making me a combo of pastries. You know, whatever you're doing that week at the bakery, so we can keep it simpler for you. Maybe start with three dozen mixed pastries or cookies. Do you think you can handle that?"

"I do. That actually sounds perfect. And if you ever want anything seasonal, just let me know."

A waiter approached the table, and attempted to whisper, "Monica, there's a little issue in the kitchen and Josh asked me to come get you."

"Okay. Well, I'm excited about this. I need to go put out a fire, but I'll be back. Enjoy. Order something from the menu if you'd like."

"Thank you," I said, nodding at Monica before she stepped away. "Your mom is really sweet. I like her."

"Yeah. She's one in a million. Always has been. But she's also nosy as hell. Sorry she grilled you," Ford said. He wore dark jeans and a white button-up. Only he could make casual clothing look formal.

"It's no problem. I have nothing to hide." I leaned over and grabbed a few crackers and some cheese and placed them on my plate, before digging in.

"I'm sorry about your grandmother," he said, gazing off at the grape fields.

"Thank you. She was an amazing woman."

"And where's your mom now? Do you keep in touch with her?"

"I try not to," I said with a laugh, and his head turned to look at me. "It's always better when Valentina DeLuca is not around, trust me."

"Really?"

"Really. But she knows about the bakery, so Gramps said she's been inquiring about me, which is never good. But I know how to handle her."

He studied me. "That can't be easy on you."

"Who said life was easy?" I said.

Wasn't that the damn truth.

Life had never been easy.

But that hadn't stopped me before—and it wouldn't stop me now.

nine

. . .

Ford

I'D SPENT the day putting out fire after fire in the press. One of my top reporters had been working on a political piece, and to say things were getting tense would be an understatement. Exposing a corrupt politician never went over well, but it didn't mean it didn't have to be done at times. Montgomery Media was one of the strongest in the industry, and we didn't print stories unless we were one hundred percent certain they were true. And we had the facts to back it up. Still didn't mean everyone was going to like it.

There was a knock at my office door.

"It's open," I said, staring at my computer screen.

"Hey." Harley walked in holding a pink bakery box and a cup. "Jack told me you're dealing with a lot of drama, so I thought you might need a little refined sugar to get you through the day."

Her hair was pulled back in a ponytail. She had pink icing on her cheek, which was not out of the norm for her. I'd never had a friendship with a woman, outside of Chanel, who was more like a sister to me. But Harley DeLuca made it easy. I talked to her every morning when I stopped in for coffee, and after our trip to Napa, I'd actually say we'd formed a friendship. She whined about the fact that I had Jerome offer her a ride home every night, but she'd come to be someone I worried about. And for whatever reason, she seemed to do the same for me.

I laughed. "You know I've eaten more sugar since meeting you than I probably have in my entire life."

She rolled her eyes. "Relax, Montgomery. It's a few cookies. Your pearly whites are still gleaming."

She dropped in the seat across from my desk and pushed the box toward me.

She'd never come up to my office before, so this was a first.

"Hey, are you working late tonight? I wanted to run something by you and thought maybe we could grab dinner up the street," I asked.

"Dinner seems sort of date-ish, no?"

I crossed my arms over my chest. She was right. I usually took the women I dated to dinner, but I didn't feel like it lately. I liked her company, and I was all about trying out this friendship thing. She'd helped me through the anniversary of my father's death, which was always the darkest time for me, and I was comfortable with her.

"You don't go to dinner with Molly?" I reached for my water bottle and took a long pull.

"Of course, I do. But don't you usually take your *ladies* to dinner? Molly tells me there are pictures of you all over the media with different hoochies a couple nights a week. I don't want to be mistaken for a skank."

I choked on my water, and she tossed me a napkin and reached in the box to help herself to a cookie. I coughed until I cleared my throat. "Jesus. I'm glad you're getting your social media updates from Molly. But for the record, she must have failed to tell you, there's already been a photo of you out there with me."

"Shut the front door," she shouted, pushing to her feet in a huff.

"Is it that offensive being seen with me? Christ, most people love the publicity. And it was only once."

"What were we doing?" She dropped back down to sit.

"We were standing beside my car a few days ago. It's not a big deal. It obviously didn't warrant a lot of attention if Molly didn't see it. My publicist just lets me know of any photos that go public."

"I'm not looking for a ride on the Montgomery train of endless women. I have a bit more respect for myself."

"Good to know. So, dinner? You're the one who convinced me to embrace this friendship. Now I'm all in, so you can't take it away. If it makes you feel better, I can invite a woman back to my place after dinner for a little fun." I wriggled my brows.

She slapped the desk. "You're truly disgusting. Don't do me any favors. I'll be closing shop at eight. I'll meet you downstairs."

"Thanks for the treats, even if you're trying to kill me."

"My pleasure," she said before moving to the door.

"Harley," I called out.

"Yeah?"

"You've got icing on your cheek. Clean it up before dinner. I'd hate for you to look like a hot mess if we get photographed together." I smirked.

"You annoy me, Montgomery."

"That's the goal."

I heard her laugh as she stepped out of my office, and I couldn't help but smile.

And that pissed me off.

My phone vibrated with a new text.

Shawna ~ Hey there, handsome. You free tonight? Dinner and drinks?

That was code for sex. Shawna and I got together every couple of weeks. But I wasn't feeling it at the moment.

Me ~ Sorry. Too much going on at work right now. Can't get away.

She sent me back a sad face emoji, and I set my phone down to turn my attention to my computer.

Harrison stepped in my office, and I ran a hand over my face. I had a shit ton of work to do, and the interruptions needed to stop.

"Governor Soto is threatening a lawsuit over this story." He dropped to sit in the seat Harley had just vacated and reached over to grab a cookie.

"Our legal team is getting ahead of it. It's to be expected. What's happening at the winery? Did you put that little fire out?"

Chef Peter had apparently banged a waitress and then tried to act like it didn't happen. She'd refused to come to work until he apologized. I was thankful that my brother handled all the drama at the winery. Harrison had a knack for putting out fires.

"He's meeting with her now. The guy is an asshole, no doubt about it. I think she actually likes him and that's the problem. I met with each of them and I think it's going to be fine. This should be cleared up in the next few minutes. Endless bullshit, right?" he said, running a hand through his hair.

"Yeah. It's always something. You heading back to Napa now?"

"Yep. I'm going to grab Jack, if I can get him out of the bakery. He's frosting cupcakes again," Harrison said with a laugh. "He claims it's his happy place."

I shook my head. "Ridiculous."

"I was surprised to see Harley up here. You two are getting friendly, huh?" He raised a brow and smirked.

"What is that supposed to mean? We're business partners—and friends, I guess."

"I think it's great. It's just so unlike you, that's all."

There was a knock at my door, and Sam informed me that Edward was here, and my brother moved to his feet.

"Send him back," I told Sam before hurrying my brother out of my office. He didn't need to be part of this meeting.

"Ford, how are you?" Edward was in his mid-fifties, tall and stocky. He ran my security and did investigative work for me as well. The guy was stealthy and dependable.

"I'm well. Please, take a seat. What did you find out?" I asked. I'd had him look into Harley DeLuca's mother as I was concerned after what she shared with me at the winery. I'd become friends with Harley, and I wanted to make sure she wasn't in danger. And we'd also invested in her business and we needed to know what our risks were. Unlike my brothers, I was more than aware that the world was a bit jaded, and I wasn't about to get caught off guard by anyone. Ever. We'd run a thorough check on Harley when we agreed to invest, and she'd checked out.

"Damn, Valentina DeLuca is into a lot of dark shit," he said.

"Meaning?"

"From what I can tell, she started out as an escort at a young age. Got knocked up by a rich dude, who I don't believe was involved at all in Harley's life. It looks like there was some form of payout at the time, but it's not traceable. She's been in and out of her daughter's life, but it appears Harley's been raised mostly by her grandparents."

This was all stuff Harley had shared when my mother asked her five thousand questions.

"And where is Valentina now?"

"She lives with a guy who is known for running both drugs and women. Let's just say he's a bad dude. And with all the publicity your brothers did regarding the bakery, it looks like Valentina has Harley on her radar. She's made a few visits to the grandfather's house but obviously doesn't know where her daughter's staying right now. But in all honesty, Valentina could easily have someone follow her home to figure out where she lives, or simply pay her a visit here."

"Jesus. Fucking Jack and his brilliant ideas. He's put a target on her head."

"Unfortunately, I think you're right. But I will say, this isn't new for Harley. There were a few instances at Berkley where the police were called, due to some sort of domestic dispute around Harley. She never pressed charges, but she did have a few hospital visits for broken bones and other injuries. I think she's probably been dealing with her mother's issues most of her life."

I shook my head. My hands fisted on my desk. How the hell do you bring this shit to your daughter's doorstep? Harley was trying to do something good with her life, and she was working damn hard. It pissed me off.

"Yeah, you're probably right. Thanks for looking into that. How about we get someone to stay back a bit but look out for her? I don't want her to know about it, but I don't think we have any options right now."

"You got it, Ford. I've got just the guy for the job. She won't even know he's there, but he'll be around just in case someone tries to pay her a visit."

"Thank you. I appreciate it. Keep me posted." I shook his hand and walked him to the door.

I had an innate need to protect this girl, for whatever reason. She'd helped me through a dark time, and I wasn't going to let anything happen to her. Her mother wasn't going to come in and fuck up everything Harley had worked for. Not on my fucking watch.

I spent the rest of the day in meetings, dealing with crisis after crisis. I glanced at my watch and realized I was already late as it was a few minutes after eight. I made my way downstairs and found Harley still working. Hell, I expected her to be annoyed that I was late, but the girl's work ethic rivaled my own.

"Oh, hey. Is it already eight?" she said, untying her apron and dropping it on the counter. She walked to the sink to wash her hands.

"Yeah. You hungry?"

"I can eat," she said with a laugh. "But let's just go somewhere easy. I know a great ramen place."

Ramen? Noodles? Was she serious?

"It's up to you. I thought we'd go to Brown's up the street."

She laughed. "Of course, you did. Because everyone needs a three-course steak dinner after a long day at work. That's probably why you get photographed everywhere. You go to swanky places. There aren't a lot of photographers outside of the ramen place. Come on, broaden your horizons, Montgomery. Let's keep it simple."

I rolled my eyes as we made our way outside. "Fine. I've never had ramen."

Harley gave Jerome the directions and laughed. "You're kidding me right now. Where have you been living? Under a rock? Ramen is the best. It's yummy, affordable goodness."

I laughed. "A steak is pretty damn good too."

"It's overrated. Overpriced. You have to dress a certain way. Ramen places take you just as you are."

I rolled my eyes. "That's ridiculous. But I'll try it. Next time we're getting a steak."

"So cocky. Already assuming this friendship is in the bag. I could be sick of you by morning, Montgomery."

"If I were a betting man, I'd say that's doubtful," I said.

We made our way into the odd storefront restaurant and found a table in the back. You had to seat yourself, which was not the norm at the places I dined, but I'd bite my tongue. I had shit I needed to discuss with her and starting off in an argument was not a good plan.

"How about I order for us? Seeing as I have the menu memorized and all. I take it you eat anything outside of refined sugar?"

"I'm not a huge fan of white flour, but since you insisted on eating at a noodle house, I'm guessing I'll have to forego that rule as well." I rolled my eyes and tossed the menu to the side.

She laughed as our waitress approached. Harley ordered us two bowls of her favorite slop.

"Do you have a nice bottle of white?" I asked the server.

"Um. No. We have wine by the glass."

My jaw hit the ground because what restaurant doesn't offer wine by the bottle? Hell, you can purchase a bottle of wine at a drugstore. Wasn't this place in the food business? Wine was a necessity. Harley chuckled before speaking, "We'll take two white spritzers."

"What the hell is that?" I whispered as our waitress glared at me and walked away.

"It's delicious. It's like a White Claw."

"I don't know what that is."

"Ah, Montgomery. You really need to live a little, my friend. You're going to love this."

"Fine. I'm sure I'll suffer later, but it's fine. I wanted to discuss a few things with you."

"Yes. You mentioned that. What is it? You want me to cut sugar as an ingredient in my pastries?" Her head fell back in laughter. She really was pretty. Hardly a stitch of makeup, her dark hair pulled back in an elastic and trailing down her back, and her brown eyes twinkled with flecks of gold and amber—fucking gorgeous. Her lips full and her smile contagious.

I leaned back in my seat which was designed for a *little person*. It barely supported my weight and creaked every time I moved. Annoying as hell.

"So, because we've partnered up, I had to look into your financials a little deeper."

She sat up, spine going stick straight, and her face hardened. "You what? You're spying on me?"

"I'm not spying on you. I'm doing my due diligence."

"Yeah, that's what rich people say when they snoop into other people's business. If you want to know something about me, just ask. Don't go behind my back." I was stunned by how angry she was. I hadn't expected that. Hell, I hadn't even told her that I'd snooped into her personal life as well. I'd definitely be keeping that to myself. Investigating her finances was common practice in the business world, especially when we were partnered up.

"Will you relax? This is not rich-people snooping. This is standard business operation, Harley. You're leasing a space from me, and I've invested in you. I don't just jump in without doing my research."

"Bullshit. Our contract is written up in a way that you have nothing to lose by our joint venture, only something to gain. If I don't deliver, you can bail. You're just making up an excuse for getting in my business. If you want to know something you best come to me, or you can call this friendship done." She leaned back and crossed her arms over her chest. Jesus. She was such a badass sometimes, I almost forgot this was a twenty-three-year-old woman who also happened to be small in stature. But her presence was—massive. As was her strength. Harley DeLuca was a force to be reckoned with. I suppose she'd have to be considering all her mother had put her through.

"Listen, you want to own your own business, this comes with the territory. Anyone who invests in you is going to do their research on you. And you claim you're an open book, so what's the problem?" I asked, studying her intently.

"I'll tell you what my problem is, Montgomery." She paused when our waitress set down our odd cocktails. "I've been around enough shady people in my life, I'm not looking for shady friends."

I laughed. I'd been called a lot of things, but shady was not one of them. I reached for my wine, or whatever the hell this was. It was carbonated and served over ice with a straw. "I can assure you, I'm not shady. If I were shady, I wouldn't be telling you about it, would I?"

"Stop staring at it and just try it, you pretentious princess," she said before reaching for her drink and taking a huge sip. She sucked half the cheap concoction out of the glass. "You bring up a valid point, but it would have been a lot simpler if you'd just come to me first."

"Moving forward I will come to you with concerns," I said, taking a small sip of my cocktail as I scrunched my face at how sweet it was. "My god, what is this?"

Her laughter carried around the restaurant, and I couldn't help but laugh. "It's a spritzer, and it's delicious."

"My family owns a winery, for God's sake. This is terrible."

She covered her face with her hands and continued to laugh. "You are such a prima donna, I can't even handle it. Okay, so let's hear it. What's this big concern you have?"

"You took a loan out at a high rate and used your grandfather's home as collateral. That's not wise."

"Jesus, you really do your homework. I'm quite aware that it wasn't a perfect scenario, but it is what it is. It was my only option. I mean... *I'd hate to have to dip into my trust fund.*" Her voice dripped sarcasm.

I rolled my eyes. "I get it. You didn't have a choice. But you have partners now, and we can offer you better options."

Our bowl of carbs was placed in front of us. I'd be lying if I didn't admit it smelled delicious, and my stomach rumbled.

Harley used her chopsticks and twirled the noodles around. "And what are these mysterious options?"

"We take over the loan. I'll adjust the rate, make it much more reasonable, and you don't need to have your grandfather's house as collateral."

She set down her chopsticks and used her napkin to dab at her mouth. "What would I give you as collateral?"

"I don't take on risky investments. This is low risk. You don't need collateral. You're selling something that I believe in. It's a long-term investment for me. And I own a piece of the company, so obviously I want it to succeed."

Her dark gaze narrowed. "Why would you do that?"

"Because it's good business."

"Bullshit," she said, piercing me with her stare. "I'll consider it if you tell me why you'd make me an offer like this."

"Because I believe in you."

"You've only known me a couple weeks. How do you know I won't let you down?"

"I don't, but I'm a good judge of character. Your work ethic is impossible to miss, your product has a line forming out the door every morning, and I think you're going to do big things."

She nodded, most likely processing my words. I got the feeling she didn't trust easily.

"Well, this was not what I was expecting. Thank you. Can I sleep on it?"

"I'm not sure what there is to sleep on, but sure. We aren't going to do anything tonight anyway," I said, taking another bite of the delicious ramen.

"How is it?"

"It's actually damn good," I said with a laugh.

"Stick with me, kid. You'll learn all sorts of new things," she said. A big grin spread across her pretty face.

I chuckled and took a sip of my odd cocktail. It was growing on me, just like Harley DeLuca.

This friendship was full of surprises.

ten

. . .

Harley

THE MORNING RUSH had come and gone, and Molly and I were cleaning up and getting ready for the next surge of customers at lunch.

"You and Montgomery sure are getting cozy," my best friend said with a smirk.

I threw a dish towel at her and walked back behind the counter to refill the pastry display.

"We're friends. He's not my type, and I'm definitely not his."

She sauntered into the kitchen and dropped the dirty rags into our makeshift hamper. "So, you don't think he's hot?"

"Ford?" I said, trying to gather myself a bit before I answered.

"Um. Yeah. Your new bestie."

"Sure. He's attractive, if you're into that richy-rich, formal look, which I'm not. But yes, he's a good-looking guy. No doubt about it. All three of them are. But I'm friends with all of them."

"I believe you're friends with Harrison and Jack. They are needy little fuckers, always coming to you for advice." She chuckled. "But it's different with Ford. The way he looks at you, my god, girl, I want to grab some popcorn and sit back and enjoy the show when he's in here."

"You're ridiculous. It's called friendship banter." I rolled my eyes.

"It's called hot, steamy, sexual tension, my friend. Are you honestly telling me you don't think about it? You know, spending a night in Ford Montgomery's bed?"

"Hell no. I don't do friends with benefits. You know that. And he doesn't *do* relationships. So it's out of the question."

"I'll bet he'd like to *do you*, though," she said, raising one brow at me in typical Molly-dramatic-fashion.

"Not my thing," I said as the door chimed. I was thankful for the interruption.

Sure. Ford was hot. Sexy as hell. Attractive. All of those things. But he had a reputation, and he'd been pretty open with me about who he was. It would never work. Did I ever think about kissing him when I stared at his full lips? Yes. I wondered what it would feel like to press mine against his. To taste and explore.

Holy shit.

This was so not me.

I needed to put some distance between me and my new bestie. I was starting my day and ending my day with this man a few days a week. We'd been to dinner several times since the noodle house. He called our dinners *business meetings*, and I didn't mind at all. I liked talking to him. I liked hanging out with him. But I didn't believe in gray areas. You were either all in or all out. And Ford would never be all in—so I was all out, as far as ever crossing a line romantically.

I didn't believe in using sex as a tool. I'd grown up with a woman who sold her body for drugs and cash, and I'd spent my entire life trying to be the opposite of her. Sleeping with Ford would be strictly sexual, and I wouldn't go there. Not that he'd tried anyway. He hadn't. Maybe he wasn't attracted to me that way. That would only make it easier for me not to be tempted.

I made my way back out to the front room to see Molly's boyfriend, Oscar, with an attractive guy beside him.

"Hey, you finally made it in," I said, coming around the counter to give him a hug. Molly came sprinting past me and jumped into his arms.

"Oh, hey, I'm Jared. I work with Oscar. Been hearing great things about this place, so we took an early lunch and Ubered over." Jared was tall with light brown wavy hair. He had dark eyes, and a very handsome face. Molly had been talking about him for weeks and I kept putting off the double date.

"I'm Harley. Nice to meet you. And thank you, so far, so good," I said, sounding like a total doofus. My flirting game was weak.

"Well, what do you recommend? It all looks so good," Jared said, but his eyes scanned my body as the words left his mouth.

Wowsers. Jared's flirting game was on point.

I chuckled and moved behind the counter. "It sort of depends what your preference is. The donuts and the cupcakes are our best sellers."

"It all looks sweet to me." He bit down on his lip and his gaze locked with mine. "Why don't you surprise me with a few things?"

I put one of everything in a box for him and tied some twine around it to buy myself some time. I could feel his heated gaze on me.

Jack came waltzing through the door from the lobby. "Hey, I need to talk to you."

He was all worked up, and Oscar and Jared both turned to look at him.

"Um, sure, yeah. Give me a minute."

"Jack, this is my boyfriend Oscar," Molly said, turning to face him. "And this is his coworker Jared."

"Oh, hey, nice to meet you both. Well good. Since you aren't real customers, I need to run this by Harls." Jack shook hands with both guys and then came around the counter and helped himself to a donut.

"They are real customers," I hissed. "What is your problem?"

"That chick up in marketing, the one I took out last week," he said, pausing to chew. "She just slapped me across the face."

He turned his cheek for me to see it, and there was a slight pink to his skin, but he was being very dramatic considering he was a big, tough football player.

"And why did she do that?" I asked as I handed the box to Jared and my gaze locked with his again.

"Who the fuck knows? She said Sierra, one of the interns, told her we hooked up this weekend." He was in a huff, and it was hard not to laugh.

"Did you hook up with Sierra?" I questioned him further.

"Yes. Have you seen her? She's fucking hot."

I shook my head and smacked him in the chest. "Serves you right, playboy. Don't dip your pen in the company ink."

"I don't technically work here. I'm PR for the company. None of them work for me," he said defensively.

I pushed up on my tiptoes and patted his cheek. "No. But they both work for the company you own, and they know one another and it's just…" I paused to find the perfect word. "It's shady. And slimy. And sleazy."

Okay, I found three perfect words that fit the situation.

He gasped dramatically but kept a smile plastered on his face. "That's hurtful, Harls. I wasn't exclusive with any of them. I said I wanted to keep it casual. They both agreed."

Jared laughed now. "Looks like they compared notes and had a change of heart."

I smiled at him. "Agreed."

Jack looked between me and Jared and then winked at me. He dropped to sit at a table and Oscar and his friend said their goodbyes.

"It was nice to meet you, Harley. I'll definitely be back." Jared smiled before walking out the door.

Jack howled as soon as the door shut. "That dude is into you, Harls."

Molly's eyes were wide, and her grin spread clear across her face. "I agree. And he's freaking hot."

I laughed. "You two are ridiculous. Okay, we have about five minutes before this place starts getting packed. Here's my advice. Don't sleep with people who know one another."

"How am I supposed to do that? Do I give a list to every chick I hook up with of the girls I've been with in the past?"

"Maybe just the ones you've been with that week," Molly said, moving behind the counter.

"Isn't it enough when you establish where it's going before you hook up? I mean, I always have the talk before anything happens. I'm not a total douchebag."

I smiled. It was impossible not to love him. Jack was sweet under all that testosterone. His boyish charm and good looks garnered him endless attention. More than he knew what to do with, apparently.

"Tell me what you say to them?" I asked, curiosity getting the best of me. I always wondered how these casual flings went down.

"I just say, *hey, you're hot as fuck. I'm not looking for anything serious, but I'd like to take you home.*"

Molly and I both fell over in a fit of giggles.

"Does that really work?" I asked. "And you definitely weren't clear enough. Do they spend the night?"

"Yes. I'm a huge cuddler, Harls."

"Well, no wonder they get pissed off," Molly said, shaking her head. "Mixed signals, Montgomery. You can't cuddle a chick all night and expect her to think you don't want to see her again. That's so intimate."

"You two never cuddled a one-night stand before?"

"I've only had two one-nighters—and no, we definitely didn't cuddle. It was wham-bam-thank-you-ma'am. And I'm not complaining. I was smiling when they left. But we sure as hell didn't spoon all night." Molly wiped down the counter and looked to me.

"I've never had a one-night stand, sorry. But no, I don't think cuddling comes with a casual romp."

"You're serious? I like spooning," Jack whined as the door opened, and he pushed to his feet and rubbed his cheek.

"You need to change your game, player," Molly said as I greeted our customer.

"Damn. See you later."

I ignored him and focused on the crowd that filled the bakery in a matter of ten minutes. Molly and I hustled to make drinks, fill orders, and ring up our customers. The second half of the day moved by in a blur.

"I'm going to the back to put some cookies in the oven for tomorrow," Molly said.

"Sounds good. I'll start cleaning up out here."

"Cool, let me know if you need me." She moved to the back room.

The door chimed, and my jaw hit the ground at the sight of my mother. It had been over a year since I'd seen her. She looked—terrible. Gaunt. Unhealthy. Rough.

"Baby girl, look at you. Gram would be so proud."

I sucked in a long breath and stayed where I was. Having the counter between us made me more comfortable.

"Hello, Mother. What can I do for you?"

"That's it? No hug. No greeting. I'm just a regular customer?"

"The last time I saw you I ended up in the hospital, so I think we can do without the hugs, yeah?"

"Baby, that wasn't my fault. Damon was in a mood that day, you know? And you tend to piss people off with that high and mighty attitude of yours. Like you're so much better than us," she said. Her blonde straggly hair looked like it hadn't been washed or brushed in days, her dark gaze resembled mine and I hated it. She was thin, and her skanky outfit barely clung to her lithe body. She wore a purple lacy bodysuit and black jeans. And yes, her pimp slash drug dealer, was the devil in more ways than just in name.

"Oh, did I? Gosh, how terrible of me. While your boyfriend was beating the shit out of me, and you were stealing my graduation money from my purse, I can't believe I had the nerve to make you feel small. Hmm… I'll really need to work on that." I seethed sarcasm. This woman was pure evil.

"Baby," she said as the door swung open and a large man walked toward her. He wore a black suit and a white button-up. He had an earpiece and appeared to be listening as he held his hand over his ear, before moving beside my mother.

"Ms. DeLuca, I'm going to have to ask you to leave. You aren't welcome here." His voice was deep and intimidating. "I'll count to three. You either walk out on your own, or I'll assist you to do so."

"What is this? How dare you," my mother balked.

"One."

"Baby, are you going to allow him to speak to me like this?" she shouted, staring up at the large man who showed zero emotion on his face.

"Two."

I didn't try to stop it, though I had no idea who he was. But I didn't want her here. I wasn't sure how he knew that, but I'd find that out after she was gone.

"I'm leaving. But we're not done, baby girl. I'm in some trouble and I would hate to have to turn to Gramps. But you're leaving me no choice," she said, her gaze locking with mine.

Fear wracked my body.

My heart raced.

"Three." The man wrapped his large hand around her bicep and turned her toward the door.

"I'm going to sue you. You can't kick me out of a public place."

"I certainly can. This is private property and you've been asked to leave. Don't come back." He opened the door and escorted her out. He stood there with his arms folded, watching as my mother walked away.

What the actual hell?

I stormed outside, seeing my mother in the distance. "Who are you?"

"Security."

"For whom?"

"I work for the Montgomerys," he said, staring down at me.

"And now you're kicking out my customers?" I shouted, dropping my hands to my hips.

"I'm kicking out your mother, yes."

"Under whose authority?"

"I'm not at liberty to discuss that with you." He crossed his arms over his chest.

"Oh, really? You just get to kick people out of my bakery without telling me why?"

"You certainly didn't look like you wanted her there. I'm not sure why you're complaining."

I huffed. "Because I'll kick people out if I need to. I can handle my own business."

He looked down at me with a condescending stare and I stormed inside. Molly was standing between the kitchen and the dining room. "Well, that was interesting."

"Can you cover things? It's slow right now. I need to go take care of something," I said, tossing my apron on the counter and moving to the door which opened to the lobby.

"You got it. Go get 'em, Harls. How dare he try to kick your evil mother out of the bakery for you? The nerve of some people," she said with a laugh as I marched out the door.

I waltzed right back to Ford's office. I didn't stop to check in with his assistant. The man never gave me that respect. He just walked in my kitchen like he owned the place. Well, he kind of did, but this was a respect thing. I pushed his door open, and he glanced up from his computer before I slammed his door shut behind me.

"Who the hell do you think you are?" I shouted, resting my hands on my hips.

"What are you talking about? Calm down."

"My mother just got escorted out of *my* bakery. You want to explain that to me?" I dropped to sit in the chair facing his desk.

"I don't know why I need to, but sure. Your mother is a danger to you. She isn't welcome here." He folded his hands on his desk and stared at me.

"You don't get to decide that. I do. I would have kicked her out," I said, anger spewing from my body. How dare he?

"I don't think so, Harley. We gave you five minutes to react. You didn't. So he escorted her out."

"You were timing me?"

"No. I was on the phone with Calvin. *He* was timing you. He does this for a living, you know. He's damn good at his job. So, you should have just said thank you, not raised your voice at him."

"My mother is none of your business."

"You rent a space in my building. I own a stake in your company. *You* are my business, which makes her my business."

"You pompous, entitled, smug—" I paused to think of more offensive words, and he waved me on with his hand. "Condescending, arrogant, bastard. No. You're a fucking asshole, that's what you are."

"Wow. Do you speak to all of your friends like this?"

"Friends don't get in one another's business, Montgomery," I said, turning and storming out of his office.

I fought back the tears in the elevator. I would not cry. I wasn't a baby. I'd been through far worse than a visit from my mother and Ford Montgomery's attempt to get in my business. I didn't even know why I was so mad at him, but I was seething. Maybe it was because it meant he'd snooped into my personal life. Maybe because it scared me that he was trying to help me. I didn't need his help. Nor did I want it. I could take care of myself. When I walked into the bakery, I leaned against the door for a little bit to compose myself.

He'd looked into my mother. He knew what she did. Who she was. Maybe it was the thought of him knowing my deepest, darkest secret.

And the shame that came along with being exposed.

eleven

. . .

Ford

JESUS. Could this day get any worse? Harley had stormed in my office like a lunatic. I was trying to protect the girl, and she'd ripped my head off.

"You got a minute?" Jack poked his head in, and I fought the growing irritation.

"What are you doing here? I thought you were in Napa with Harrison?"

"Well, no. I'm having some girl drama, so I stayed to smooth it over. It's all cleared up now," he said, dropping to sit in the seat across from me.

"I don't know what that means, nor do I care."

"Good to know, brother. Thanks for the support," he said, crossing his arms over his chest.

"I'm busy, Jack. You said you took care of it."

"I did. I've got two cases of our best wine shipping out to two ladies that will remain nameless, and I'm taking them each to dinner next week. Once we talked it out, I offered the wine, they both said they'd like a repeat on the Jack mobile, if you know what I mean." He wriggled his brows.

"Jesus. Why do I need to know this?"

"You don't. I just wanted to know if you always have a clear, concise conversation before… you know, getting down to biz."

I pinched the bridge of my nose and closed my eyes. "Sure. There's no secret about what I'm looking for. I only date people who want the same thing."

"Well, I thought I was doing that too. But Harls and Molly told me they don't spoon with one-night stands. Actually, scratch that. Harls has never had a one-night stand, but she said she doubted cuddling would be part of the deal. Molly said she's never spooned a one-nighter. So, there you go. Live and learn, right? That bakery was a damn good investment, for more reasons than pastries."

How were we related? I wondered this all the time. The shit that came out of his mouth alone, left me mystified.

"You asked Harley about who she's slept with?" It was the only thing that came out of his statement that mattered.

He barked out a laugh. "I figured that would get your attention. We were chatting. She helps me with my shit. But I should give you warning—Molly's boyfriend, Oscar, brought some dude to the bakery today. He was practically drooling over our Harls, so if you're inter-ested, you better get cracking, brother. This guy is about to make his move. I know when someone's getting ready, and the dude was ready."

"Please shut up," I said, pushing to my feet. "I have a meeting. You need to go. Keep your goddamn dick in your pants when you're at the office."

"Ooh, someone's irritated now." He saluted me and laughed.

I flipped him the bird before we both exited my office and I made my way to the conference room.

The thought of someone making a move on Harley bothered me. It pissed me off. We were friends. I was protective of her, and I didn't want some piece of shit putting the moves on her.

The rest of the day was just as aggravating as the first half. When I exited the building, the lights to the bakery were off, and I met Jerome outside. He told me Harley refused a ride home, but he followed her to make sure she made it safely.

Stubborn girl.

I closed my eyes, and my phone vibrated.

Blaire ~ Hey, are you in the mood for some company? I'm home and feeling lonely.

Same game. Different night. I didn't answer. I wasn't sure if I was in the mood for company yet. It had been a while, but for some reason it hadn't been important lately. I'd shared a couple dinners with Harley, and she'd been a distraction. But it wasn't like I could fuck her. She'd made it clear. We'd both agreed that was off the table. So why the fuck did I feel guilty about being with anyone else? Hell, it sounded like she was going to have some guy hitting her up to go out.

My phone vibrated again, and I expected to see Blaire's name. But the text was from Edward.

Edward ~ We've got an issue. Call me.

I dialed the phone and he picked up immediately. "The guy I have tailing Harley said she just left her apartment carrying a baseball bat when she got in her car."

"What? It's ten o'clock at night? Where in the hell is she going with a baseball bat?"

"The hell if I know. He texted you and sent his location so you can track him. He's right behind her. Looks like she's heading to Oakland."

"Christ. Stay in touch." I ended the call and told Jerome to get on the same freeway Harley was on. I wanted to be close just in case there was a problem.

I couldn't call her, she was already pissed at me, for god knows what. Keeping her piece of shit mother away from her. Yeah, that made me an asshole.

I directed Jerome to get off the freeway when my phone rang.

"Hello, Mr. Montgomery, this is Calvin. She's out of the car. How would you like me to proceed?"

"Goddamn it. Is she at a house?" I knew her grandfather lived in Oakland, but why would she bring a bat to his house?

"Yes. It's a small, private residence."

"Does she have the bat with her? Do you see anyone else there?" I asked.

"Yes, she got out of the car with the bat in hand. She's hiding on the side of the house behind a bush. I do see a car half a block up that just pulled over. Not sure if it's related."

"I'm almost there. Keep your eyes on her, and only step in if someone gets near her."

I had Jerome turn off the lights when we pulled down the street that I assumed Harley's grandfather lived on. I stepped out of the car and heard shouting up ahead. I took off running. The driveway I sprinted across was full of potholes, and it was difficult to navigate in the dark. There were no fucking lights on this creepy-ass street, but I continued to run toward the house.

"Get the fuck off me," a loud male voice shouted, and I ran faster.

"Who the fuck are you?" I used the flashlight on my phone to make out what was happening. Harley had one arm around a woman's neck that I was fairly certain was her mother. The woman looked like a strung-out junkie. Harley held a bat in her free hand, while Calvin had a man pinned to the side of the house. Harley's eyes locked with mine, and for the first time today, she didn't look pissed. She appeared… frightened? Embarrassed? I couldn't place it.

"What the fuck is going on?"

"I found these two sneaking up on Harley, so I interceded," Calvin said.

"I had it handled." Harley glared at Calvin before tightening her grip on the woman's neck.

"Man, do you have a search warrant? You can't just hold me against my will," the dumb fucker Calvin had pinned to the wall said.

I moved forward and pressed my forearm against his throat. "We don't need a search warrant, you piece of shit. Stay the fuck away from her. Do you hear me?"

"This is my girl's family home," he said with a laugh, and the light shone on his mouth made it clear he was missing several teeth.

"This is my grandfather's home, and she's not welcome. You came here to hurt him, and you called me to let me know because you knew I'd come. You can try all you want, but you're not going to touch him." Harley loosened her grip and pushed her mother to the ground, raising her bat and facing both of them.

The man laughed again. "You gonna stop me, little girl?"

Harley moved in his face. "Yeah, I am. I didn't have a bat last time you kicked the shit out of me, did I? When you two robbed me and left me in that alley bleeding and alone. You won't ever catch me off guard again, Damon."

I reached back and plunged my fist into his face, hearing bones shatter. I couldn't stop myself. Calvin let him go and he dropped to the ground as blood splattered around.

"You fucker. You broke my nose," he shouted.

I lifted him by the back of the collar and dragged him to his feet, shoving him toward Harley's mother. "I'm going to have eyes on you, and eyes on her. If you come near her again, I swear it'll be the last time. Get the fuck out of here. You've been warned."

"Fuck you for breaking my nose," Damon shouted as they both walked away quickly.

Harley stared at me for a long moment before speaking. "I need to stay here to make sure they don't come back."

"Calvin, you stay here for now, and I'll have Edward send someone out to relieve you."

"You got it, boss."

Harley looked the man up and down and clasped her hands together. "Thank you."

"Not a problem."

I took her hand and led her over to where Jerome stood beside my car. "You can head home. I'm going to ride with Harley."

"Everything okay?" he asked.

"Yeah, for now."

We walked back to her car and I dialed Edward and asked him to send someone out to Harley's grandfather's house to relieve Calvin. I climbed into her tin can of a car and laughed as I buckled up.

"Something funny?" she asked as she started the engine.

"Just not sure this seat belt would do anything if we got in an accident. Could you not find a *smaller car*?"

"It's a classic. I love it." She drove in silence and parked out on the street in front of the dry cleaners.

I followed her inside and dropped to sit on her couch.

"Thank you for showing up tonight," she said, dropping to sit beside me.

"It's painful for you to thank me instead of being mad at me, isn't it?"

"It is." She laughed. "I do think I could have handled myself, but truthfully, you showing up and having Calvin stay there gives me peace of mind. I don't even want to know how you knew where I was, do I?"

"Calvin has been watching out for you. Your mother is dangerous, Harley. Obviously, you've been pulled into her shit before, so this isn't new for you. But taking a baseball bat to meet with a drug dealer or pimp, whatever the hell that asshole is—it's not safe. You need to tell me when shit's going on, okay?"

She rolled her eyes. "Listen, Montgomery, I appreciate you, I do. But I've been surviving for a long time without you. I'm very capable of taking care of myself."

I moved closer to her and tucked the loose piece of hair that had fallen from her ponytail behind her ear. "I don't doubt that you can take care of yourself. I'm just here to tell you that you don't need to."

She sighed, her gaze locking with mine. "So, you're going to have someone watch out for Gramps? For how long? I mean, we can't keep this up forever."

"For as long as we need to. It's not a big deal. Edward runs security for me and the family. He has a great team. Let me figure some things out, okay?"

"Why are you doing this? I mean, what do you gain from helping me?" she asked, her gaze searching mine.

"We're friends, right? I have the resources to help you, so why wouldn't I?"

"I don't like owing people, that's all," she said, folding her hands in her lap.

Her nearness had my heart racing. My heart didn't race for women. Usually I knew what was going to happen. It had always been a sure thing, so to speak, when it came to the opposite sex. Harley was different.

"You don't owe me. This isn't something I plan on collecting from you. Would it be so bad to just let me do something nice for you?"

She licked her lips, and I fought the urge to reach down and claim her sweet mouth.

I wanted to.

"It's slightly tragic, but I guess I'll get over it for Gramps' sake."

I laughed, which caused a large grin to spread across her face. And I couldn't take it anymore. I leaned down and covered her mouth with mine. I wanted to claim her. Taste her. Make her mine.

Her lips parted and my tongue dipped in.

So fucking sweet.

A little moan escaped her, and I pulled her onto my lap, so she was straddling me. She pressed into me, making it impossible to miss just how much I wanted her. Needed her.

Needed her in a way I'd never needed anyone.

Anything.

She ground up against me, tangling her hands in my hair and angling her head so that I could take the kiss deeper.

"Fuck, I want you so bad, Harley," I said against her sweet mouth before her hands moved to my chest and she pushed me back.

"Oh my god. No. What the hell are we doing? What is this?" she asked, moving off my lap to sit on the other end of the couch, which wasn't saying much seeing as her couch was made for little people.

I turned to face her, not sure what to say. "What do you mean? I'm attracted to you. You're attracted to me. We're friends. What's the problem?"

"I don't do *that* with friends." Her face hardened as her gaze locked with mine.

"You don't ever act on physical attraction?"

"No. I don't." She crossed her arms over her chest.

I scooted closer to her and reached for her hand. I needed to touch her. Longed to kiss her again. Taste. Explore. "Harley, you're over-thinking it."

She pulled her hand away and pushed to her feet. "No, Montgomery. You're *underthinking* it. It's not my thing. And I've worked hard to never cross that line, and I'm not doing it now. Not even for you."

I pushed to stand and moved in her space. "Cross what line? What are you talking about?"

"My mother trades her body for money and drugs, and god knows what. She tried to pull me into her world more times than I can count. I don't view sex as a form of payment, nor will I ever use my body as a trade for something."

I shook my head and moaned. "Good Christ, that's not what this is. I want you. Not because you owe me, or I expect anything in return. Because we're attracted to one another. That's different."

"Not for me. No. I don't mix the two."

"So, you just never have sex then?" I said with a smirk. Half teasing, half curious.

"Not often. I waited twenty-one years to have sex for the first time because I was so terrified of trusting anyone. It's the one thing I had control of in my life. And trust me, my mother brought creepy, dirty, scary men around me for years. They'd hit on me and try to offer me things—" She paused and swiped at the single tear trailing down her face. "And I trusted Todd after we'd dated for months. And even he turned out to be a huge disappointment. So, I'm certainly not jumping into something with someone who doesn't even believe in dating. *I don't share.* It's not my thing. I'm not looking for a casual romp in the hay. Hell, I'm not looking for anything if I'm being honest, but I can't just have sex with you. I can't. I won't."

I put my hands on her shoulders. Jesus. I was ashamed for suggesting it now. "I get that. I wish I could tell you that I could give you more than a night of pleasure, but I can't. I respect the hell out of you, if that counts for anything."

"Yeah. Thanks. So, you better get going then."

"I'm not going anywhere. Calvin is heading home after your grandfather's replacement arrives, so I'm staying here. I'll just stay on your ridiculously small couch again. Or you could come to my place, where there are actual bedrooms and we could each have a bed. It seems cruel to put me on the world's shortest couch with an incredibly painful case of blue balls."

Her head fell back in laughter. "That's rich, Montgomery. I am not sleeping at your place, but nice try. You know you don't need to stay here. I can take care of myself. I highly doubt Damon is going to do anything tonight with a broken nose."

"Not happening. It's Friday, so at least we don't have to go to work tomorrow. I'll be fine."

"Goodnight," she said, leaning forward and hugging me quickly before pulling away and heading to the bathroom.

"Goodnight."

I knew I wouldn't be getting any sleep.

My adrenaline was pumping from our night.

My painful erection strained against my pants.

And I couldn't get my mind off of the girl sleeping five feet away from me.

twelve

. . .

Harley

THE NEXT MORNING was very entertaining. Seeing Ford Montgomery's legs hanging off my couch, and how peaceful he looked when he actually slept. Thoughts of the night before clung to me. That kiss. I'd never had a kiss quite like that. With so much want and desire fueling it. The way he'd claimed me. He'd kissed me like he was possessed with need.

And I liked it.

That's the worst part—I liked it a lot.

But my heart would never survive a man like Ford Montgomery. He'd make me feel special for one night and then move on to the next woman tomorrow. I had no desire to feel dirty. Or used. Two things I stayed clear of. So, we'd have to be friends, and I'd just try to block out that kiss. It had awakened something in me, and now I found it diffi-cult to look at him without staring at his mouth.

"Tell me why I'm going with you to your apartment?"

"Hmmm… I don't know. Because someone tried to attack you last night and you can't leave your apartment without a baseball bat."

"I don't need a babysitter, Montgomery. You must have better things to do today than look after me."

"I'm not a babysitter. I'm a fabulous best friend though, aren't I?"

I laughed. He was ridiculous. "You're all right."

I pulled into the garage beneath his building, and he guided me to a parking spot right near an elevator. We moved out of the car and he slipped a key in the elevator before we stepped on. He hit the button that read PH, and I couldn't help but chuckle.

"Of course, you're in the penthouse. It's so you." I rolled my eyes.

"Hey, you're also on the top floor of your building."

I laughed. "I'm sure they're exactly the same."

When I stepped off the elevator, my jaw hit the ground. Floor-to-ceiling windows replaced the walls, with views overlooking the entire city. The shiny white floors glimmered in the sunlight as I followed him inside.

"Make yourself at home. There's coffee, juice, food in the fridge. Let me grab a quick shower and change my clothes."

I licked my lips at the mention of him showering and tried to calm my breathing. We were friends. We'd established that.

"Okay, don't worry about me. I'll just be wandering around aimlessly in your palace."

He rolled his eyes. "Just chill out for a few minutes. There's a library you might like down that hallway. I noticed you have a lot of books."

My bat senses were on high alert. Nothing got to me quite like a good library.

"I'll go check it out. Take your time, I'm fine."

I heard him chuckle as he disappeared down the hallway. But, wow. Ford Montgomery's apartment was not like anything I'd ever seen. Not even in magazines or on TV. This place was a palatial masterpiece. I started my self-guided tour in the kitchen. It was a chef's dream, though I doubted Ford did a lot of cooking. I snooped around the cupboards, wondering what it must be like to have so much storage. Talk about a great place to cook a Thanksgiving meal for your hundred closest friends. The space was massive. Two large islands with white marble counters sat in the middle of the kitchen. The cupboards were gray and the island black. It managed to be masculine, yet classic and tasteful. The appliances —I couldn't even focus as I took them in. Top of the line. State of the art. Best of the best. All of these terms flew through my mind as I checked out the Viking oven and cooktop. Ford's refrigerator was stocked. I knew that without even opening the door because the doors on his refrigerator were clear glass. Something you'd see in a restaurant. Full bottles of Pellegrino lined one entire shelf. Bottles of Montgomery Vineyards wine were on a shelf of their own. Fresh produce was organized in glass bowls and baskets. My god. Who the hell organized this? There was no way he could keep up with this with the hours he worked. Something came over me and I pulled one door open, took a lemon out of the basket, and placed it on the bottom shelf near the sparkling water. I laughed as I closed the door, just picturing him gasping at the out-of-place lemon.

"Hello, there," a voice said from behind me, and I spun on my heels with a gasp.

"Oh my gosh. I'm so sorry. Hi. I, um, I, well, I was completely ogling this refrigerator if I'm being honest," I said to the woman standing in front of me. She was older, maybe mid-fifties, dark hair slicked back in a bun and her kind gaze locked with mine.

"Nice to meet you. You must be Harley, Ford's friend. He texted that you two would be here soon. I'm Helena. I keep this place running." She reached out a hand and shook mine.

"Yes, I'm Harley. It's nice to meet you. So you must be the one that keeps this refrigerator looking like a piece of art instead of a source of food." I chuckled.

"Yes, thank you. We do our best. It's not a one-man show, but I'm the only one here on Saturdays. Can I get you something to drink?"

"No, I'm okay. I was just going to wander around and go check out the library, if that's okay? I don't want to get in your way," I said.

"Of course, it's okay. Head right down this hallway," she said, leading me through the enormous home and motioning me in the direction of yet another hallway. "If you enjoy reading, you're going to love it. It's really something."

"Okay. Thank you. It was nice to meet you. I'll see you in a little bit." I waved awkwardly because I didn't know how to act in this place. It was a mansion up in the sky. He had a staff. A refrigerator that belonged in a museum. Sans the out-of-place lemon that I was hoping Helena wouldn't move.

I peeked in the first door on the right, and dark cherry flooring with floor-to-ceiling bookcases lined the space. There were floating ladders on each wall so that you could reach the higher shelves. I walked the room taking in the incredible collection of books. The classics, biographies, non-fiction, and fiction books lined the shelves. Encyclopedias and geography books. There was an entire section of historical non-fiction. There were endless genres to choose from. He was more eclectic than I would have guessed with some of the pop-culture covers I noticed. I climbed the ladder to check out his classics. I ran my fingers along, grazing the spines as I let the ladder move me across the wall. Unbelievable.

"I figured I'd find you in here," Ford said, startling me from my literary coma.

"Wow. Just, wow. This is quite the collection."

"Thank you. Yeah. It was a hobby I shared with my father. We'd spend hours in our library reading together when I was a kid. He favored biographies and I was drawn to anything action and adventure related."

I made my way down the ladder and back to the floor, noticing a photo of Ford as a young boy standing beside a man.

"Who's this? Your father?"

"Yeah. That's when I was maybe ten or eleven," he said, and I didn't miss the tension in his voice.

"You look a lot like your father. I thought he looked familiar and then I realized it's the resemblance."

"Yep. I was the mini version of him. He's a good-looking son of a bitch, right?" He laughed, and I knew he was trying to lighten the mood. I knew that Ford struggled with the loss of his father, even if he tried to act stoic.

"It's okay to miss him, you know. It sounds like you had a great father, and I'm sure losing him was traumatic. It's okay to be sad about it. You don't have to put on a brave face for me." I shrugged.

"I'm not," he said, dropping to sit on the leather couch in the center of the library.

I sat beside him. "Whatever you say, boss. So, now what? You do know I need to get back to my regular life, right? I can't hide out with you all weekend. I have things to do."

"Such as?"

"I'm not going to list everything. It's ridiculous. It was nice of you to show up last night, but honestly, this isn't new for me. I can handle it. You really don't need to worry," I said, shrugging as I faced him.

"Why are you in such a hurry to go home? What, do you have a date? Jack told me Molly's boyfriend brought some guy to the bakery and he was hitting on you."

I laughed. Ford Montgomery appeared—jealous. It was quite the sight. His gaze searched mine, and my heart squeezed a little. But it made no sense.

"We're going out this week. A double date sort of thing. I hardly know the guy, but I'm open." I raised my brow in challenge. He wasn't going to tell me what to do. You can't tell someone that you don't want to date them and then expect them not to date anyone else.

Before I realized what was happening, his mouth was on mine. Delicious and warm. His tongue moved in, tasting and exploring. His fingers tangled in my hair, and he groaned into my mouth. My entire body tingled. Goose bumps covered every inch of skin. My fingers found his damp hair, and I pulled him closer. My brain fired off warning bells, and I pulled myself from the moment of pure bliss.

I shoved him back and pushed hard against his chest.

"What the hell, Montgomery?"

He had a dopey grin on his face and stared down at me. "What? I like kissing you."

I pushed to my feet, anger coursing my veins. "Seriously? We talked about this. You don't date. And I don't do this. Whatever this is."

"Kiss people for pleasure?" His tone oozed sarcasm.

"I don't make out with people I'm not dating, playboy. Get a grip. Go call one of your ho-bags but leave me out of it." I stormed out of the library and down the hall before he caught up with me.

"Harley." His deep voice came from behind me.

"What? What do you want from me?" I asked, turning around to face him.

He invaded my personal space, running a hand through his hair. "I don't fucking know."

"Well, you don't get to take what isn't yours just because you feel like it, Montgomery. And where I come from, friends don't have sex. And for the record, I don't owe you anything, and my body is off-limits," I hissed and turned to storm away.

He wrapped his hand around my bicep. "Oh no you don't. You don't get to make a bullshit statement like that and then stomp out of my home. I'm not kissing you because I think you owe me something, nor do I think your body is a form of payment. Don't insult me, Harley. I can have sex with a multitude of women if that's what I'm looking for. But I kissed you because, well, I wanted to. I like you. It's an unfamiliar feeling for me, and I don't know what it means, but I know that I want you."

Was he for real? "Wait. That's your actual defense? You can sleep with a multitude of other women? You think that makes me feel, what? Flattered. That you have your pick of the litter and you've chosen me today. Fuck you, Ford Montgomery. I don't have time for you to sit around and decide what you want. If you wanted me bad enough, this wouldn't be a discussion. But you want me today and someone else tomorrow, and that does not fly with me, buddy. So, go find yourself a willing companion. I'm out of here. Your babysitting shift is over." I poked him hard in the chest before turning down the long hallway.

"Edward has someone waiting downstairs to follow you home. Someone will be looking out for you round the clock, just so you feel safe." His voice was low. He sounded wounded, but I wasn't falling for it.

"Well, thank you. But I wasn't worried about it. I've survived a long time without you. I certainly don't think I need you now."

"You're overreacting, but okay. You know, Harley, just because someone is attracted to you doesn't mean that they think you're a prostitute. You have a pretty warped sense of what relationships are."

I turned back to face him. Did he really think I'd fall for his shtick? "Is that so? Okay. Educate me. So, you have ladies that you get together with often?"

"Yes," he said, crossing his arms over his chest with confidence. His dark hair a bit disheveled, and his sapphire blues locked with mine.

"Right. So, do you just see one at a time? Consecutively?"

"No. But they are aware of the situation. They know we aren't exclusive."

"Ah. I got it now. So, you sleep with multiple women, but they're aware?" I said, moving closer to him.

His lips turned up in the corners like he'd just helped me realize what a great idea this was. "Exactly. No one gets hurt."

"Do you talk on the phone with them during the week?"

"No," he said, running his fingers and his thumb over the scruff on his jaw.

"So, no emotional relationship. You meet them for sex?" I said, staring at him hard.

"Sometimes we go to dinner." He shrugged. Clueless bastard.

"Do they come to your place? Spend the night?" I asked. Now I was just curious about this arrangement he had with multiple women.

"Never my place. I don't bring women here. I go to their place. And I never spend the night."

"Wow. *That's so tempting.*" I paused to roll my eyes. "Not interested. At all. I may live above a laundromat and have a piece-of-shit mother. I might have the world's smallest couch and the crappiest car, but I'm proud of everything I have. And the day I agree to a relationship like what you're offering will be the day I've thrown in the towel. It's cheap. It's gross. And I think I'm worth a hell of a lot more than just being some girl who gets to fuck a rich guy."

"Good Christ, that is not what I'm offering you." He put his hands up defensively.

"Well, what then? Where are you wanting this to lead? You just want to be friends that make out? How long would that last? Because it sure as hell felt like we were about to rip one another's clothing off last night. And again today. Then what? I explained to you that that isn't my thing. You said you understood. But here you are kissing me again. What, are you just hoping to catch me at a weak moment, and I'll give in? And then we'll hate each other?"

"No. That's not what I'm doing. I just, well, I just…"

"You just what?"

"Well, I like you."

"And that's why we're friends. I need to go. Thanks for your help last night. I'll see you on Monday." I didn't turn back this time when he called my name. I needed some distance from this man. This couldn't go anywhere, and I needed to draw that line in the sand for him before we crossed one that we couldn't take back.

Ford Montgomery needed to stay in his lane.

I needed to stay in mine.

And we'd have to figure out how to be friends without crossing over.

thirteen

• • •

Ford

THE WEEKEND SUCKED after Harley basically called me a whore and stormed out of my place. I'd gone to dinner with Blaire Sunday night to make up for leaving her hanging the night I'd gone to find Harley. It had been a typical date for us. A nice dinner, a great bottle of wine, some small talk and a little flirty banter. But when we'd left the restaurant and I'd agreed to meet her at her place, I'd gotten a migraine and decided to go home. She wasn't happy, and I really didn't care. I'd texted Harley a few times, but she ignored me. She was clearly putting distance between us, and fuck if I wasn't going out of my mind.

I stopped in for coffee Monday morning. "Hey, how was your weekend? I tried you a few times."

"Yes, well, I was busy. I do have other things going on, Ford. I don't just sit around waiting for you to call me, you know."

Jesus. She was still pissed. I tried not to stare at her pouty full lips as she hissed at me. She tossed the dough around on the counter and I leaned against the wall, crossing my legs at the ankle. "Ah, I see. Can we grab dinner tonight? I'll even go to the noodle house if you want."

I needed to spend time with her. I craved it. Craved her.

She raised a brow, and turned over a giant ball of dough, shaking flour all over it. "I'm going on a double date tonight. With an actual grown up. Not someone who just wants to sleep with me, but someone who wants to get to know me."

My jaw clenched. "I already know you. I just happen to want to sleep with you, too."

She huffed and rolled her eyes. "Right. Well, I'm going out with someone who doesn't want to sleep with me, *and* the rest of the women in the city."

"Is that so. You asked him that?"

"That is so, and I don't have to. Because he's *normal*." She smirked. "Perhaps you should call one of your lady friends who just sits by the phone waiting for you to grace them with your big penis."

I coughed and coffee shot all over her counter and down my shirt. "Damn it. You're really pushing it today, Harley."

I reached for some napkins and she used her towel to clean up the mess on her work counter. "Good. I suggest you get used to it."

"I'm not playing this game with you. If you can't handle us being friends, then we can call this done," I said, my voice harsher than I expected. I mean, we'd kissed twice. It was harmless. Mind-blowingly good. But harmless. She was blowing this way out of proportion. Because she was fucking sexually frustrated. She wanted me as bad as I wanted her.

"Don't threaten me with a good time, Montgomery," she said. Her arms crossed over her chest and she raised a brow in challenge.

I tossed the napkins in the garbage and made my way out of there. I was done trying to talk sense into this woman. I couldn't. She wanted something I couldn't offer, and I wanted something she couldn't give me. In the business world, it would be a no-brainer. Go a different route. Find someone who could meet my demands. The problem was, I didn't want to.

My day took off, and I tried to shake off my bad mood. Harrison and Jack both came by eating pastries, which only pissed me off more. Fuckers. They were always hanging out with her, and she was never mad at them.

I finished my last meeting of the day and sat at my desk answering emails. I checked my phone a few times to see if Harley texted to try to put this behind us, but she hadn't. And I was tempted to fucking text her and apologize. But I wouldn't. Two could play this game. Stubborn was my middle name.

"Hey, you still here?" Harrison asked, stepping in my office.

"Yes. What are you doing here?"

"Mom had things under control at the winery, so I've been up in the newsroom working on a few things with Eileen. You okay?" he asked. "You seem off today?"

"I'm fine," I said, my tone harsher than I meant it to be. I was in a foul mood, and I wanted to be left alone.

"Funny. Harley's in a mood too."

"Meaning?" I asked, leaning back in my chair, not hiding my irritation.

"Meaning—get your shit together, brother. You like her. Admit it."

"I did admit it, you asshole."

"And?"

"And, nothing. She wants the whole nine yards. That's not my thing. So, it can't go anywhere. It's better to stay friends. This will blow over," I said.

"Ah, I see," the smug bastard said. "So, you're fine with her going out with that dude, Jared tonight? Jack met him. Said he's a cool guy. They're going to Blaze apparently."

He was giving me the details on purpose. Trying to get a reaction out of me. We owned a few clubs in the city, and Blaze happened to be one of them. He knew it would irritate me that she was going on a date to a club we owned.

"Thanks for that. I need to get to work." I stared at my screen and let him know I was done with this conversation.

"You know, Ford. You used to date. I don't know why you suddenly think you can't be monogamous."

"Says the guy who hasn't had a real relationship since Laney Mae," I said, tossing her name out there knowing it would piss him off.

"That's because I haven't met anyone worth being monogamous

with since Laney. And I have to live with the fact that I let the best thing that ever happened to me get away. You don't. But thanks for bringing her up. Nice touch, asshole," he said, pushing to his feet and heading for the door.

I pinched the bridge of my nose and closed my eyes. "I'm sorry. That was a dick thing to say. I don't know what I'm doing with this girl. I don't know what I have to offer, you know? I'm not the same guy I was when I dated Madison."

He turned around to face me. "Yeah, you are, Ford. You've just been punishing yourself for a long time. I think it's time to let it go and start living your life. Do you like her? I mean, do you *really like* her?"

"Yeah."

"Well, the brother I know doesn't sit around and do nothing when he wants something. He's a fighter. He's not afraid to admit when he's wrong. Stop being a pussy and go after her."

I scrubbed a hand down my face. "I'll think about it. Goodnight."

"I wouldn't wait too long, brother. Girls like Harley don't come around often. Don't be too stubborn to recognize that."

I nodded. I knew he was right. But I just didn't know what to do about it. I'd been out of the dating world for five years, and I wasn't all that good at it when I was in it. I mean, my girl ended up in bed with my best friend. I clearly wasn't great boyfriend material. I never cheated. That was never the problem. But now—now I was used to this lifestyle. Letting my dick do the talking, not my head. And certainly not my heart. Hell, I didn't even know if I had a heart anymore.

I left work and noticed the bakery was dark. She'd already left. She had a date, after all. Fuck. My blood boiled at the thought of anyone kissing her. Touching her.

My phone vibrated when I slipped in the car.

"Hey Edward, what's up?"

"So, I've got eyes on everyone as asked. That Damon character didn't stay down for long. He and another dude are parked outside of the restaurant Harley and her, er, friends are at."

"Are you fucking kidding me with this guy? How stupid is he?"

"I think he's pretty fucking stupid. What do you want me to do?"

"Let's just track him for now. Stay on him. Let's see what he does. If he makes a move, intercede. I want to be kept abreast of all movements."

"You got it, boss. I'll be in touch in a bit."

I ended the call and told Jerome to pull up at the noodle house. I called in an order to go and jogged in to get it. When I returned to the car Edward informed me that Harley and her friends had moved to Blaze, and Damon and his douchebag companion had just entered the club as well.

My pulse raced, and it took everything I had to contain my anger. I directed Jerome to drive over to the club, and told Edward to meet me there, as I dialed our general manager over at Blaze.

"Hey, Ford, what's up?"

"There's a girl there. Just arrived a few minutes ago. Small, dark hair, very pretty. She's with a blonde and two dudes."

"Yep. I've got eyes on them. You want me to ask them to leave?" Charlie asked. The dude was as good as you got for managers. He ran a tight ship, and the employees respected him. He was honest and loyal, and I couldn't ask for more.

"No. Just keep your eyes on her. There are two guys that just walked in behind them. One has a broken nose. I don't want them near her. You can escort them out after I leave. I'm on my way now, but I don't want to make a scene before I get there. The two shady asshole dudes are not allowed in the club again. Got it?"

"Yes. I'm on it. I've got eyes on them now. See you in a bit."

Jerome pulled up out front and followed me inside, and as soon as I arrived two security guards flanked either side of me. I scanned the club. It was a large warehouse that had been turned into an upscale downtown nightclub. Modern lighting and fixtures spanned the large space. I spotted Harley on the dance floor with the guy that I assumed was her date. She was shaking her ass and he was looking at her like he wanted her. My blood boiled. Not happening.

I stalked across the room, unsure of what my plan was. But I wasn't leaving without her.

I wrapped my hand around her bicep. "Say goodnight to your date."

She stopped dancing and blinked up at me. Complete disbelief on her face. Molly chuckled to my right and I gave her a nod.

"What are you doing here?" Harley gasped, yanking her arm away from me.

"I'm taking you home. You were followed here."

Her eyes scanned the room and she shook her head. "I can take care of myself, Montgomery."

I bent down, grabbed her by the back of her legs and tossed her over my shoulder. Her date watched with his jaw on the ground, and Molly put an arm around the guy and smiled at me. Harley punched my back and shouted, but I couldn't make out her words over the loud club music. No one missed a beat. People continued dancing and drinking, and whatever the hell else these people did. The guys at my side helped me easily make my way to the door without a problem. Once outside, she slapped at my backside again and yelled out to the bouncer.

"Hello. Are you seeing this? I'm being kidnapped. Aren't you supposed to do something?"

"Have a good night, Mr. Montgomery," the bouncer called out. The guy knew me and was more than aware that I was not a guy who'd take a woman home against her will. Hell, I was usually trying to sneak away to escape some of these chicks that hung out here.

I tossed her in the car and pulled the door closed once I was inside. "Will you calm the hell down?"

"Calm the hell down? I was on a date. You just can't stand the idea of me being with someone else, can you?"

"I don't particularly care for it, no."

"You pompous ass. You don't want me, but you don't want anyone else to have me. So, you think you can just storm in there and yank me out when you feel like it?" She continued shouting, and I closed my eyes and put up the window so Jerome wouldn't hear our conversation.

"Stop shouting. Damon and some other scumbag followed you to dinner and they were in the club with you. I had to get you out of there."

She fell back against the seat beside me and remained quiet for a minute before speaking, "Oh."

"That's all you have to say about it? Oh."

Her eyes glanced down at the to-go bag with my dinner sitting on the seat across from us. "Oh my gosh. You went to the noodle house. I knew you loved it."

"You sound so surprised. I offered to take you there tonight. But you turned me down."

She turned on the seat to face me. "No, Montgomery. You turned me down. Don't twist this."

I scrubbed a hand over my face. "I didn't turn you down. I just didn't know what I wanted."

She studied my face. Her gaze intense. "And you know now?"

"I don't fucking know, Harley. I'm not good at this."

"You're not good at what?" she asked.

I wrapped my hand around her neck and pulled her close. My mouth covered hers. I was like a dying man in the desert and she was the body of water I needed to survive. I pulled her onto my lap and kissed her deeper. She didn't pull back. She slipped one leg on each side of me, straddling me. Desperate and needy. I tangled my fingers in her hair, angling her head so I could take the kiss deeper.

She pulled back but didn't move off my lap. Her labored breaths came hard and fast. Her desire-filled gaze locked with mine.

"What is this? What are you doing?"

"I don't fucking know. But I want you," I said, and she tried to slip off my lap, but I held her there. "This isn't about sex. Well, it's not only about sex. I want you. All of you. I hated the idea of you being with that guy. I like spending time with you. Talking to you. And I missed you today. You weren't speaking to me, and well—I hated it. I fucking hated it, Harley. And I was glad when Edward called to say those two douchebags were in the club."

"Why?" she whispered.

"Because it meant I had an excuse to come get you."

She smiled and ran her fingers through my hair, her mouth so close I yearned to taste her. "What does this mean?"

My gaze locked with hers. Dark and stormy. "I don't fucking know. I can't promise you I won't mess up. But I can promise you I won't be with anyone else. Only you. I only want you."

Her mouth crashed into mine and she ground up against me. My desire impossible to miss. My hands moved to her hips to stop her from moving.

"What's wrong?" she asked against my mouth.

"I figure we better take this slow with you thinking I only want sex. And well, with you grinding up against me like that, things are going to progress very quickly if you don't take it down a notch."

Her head fell back in laughter and we pulled up in front of my building and she moved off my lap.

"Good idea. So what now?"

"Sleep over. We don't have to do anything. We can share the noodles and I don't know, what do regular people do when they aren't working or fucking?"

She rolled her eyes. "We can watch a movie?"

"Sure."

"I thought you didn't bring girls to your place?" she asked once we stepped on the elevator.

"I don't. But you're not a regular girl."

She smiled, and for a minute it looked like her eyes watered. Harley didn't strike me as a crier, and I doubted she did it often. "Good to know."

"Is Helena here?" she whispered, like we were two teenagers sneaking into our parents' home.

"No." I laughed. "We're all alone. She'll be here early in the morning though. And she left dinner in the oven."

Harley flipped on the lights and walked into the kitchen, opening the oven. "Oh my gosh. She left you this gourmet dinner, and you stopped for noodles?"

"I guess I missed you."

"I saw you this morning," she said, one brow raised.

"It wasn't enough. And you barely spoke to me."

She nodded. "Yeah. You hurt my feelings."

"I'm going to try really hard not to do that again. But Harley, I've never really had a successful relationship with a woman."

"Because you have a wandering eye?" she asked, jumping up on the counter to sit.

"No. I'm not that guy. Hell, if I wanted other women, I wouldn't be pursuing you. I'd keep things the way they were. But I do work a lot, and that's caused me issues in the past."

"I do too," she said with a shrug.

"And I don't share. So, this works both ways, Harley."

"*Okay, Ford,*" she mocked. "Monogamy is not a problem for me. But trust is. I have a hard time giving it. But when I tell you I'm all in, I mean it. And I expect the same in return."

"Fair enough. So you're mine."

She smiled. "We're really doing this? Just like that?"

"It wasn't really just like that. It took some time. But yes. And I want you to stay here as often as possible." I moved to stand between her legs, and she tangled her hands in my hair.

"No. You don't get to start bossing me around just because we're dating. That's not how this works."

"That's exactly how this works. Relationships are all about compromise. I have the bigger place, so it makes more sense to stay here. Not to mention it's a hell of a lot safer," I said, grazing her lips with mine.

"I'm not dating you for your big… place." She pulled back and wriggled her brows. "I worked hard for my own apartment, and I like it. It's mine, you know? And we don't need to stay with each other every night. Hell, you haven't stayed the night with a woman in five years, right?" She chuckled, and I yanked her from the counter, and her legs wrapped around my waist.

"That was by design. You're different. I want you with me. All the fucking time. Careful what you wish for, Harley DeLuca. I'm a possessive man."

"Is that so?" she asked as her head fell back in laughter.

"It is."

"Good luck with that, Montgomery. I march to the beat of my own drum. Always have. Always will."

"We'll see about that," I said, walking her to sit on the couch.

I wanted to go to the bedroom. It was late. We were both tired. But I didn't want to push her. She had some triggers where sex was involved, and she was going to have to make the move now. It was unnatural for me to hand over the reins, but I knew she needed them.

And for whatever reason—I wanted to give her what she needed.

I wanted to give her everything.

fourteen

. . .

Harley

WE SAT on the couch for a while and shared his noodles. I was anxious about all that happened tonight. I'd sent Molly a text and asked her to apologize to Jared for me. I felt terrible about the way I'd left, but I'd already established early on with him that I wasn't interested in anything more than a friendship. My head was too focused on one particular Montgomery brother. It had been since the day I'd met him. I didn't know why. We were so different. Yet something pulled me toward him. He made me feel things I'd never felt.

Like I belonged.

Like I was special.

Like I actually mattered.

And now he wanted to date me. I didn't know how that would work. Ford didn't have a great track record, and I wasn't the most trusting person on Earth either. The combo would most likely be disastrous, but for some reason… I wanted to try.

"So, what should we do? It's after midnight. You want me to sleep here tonight?" I asked, turning to face him where we sat on the couch.

"I want you to sleep here every night."

I rolled my eyes. "Not happening. Let's take this one night at a time. I'll sleep here tonight. But I'm not having sex with you."

He chuckled. "Of course, you're not. That would be far too easy."

"I'm anything but easy," I said as he pushed to his feet and pulled me into his arms.

I wrapped my legs around his waist, and he carried me down the hall. I whistled when we entered his ridiculously large bedroom with floor-to-ceiling glass and views of the city. The moon brightened the dark sky, and I turned to gaze out the windows.

"That's some view."

"I like this view better," he said as his gaze locked with mine.

"Such a smooth talker. Do those lines really work?"

He laughed. "I don't use lines. Never have. And you're the first woman to ever sleep in this bed, or in this apartment."

I buried my face in his neck. It was too much. Ford Montgomery's presence was overwhelming at times. Like he was reaching into my chest and squeezing my heart. I'd never experienced such strong feelings for another person. Our connection was—powerful. And terrifying at the same time.

"Well, thank you for having me. Can you set me down, and loan me a T-shirt to sleep in?"

He smiled. "Of course."

We both stepped into the bathroom and I was thankful that I had a hair tie in my purse. I wrapped my hair in a high bun on top of my head and washed my face. I glanced at the oversized tub. "Wow. I've never seen such a big bathtub."

"Yeah. It's never been used."

I gasped. "Seriously? That's crazy. I don't know if you know this about me, but I don't take showers. I actually hate them. I only take baths."

He turned to face me. "Really? I don't think I know anyone who doesn't take showers. Although I guess I've never asked."

I laughed. "Yeah. It's just always been my thing. Mom and I lived in a motel for a while when I was young and they didn't have a tub, and I was so depressed. I couldn't wait to get to Gram and Gramps' to take a bath. It's always just been my happy place, I guess."

He cocked his head to the side. "Maybe we can take one together. When you're ready."

I bit down on my bottom lip. "You want to take a bath with me?"

"I want to do everything with you," he said. It was honest and vulnerable and my heart burst into a million traitorous pieces.

"Maybe." I followed him back in the bedroom and climbed beneath the sheets. I was having a sleepover with Ford Montgomery. And his bed was like a cocoon of softness. Lush fabrics, and the coziest comforter.

He flipped off the lights but left the shades up on the windows. The stars twinkled and the moon shined just enough for me to make out his features. We both rolled on our sides to face one another.

"I'm glad you're here. I'm sorry for taking a while to figure it out." He stroked my cheek with his fingers, and chill bumps covered my arms.

"That's okay. I'm glad you came around," I said.

"You said your mom and you lived in a motel when you were young. Tell me about your time with her. Was she always on drugs?"

"Apparently she stopped during her pregnancy and for the first year after I was born. I know that my father, or my sperm donor, gave her a chunk of money to get herself together when she got pregnant. He didn't want to be part of my life. She was an escort at the time, or at least that's what she calls it. So I guess that makes her a prostitute because she obviously slept with a rich client," I said, pausing. Talking about my mother was uncomfortable. Not because I didn't trust Ford, but because I was ashamed of where I came from. A shame I'd been trying to hide my entire life. Like this permanent dark cloud that followed me everywhere, no matter how far I tried to run from it.

"You've never met your dad?" he asked.

"Once. After I graduated from high school. My mom finally told me his name, but only because she wanted a favor. She asked me to follow him to a restaurant and confront him there. I'm mad at myself for going. But the truth is, I wanted him to see that I was just fine without him, you know? It sounds so stupid now. But in a sick way, I wanted to impress him. I wanted to be accepted by a man who never wanted me."

"That doesn't sound stupid at all." He stroked my hair. He was close enough that his warm breath tickled my cheek.

"Well, it was an epic failure. He had no interest in knowing me. I was leaving for Europe the day after my high school graduation. I'd saved money for years from my summer jobs to take the trip with a few friends. I was going to be attending Berkley on a full-ride when I returned, and I guess, I don't know, I wanted to shove it in his face. Let him know I'd done well on my own, even though he'd left me with an addict to fend for myself."

"Jesus. What a bastard. Was he surprised to see you there?"

"Yes. And not in a good way. I marched up to his table and told him my name. It took him a minute to process. He was at a table with some friends, and they got up and excused themselves. He offered me money, and basically just wanted me to go away. He wasn't interested in my accomplishments or who I was. He was only concerned about being exposed."

"What a piece of shit. How did it end?"

"I thought I'd leave feeling on top of the world, you know? I thought I'd tell him off and it would feel really good. But it didn't. It made me feel small and I hate him even more for that. It was better when I hadn't met him. I romanticized it in some ways. I imagined he didn't know what he was missing, and that he'd regret it. That he'd feel bad about the situation he left me in. But he didn't. He just wanted to pay me to go away. It was all he had to offer me. He didn't want to know about where I was going to school or that I was a great student. He treated me like I was insignificant, and that was tough to swallow." It was weird to talk about this with Ford. I didn't talk about it with anyone. Molly knew I'd met my father once, and that it had been an epic failure, but that was as much as I'd ever shared with anyone. Todd knew I didn't have a father, and he'd never really inquired about it. I didn't know why I was sharing all of this now, but Ford wanted to know, and it actually felt good to tell him. To get it off my chest.

"What kind of man abandons his child?"

"Not a good man. Tell me about your father," I said, and he stilled before speaking.

"He was a great man. I wish you could have met him. He was an amazing husband and father. He lived for his family. He was dedicated to Montgomery Media but never at the expense of us. We ate dinner together every night. He never missed one of Jack's football games. He took mission trips with Harrison. And he and I, we shared a special bond."

"He sounds amazing. What did you two do together?" I asked.

"We both had a love for reading. I'd find new books and couldn't wait to share them with him. He had so much family pride. His father had started Montgomery Media back in the day, but Dad grew it into a multi-billion-dollar company. He couldn't wait to pass it on to me. He had nicknames for all of us from a young age. He called me the legacy, Harrison the peacekeeper and Jack the rebel." He paused to laugh. "He'd always tell me that I'd do big things at the company and bring my own innovations to the forefront. He believed in me, and there wasn't a day in my life that I didn't worship the man."

My chest squeezed. The way Ford spoke of his father with such adoration and love was so genuine and real. They were clearly very close, and I knew that his father's death had been very traumatic for him.

"What was the fight about that night?"

"It was stupid, really. That's what haunts me. I'd found Madison in bed with my best friend, Garrett, and I'd lost my shit. Not even because I was heartbroken. Looking back, I don't think I loved Madison at that point in our relationship. It had run its course. But we stayed together because we had a history. Garrett and I grew up together, and I couldn't believe he would do that to me. And at the time, in the moment, I thought I loved her. I think my ego was wounded that they'd both betrayed me. It happened the night before my college graduation, so you can imagine what a fun celebration that was." He paused to chuckle. "I was set to start at Montgomery Media the following week, and my dad couldn't wait for us to work together. But I was in a dark place. I called him from the airport to let him know I was leaving and wouldn't be coming to work with him. I'd decided to go to London, and I'd start my MBA the following fall abroad. I wanted to spend the summer traveling before I started the program. I'd been admitted immediately, and I wanted to get far away from everyone and everything. It was an impulsive decision and not a rational one. Dad was fuming. He'd made a position for me and he told me that I was behaving like a spoiled rich kid. I told him he was right, and he could thank himself for raising one. Those were the last words I spoke to him. We'd never fought before. Even through all the teenage years, we'd never had a big blowup. He was an even-keeled man—always fair and reasonable. But I'd lashed out. I'd been mad at the world at the time."

I ran my fingers through his hair and swiped at the tear running down my cheek. Damn if this man wasn't making me a sappy asshole. "He knows you didn't mean it. You and your dad shared a special relationship. I'm sure he felt bad for getting upset with you. You'd just found your girlfriend and your best friend in bed together, which by the way, total asshole thing to do. It was still raw for you. You probably would have been more rational a few days later, but you weren't given that time."

"Yeah. He was killed that night. I got the call when I was sitting in a hotel room in London. It haunts me to this day, you know? He and Hanky were in a terrible accident. They were arguing. Hanky tried to calm him down, make him understand that I was young and just being irrational. He told him I'd come around. But Dad was pissed and swerved off the road and hit a tree. They were both ejected. Hanky was hurt but conscious. It was a miracle really that he was able to drag himself over to Dad and dial 911 for help. Dad died in the ambulance on the way to the hospital. I never said goodbye. I never got to tell him I was sorry for what I said."

My heart ached. Most of the time I didn't believe my heart even worked like normal people's hearts did. But right now, it was wide awake and aching for this beautiful man.

"You know you can tell him all those things now. He's watching out for you, I'm sure of it."

"Yeah, that's what Mom says. I do feel him with me, but I think it's just me wishing he were here."

"You should tell him how you feel. Tell him you're sorry and that you miss him. You don't have anything to lose. And if there's a chance he can hear you, wouldn't it feel good to say it? I'm not saying to do it now, with me, but when you're alone. Talk to him. See if it helps."

He chuckled. "Yeah, I sure as shit am not having a conversation with my dead father while lying in bed with you."

I laughed. "Try it when you're alone, Montgomery. I talk to Gram all the time. It helps me feel close to her."

"Yeah? Tell me about her."

"She's the reason I fell in love with baking. She taught me how to make cupcakes before I could talk. She was the most talented baker I know. Honestly, the woman didn't measure, didn't follow recipes, she was just a natural. And she tried to make up for the fact that I didn't have a mother growing up. It was tricky because she hurt for me, I could see it in her eyes when she looked at me. But she was also grieving for the little girl that they lost in a sense. My mom had been a tough kid, at least that's what Gram told me. She had a wild streak from the start. She got in with the wrong crowd in high school, became an escort, and hid it from them. She didn't like the house my grandparents raised her in and told them she wanted more. And she sure as hell didn't want to work for things. She wanted an easy way out. Gram said after I was born my sperm donor gave her money, and she got us a place on our own and started getting involved in drugs. Apparently, she would bring me to live with them, and then come into money and take me back and it was a vicious cycle. They finally got full custody of me in middle school, because I broke down and told them the things I was exposed to." I cleared my throat at the memory.

He pulled me closer, wrapping his arms around me tight. His chin rested on top of my head. "What kind of things?"

I heard the hesitation in his voice. I squeezed my eyes closed. I'd never talked to anyone about it aside from Gramps and Gram, and that was only because I was desperate to get away from her.

"Scary things. Creepy men. She'd take me with her to score drugs and then she'd pass out in an alley and I'd just have to sleep out there with her. But when I got to an age where her clients were interested in me, that's when it got really scary. That's when I learned to fight. One night, this guy was at our apartment and he came into my room where I was sleeping. I woke up with him on top of me, and I fought like hell to get away. I spent the night hiding outside in the bushes. That was my breaking point because I knew I wasn't safe there. I hitchhiked to my grandparents' house and told them everything. And, well, they saved me."

He squeezed me tight and let out a long breath. "You saved yourself, Harley. I'm so proud of you for knowing to get away. For not being afraid to fight and fight hard. I saw that in you the first day we met, you know. I knew you were different. Special. Even though I tried like hell to push you away."

I laughed. "You were such a jerk the day we met."

"A sexy asshole though, right?" He chuckled.

I pushed back so I could see him in the moonlight. "Thank you."

"For what?" His gaze searched mine.

"For everything." I wrapped my arms around him and nestled just beneath his chin again. It was nice to feel—safe. Cared for. I trusted this man and I had no idea why, but I liked it.

I liked him.

And that was terrifying.

fifteen

· · ·

Ford

THIS WEEK HAD BEEN a hectic one. There were a ton of political stories breaking, and I was putting out fires left and right. But Harley and I had spent every night together, and to say that it was good would be an understatement. I hadn't had an actual relationship in five years, and that paled in comparison to what I shared with this girl already. She was fire and sunshine. Strong and vulnerable. All wrapped in one beautiful little package. We talked for hours every night. I'd never wanted to talk to anyone this much before, never really cared for small talk or deep conversation with anyone outside of my family. I'd always been a man of few words, but this girl—she brought something out in me. And, the whammy of all whammies—I hadn't even had sex with her yet. I didn't know what we were waiting for. We weren't seeing anyone else and we were clearly together. Hell, I couldn't get enough of her. She'd tried to go home Wednesday night to sleep in her own bed, and I'd all but had a meltdown. I thought about her when I wasn't with her, and I was happiest when we were together. How fucked up is that?

Tonight, she was making me dinner at her place, and she'd convinced me to spend the night at her little studio apartment. I couldn't fathom why we'd sleep at her tiny place when I had a much larger space, where Helena cooked for us, and it was safe and comfortable. But Harley had a way of persuading me, and I'd given in. I had more security on her than she knew, as well as a guard set up at her grandfather's house. I knew that Damon and Valentina weren't going to give up. People like them didn't just go away. They'd force you to handle them, and I was still trying to figure out how I'd go about it.

"Here you go, it's my favorite new wine," Harley said, handing me a glass of Montgomery Vineyard Chardonnay as I sat on her couch. Her apartment smelled like basil and garlic, and my stomach rumbled.

"Thank you." I took the glass and set it on the coffee table before reaching for her and pulling her to sit on my lap. "And thanks for making me dinner. You know Helena will cook whatever you want. I know you had a long week at the bakery."

She rolled her eyes before tangling her fingers in my hair. "I like to cook. And I'm excited to have you here. I know it's small. I know it's not a palace. But it's mine. And I worked really hard for it. I want to share it with you."

She kissed me quick before pushing to her feet. She moved to the kitchen and pulled something from the oven. I glanced around the place. She was right. It was very—*her*. The small space above the dry cleaners was, well, normally it would be considered a dump. But Harley had turned it into a chic little oasis. She had a small dining table set for two, with flowers on the table and a few candles lit throughout the space. I believe this is what my mother would call cozy. I'd never been one for cozy, but being here with her, was nice. I liked it. I walked over to her bookcases and admired her collection. She had a ton of books, and they were organized by genre. She took pride in everything she had. Everything she did. And I admired it. I moved across the room, studying the photos hanging on the wall beside the front door. There were wedding pictures of a couple, which she'd told me were her grandparents. A few of her as a little girl with them as well. None of her mother.

My blood still boiled when I thought about how her mother had exposed her to shit that no kid should ever see. It infuriated me. The thought of some fucking creep climbing into her bed and having to fight him off. I tried to bury that anger, because I knew it was painful for her to share it with me, and I wanted her to tell me everything.

"Dinner's ready. Come on over and eat."

"This looks really good," I said, dropping to sit at the little table that took up residence between the living room and kitchen area.

"It's my favorite. Penne alla vodka. This was Gram's favorite sauce recipe. And, in honor of my high maintenance boyfriend, the pasta is gluten-free."

"Very thoughtful. And, Jesus, this is delicious," I said after I finished chewing.

"I'm glad you like it."

"So, we're sleeping here tonight, huh?" I asked, one brow raised.

"You're not weaseling out of it, Montgomery. It's small, but it's quaint, right? I want you to spend time at my apartment, too."

"I'm teasing. I like your apartment," I said, taking another bite. I preferred my home for obvious reasons, but there isn't much I wouldn't do for this girl.

"So, I did want to talk to you about something."

"Shoot."

"Sex."

I dropped my fork on the plate and wiped my mouth. "Do tell."

She laughed. "Well, I know I told you before that I wouldn't sleep with you because you were still seeing other women. But now, I mean, we're together, right?"

"Yes. Of course."

"So, what's the holdup?" she asked, taking a sip from her wine glass.

I barked out a laugh. "I don't know. I thought you weren't ready."

She cocked her head to the side. "Yeah, probably sharing every torrid detail of my life put a damper on the whole sex thing. But I don't want to hold back with you. I appreciate you being so patient though. I know that's not your strong suit."

We both chuckled at her words. And that was the fucking truth. I wasn't the most patient man. I wanted what I wanted, and I didn't like to wait for it. But this was different. I wanted Harley something fierce, but not unless she was ready for it. Our connection was strong, but it ran deeper than just the physical.

"Does that mean you're ready?"

Her head fell back in laughter. "Well, I didn't expect to have such a formal talk about it, but yeah, I was sort of wondering why you hadn't made a move. We've slept in the same bed for a week, and we've just kissed. Which, trust me when I tell you, I've enjoyed it. But I just want to make sure you still want more."

She had a smile on her face, but something in her eyes caused my chest to squeeze. She looked vulnerable and nervous.

I pushed to my feet and reached for her, pulling her to stand. She'd never need to ask me twice. I tossed her over my shoulder and her body shook with laughter. I gently dropped her to the bed. Her dark hair fell all around her on the white bedding. She looked like a goddamned angel.

"I want you so fucking bad I'm going out of my mind. But I know sex is something you take very seriously, so I didn't want to rush you. But I'm dying here, woman," I said, propping myself above her.

"Oh yeah?" She beamed up at me with a wicked grin.

I covered her mouth with mine and moved down her neck. Kissing her everywhere. I reached for the hem of her T-shirt and she arched her back so I could pull it over her head. I pushed the straps of her lavender lacy bra off her shoulders and exposed her perfect tits. I took one in my mouth and she moaned and tangled her fingers in my hair. I reached behind her and unclasped her bra and tossed it on the floor, moving my attention to the other breast. I couldn't get enough. I could spend hours tasting and exploring her beautiful body. I kissed my way down and unbuttoned her jeans before pausing to look up at her. She pushed up on her elbows, and the heat in her gaze nearly undid me right there. She helped me yank them down her body and I paused as I took in her matching lavender panties.

"Did you wear these for me?" I teased, tucking my fingers in the lacy fabric and moving it down her legs.

"Yeah, Montgomery." Her words were breathy and hoarse. "I only have two matching sets, which is why I've had to do laundry every night at your place because I didn't know when you'd finally make your move. I didn't want to be caught in a mismatched set." She was propped up on her elbows, completely naked, with one brow raised in challenge. Jesus. This woman would be the death of me.

"We're going to have to remedy that situation and make sure you have more matching sets than you know what to do with." I stood over her and scanned every inch of her glorious body with my eyes.

Fucking perfect.

Her head fell back with a laugh. "My point was—it took you long enough."

"Oh baby, I've been thinking about this since the day I met you in that conference room. Just didn't want to rush you." I unbuttoned my dress shirt and tugged it off my shoulders, letting it drop to the floor.

Harley moved to push up on her knees and she reached for the belt on my suit pants. She yanked it off and started to undo the button on my pants. I didn't miss the tremble in her hands. I needed to remember she hadn't done this in a long time. Hell, she hadn't done this much in her life. I never really stopped to put thought into sex. I just did it. And I was fucking good at it. But I needed to be more aware with her.

Slow.

"Hey, there's nothing to be nervous about." I covered her hands with mine, pushing my pants down my legs.

"I'm not nervous," she said, looking up at me before she tugged my boxers down and gasped when she saw how ready I was. "Okay, maybe I'm a little nervous."

I kicked out of my boxers and moved her back on the bed before settling above her. "You don't need to be. I plan on taking my time."

"Oh my god," she whispered, and I chuckled as I kissed my way down her body once again. Goose bumps covered her skin and damn if it didn't do something to me. She put on such a tough front—always so stoic, but Harley DeLuca was pure sweetness. And I'd never get enough of her.

"Ford. Please," she moaned, tugging my head back up and kissing me hard.

I pushed to stand and pulled my wallet from my pants to get a condom. I covered myself and she edged up on her elbows to watch. "I won't make you wait."

She bit down on her bottom lip, and I leaned over her again, covering her sweet mouth. I settled between her legs and pulled back to look at her one last time. She smiled and nodded before tugging my head down to kiss her again.

"I want to look at you. I want to see your face when I make you mine. When I claim you in every way."

I pushed forward, slowly. She sucked in a deep breath as I buried myself inside her. And nothing had ever felt so good. Nothing could have prepared me for this.

Pure ecstasy.

Her nails dug into my back, and we moved together. Perfectly in sync. Like we were made for one another. I took my time, relishing every moment.

We were both sweating and panting. Desperate and needy.

"You feel so good, baby."

She moaned. "Don't hold back."

"Never," I said, reaching my hand between us, finding her sweet spot.

"Ford," she cried out, and her entire body shook beneath me. I leaned down to kiss her, just as I went over the edge right along with her. A sound I'd never heard left my body. She clung to me like her life depended on it.

"Jesus," I said, lying there breathless. I moved to my feet and made my way to the bathroom, tossing the condom in the trash.

When I returned, she was lying on her side, the sheet was covering her body, and her head was propped on one elbow. Her face was flush, and she flashed me a wicked grin.

"Wow," she said, wriggling her brows.

I pushed the sheet down. I needed to see her. "Wow is fucking right."

I slipped in bed beside her and we stared at one another in silence for a few minutes.

"So that was different," she said.

"How so?" I asked, pushing her wild, dark mane of hair out of her face.

"Well, I've never, *you know*." She shrugged. So goddamn sweet.

"You've never orgasmed during sex?" I asked.

She reached for the sheet and pulled it over her head. "My god, Montgomery. You just say it, huh?"

I lifted one side of the sheet and pushed my head beneath with her. "Yeah. It's just sex. You don't need to be embarrassed. I love that I'm the first to give you that pleasure. And trust me when I tell you, it'll be your first of many. I plan on repeating this a couple more times tonight."

She reached up to stroke my hair. "I never knew it could be like this."

"That piece-of-shit Todd was clearly a selfish prick."

"Yeah. In his defense, I didn't know what I was doing. It was always just quick. Not very intimate. Not like this," she said, and her dark browns locked with mine.

"Trust me, you don't need to know what you're doing for it to be enjoyable. He was just an asshole. You're already a pro." I kissed her as we huddled beneath the sheet.

And within minutes we were back at it.

Because now that I'd had a taste of Harley DeLuca, I'd never get enough.

———

It was the first Sunday in August, which meant brunch at my mother's. The first of every month, no matter what, we always dropped what we were doing to get together. And this time I'd be bringing my girlfriend along with me. Harley agreed to take the helicopter so we could have more time in bed and skip the long drive.

"It's so pretty here. I bet it was a fun place to grow up," she said as we made our way up the driveway to my mother's house. The house I'd grown up in.

"Yeah. We were always getting in trouble."

I pushed the door open, and Jack rounded the corner.

"Harls," he shouted, lifting my girlfriend off the ground, and spinning her around. Her long floral dress fluttered around her.

I rolled my eyes. "Put her down."

"So protective. I love this side of you, brother."

Harley settled back on her feet, and I intertwined my fingers with hers. I'd never been one for public displays of affection, but something about her brought out a different side of me. I didn't give a shit what anyone thought. I wanted her with me. Beside me. All the fucking time.

"Sweetheart, I'm so happy you're here," Mom said, pulling Harley in for a hug.

"Thank you so much for having me. Your home is gorgeous."

"Thank you. Ford can give you the tour. Come on in, Harrison's making mimosas." My mother led the way.

"Har-bears got a girl here, and I think the shit is about to hit the fan," Jack whispered so only Harley and I could hear him.

It wasn't unusual for my brothers to bring women to brunch. I never had, because I never stuck around long enough to have breakfast with anyone in the past.

"Who is it?" I kept my voice low.

"Zoe."

"Zoe Baron?"

"The one and only."

"I thought you hooked up with her a few months ago? Didn't she lose her shit on you?" I asked.

"Yep. And I never told Harrison about it, because I know he thinks she's hot. I'm pretty sure she ran into him last night and purposely got herself invited today. I've been sort of avoiding her these last few months and I think she's pissed. She glared at me when they arrived, making sure no one saw her do it. She's got something up her sleeve. And if Har-bear hooked up with her last night, he's going to kill me."

"Jesus. Can you not keep your dick in your pants for five fucking minutes?" I hissed, and Harley chuckled.

"Dude, she was the one who hit on me that night. I'm only human. But Harrison isn't going to be happy, so I've got to tell him before this goes any further," he said nervously as we entered the large great room.

Harrison stood behind the bar, and we beelined his way.

"Hey, so glad you're here." He came around and hugged my girlfriend before giving me a half-hug.

Harley smiled. "Happy to be here."

"Where's Zoe?" Jack asked, his gaze scanning the room.

"She's in the bathroom."

"Dude. We need to talk," Jack said, reaching for a mimosa, tipping his head back and chugging the entire glass.

Just then Zoe returned from the restroom. "Ford, hey, long time no see."

"Fuck," Jack mumbled under his breath, and I shoved him out of the way and gave Zoe a hug.

"Good to see you. This is my girlfriend, Harley."

"Nice to meet you," they both said in unison and laughed.

Mom called us to come to the dining room, and we took our seats at the long oval table. Harrison sat beside Zoe, my mother was at the head of the table and Jack, Harley, and I sat on the other side across from them.

Lorena and Celine brought out platters of food. Scrambled eggs, waffles, bacon, sausage, yogurt, and fresh fruit. We started passing the food around the table, and my mom asked Harley all about the bakery. Conversation flowed, but Jack remained quiet. Which was a rarity in itself.

"So, Zoe, it's nice to see you. It's been a while," my mother said as she scooped some fruit onto her plate.

"Thank you, it's a pleasure to see you as well. It was a nice surprise to run into Harrison last night, and I asked about you all, and he was kind enough to extend the invitation to me today."

"What have you been up to?" Mom asked.

"Well, after your youngest son took me to bed, and then called me by the wrong name the following morning even though we've known one another *our entire lives*—I've been pretty busy."

Jack coughed and spit a mouthful of mimosa across the table. Harley fell over in a fit of laughter, and Harrison's mouth hung open as he glared at our baby brother.

"You didn't want to mention this last night when we spoke?" Harrison asked Zoe.

"Nah. I thought it would be more fun this way. He's avoided me ever since, and I figured Monica would want to know what her son had been up to. I mean, at the very least, he could have apologized."

"So, you came here to tattle on me?" Jack shouted as he tried to wipe up his mess on the table. My mother sat perfectly quiet as she watched the scene play out in front of her.

"Damn straight, *Jack ass*. Pun intended, by the way."

"For the record, I avoided you because you called me an asshole and kicked me out of your house. Quite frankly—you scare the shit out of me."

"You forgot my goddamn name." She pushed to her feet and shouted.

"How many times do I have to tell you that I'm not good with names." Jack threw his hands in the air. The dude didn't have a mean bone in his body, but he managed to fuck up often.

Zoe chucked her napkin in Jack's face and turned to my mother. "Sorry for the drama, Monica. Thanks for having me. I'll see you soon."

"I'm sorry that my son was so disrespectful, Zoe. I assure you it's not something I'm proud of," Mom said, shooting a glare at Jack. I couldn't help but laugh. The little asshole got away with murder most of the time. It was nice to see him sweat every once in a while.

"Sorry Harrison. I should have been honest. But I couldn't let that little weasel get away with it," Zoe said, giving Harrison a hug.

I continued to eat, because in all honesty, this wasn't all that odd for a Sunday brunch at the homestead. Shit always went down when we all got together. Harley was watching with pure fascination and I reached for her hand under the table.

"Yeah. A heads-up would have been nice. But Jack's at fault here," he said.

"Hey. The weasel can hear you," Jack shouted, following Zoe out of the room.

"Well, that was interesting," Mom said, and we all burst out in laughter.

"I should have known something was up. The girl has never given me the time of day, and she pushed really hard to come to brunch." Harrison snatched some bacon off the plate.

"Har-bear, I fucked up. How pissed are you on a scale of one to ten?" Jack said when he waltzed back in the dining room.

Harrison rolled his eyes. "Whatever, dude. You should have just told me. But I'm glad I didn't hook up with her."

"Sorry, Mom," Jack said, moving to stand behind our mother. He leaned over her chair and hugged her, tossing a wink at my girlfriend.

Conniving bastard.

"You need to do better, Jackie boy. It's not okay. Zoe's a nice girl." Mom reached her hand back to pat his cheek.

"Welcome to the shit show, Harls," Jack said when he returned to his seat.

Harley laughed and squeezed my hand beneath the table. "This is the most entertaining brunch I've ever been to."

Harley laughed as Jack tried to win her sympathy, and Harrison joked about getting a pity hug. And just like that, my girl was a part of this family. She fit right in here.

She fit perfectly everywhere.

sixteen

. . .

Harley

THE NEXT FEW weeks were a whirlwind. Ford and I were together in every sense of the word. I'd never had a relationship like this. Overpowering and all-consuming. I missed him when I wasn't with him, which was crazy. We both worked long hours, and we spent every free hour together. We talked about everything. He convinced me to stay at his place most nights, but every once in a while we'd spend the night at my studio. But truth be told, his bathtub sold me on the place. I swam in it every night. Ford usually drank a glass of wine and sat beside the tub while I bathed, but he promised to get in there with me one of these days.

The morning rush was over, and Molly and I were cleaning up when the door chimed. I looked up to see the woman I'd met a few months ago that I'd thought was on a date with Ford.

"Chanel, hey, nice to see you again," I said. I knew how important she and her family were to Ford, and I looked forward to getting to know all of them.

"Hi there. I thought I'd stop by and say hello, and maybe snag a few cookies while I'm here." She laughed. The weather was getting chillier as fall was on its way, and she wore a thin black sweater, and black fitted dress slacks. She was the epitome of elegance. Her blonde hair was pulled back in a classic chignon, and her sky-high heels made me feel short in comparison.

Molly came out and I introduced them and let her know my best friend was currently applying to law school. Chanel offered for her to come check out her office, and Molly fluttered off excitedly. I grabbed Chanel a bag of cookies and joined her at one of our quaint little tables.

"I hear you've kind of tamed the beast," she teased, reaching in the bag and moaning when she took her first bite.

I chuckled. "I don't know about that, but we're having fun."

"I can't even get him on the calendar now. I asked him if we could all go to dinner a few times, but he seems to want you all to himself." A warm smile spread across her face. "It's good to see Ford happy."

My heart raced at her words. I was trying to keep myself reined in as this was all happening so fast. My feelings were strong where this man was concerned, and as happy as that made me, it also terrified the hell out of me. I didn't like depending on others. Nor did I want to need anyone. Life always got tricky when you put all your eggs in one basket. I'd learned that at a young age with my mother.

"That's nice to hear. And I'd love to go to dinner sometime soon. I'm looking forward to meeting everyone at the big fundraiser at the winery next month. Ford speaks so highly of your family. I know your dad really stepped up for him when he lost his father. I'm looking forward to getting to know you all," I said honestly. Ford had met my grandfather twice now, as we'd gone out to see him and taken him to lunch. And though I knew the Montgomerys pretty well, Chanel's family was a big part of his life too.

"That's perfect. It's such a fun event. Wait until you see it. No one throws a party quite like Monica Montgomery," she said.

"Yeah, Ford said it's pretty formal." I chewed on my fingernail, as I would have to find something to wear, and those events always made me a little uncomfortable.

"Yes, ma'am. Everyone is dressed to the nines. It's going to be loads of fun," she said, reaching in her bag for another cookie.

"So, I hear you've got a big case you're working on." Ford had shared that Chanel was a prominent attorney, and she worked at the hottest firm in town. She'd attended Harvard Law, and according to my boyfriend, she was a force to be reckoned with.

"Yep. And some of the old men at the firm are not happy about it. But they can suck it. I've sort of put a big gaping hole in their little boys' club, you know?"

I laughed. "Good for you. You're paving the way for all women."

Nobody loved girl power more than me, and Chanel was a badass woman. I was happy to see that we'd get on really well.

"Amen, sister. Let's get together soon. I need to get back to the office, but I'll look forward to spending some time with you at the event in Napa. And let's bully your boyfriend into sharing you with the rest of us sometime soon."

"You got it," I said, pushing to my feet as a few customers walked through the door.

She leaned over and gave me a hug before leaving.

The rest of the day was business as usual. DeLiciously Yours was swamped all afternoon. Ford texted me between meetings and tried to convince me to run upstairs and see him, but I'd yet to find a break in my day.

I pulled some dough from the fridge and started to roll out a few batches of butter cookies for tomorrow. Molly grabbed a big hunk of dough and jumped to sit on the counter.

"Damn. Who knew working at a bakery was so much work?" she said as she scrolled through her phone.

"Exactly. That's why you need to wear tennis shoes, girl. You keep trying to pull off these cute shoes."

"Hey, it's almost Fall. The booties are all the rage. I've just got to break these babies in a little." Molly held her leg up to show me her cute heeled boot.

"Fashion is overrated when you're on your feet all day. You're going to need to help me find an outfit to wear to this big fundraiser in Napa. Apparently, it's pretty swanky."

"Done. You know how much I love to dress you. You clean up well, kid," she said and we both laughed. "Ooh, look who's trending on social media."

I glanced over my shoulder to see Molly hold her phone up for me as I read the caption: *San Francisco's sexiest bachelor is off the market.* I rolled my eyes. I didn't pay much attention to any of that stuff, but I'd noticed photographers a few times when Ford and I had been out, but he always managed to shield me. We usually went back to his place, or my place, so we hadn't been out in public all that much. But apparently word travels fast.

"Harls, listen to this. It's from one of those online entertainment sites." Molly used her best haughty voice as she read, "Sorry, ladies of San Francisco, but Ford Montgomery, president of Montgomery Media and heir to the Montgomery fortune was asked recently if he was still an eligible bachelor when we caught him outside of a downtown lingerie shop. He told us he was very much off the market. Inquiring minds want to know. Who is this mystery woman he's shopping for?"

My cheeks burned pink. Ford had bought me a few matching sets of panties and bras a few weeks ago.

"Oh my gosh, these people are such creepers."

"You're avoiding the topic at hand. Is someone getting gifted lingerie?" she teased, and I turned my attention back to the cookie dough on the table.

"He bought me a few bras. It's not a big deal."

She hopped down and came around to stand by me. "I'm happy for you, Harls. It's nice to see you like this."

"Like what?" I rolled my eyes when I looked up to meet her sappy gaze.

"Less bitter and angry. Lighter. Happier."

I nodded with a laugh. "Well, at least you 're honest."

"You guys are pretty serious, huh?"

"I guess. We don't really talk about it. I mean, we're dating, and we spend a lot of time together."

"But, do you loooooove him?" She grabbed my cheeks and forced me to look at her.

"Oh my gosh, stop being weird. We're good. We don't say that." I shook my face free and pounded the hell out of the dough. I'd never thrown that word around lightly. Sure, I said it to Gramps, Gram, and Molly. And Todd had said it to me a few times over the two years we dated, and I'd always nodded and given him a "me too" as a lame answer. It's just not something I'd ever felt before for a guy.

"I didn't ask if you've said it, I asked if you love him. You know it's okay if you do. No one is going to think you're weak."

Damn, my best friend knew me well.

"Well, I'm certainly not going to say it first." I shrugged.

"I knew it," she shrieked, and I wouldn't be surprised if the glass windows shattered in the dining room.

"Take it down a notch," I said just as the door chimed.

"Damn these sugar addicts. We're closed," Molly said as she peeked out to see who was there and Harrison and Jack came waltzing into the kitchen.

"Tell me all the peanut butter cookies aren't gone," Jack said, helping himself to a hunk of dough.

"Come on. You can pick what you want before we put the rest away for the night."

Jack followed Molly out to the front room and Harrison leaned against the wall and smiled.

"What's up? You heading to Napa now?" I asked.

"Yeah. But Jack needed a treat for the short helicopter ride." He shook his head.

I laughed. "I've never seen anyone consume more baked goods and never gain so much as a pound."

"Yeah. It's his freakish metabolism." He chuckled. "So, you and Ford are doing well, huh?"

"What? Yeah, sure," I said, feeling my face heat again. Sheesh. Everyone was inquiring about him today.

He barked out a laugh. "Damn, you guys are perfect for one another. You're both so fucking stoic and private. I just wanted to thank you."

"Thank me for what?" I asked, wiping my hands on my apron and studying him.

"For bringing my brother back to life. I'm seeing the old Ford again and it's nice." He ruffled the top of my hair and kissed my cheek.

I bit the inside of my cheek and let the words sink in. He'd brought me to life as well. But it wasn't the old me, it was the new me. I was happy. Truly happy. For the first time in as long as I could remember. Maybe forever. I wasn't worrying about tomorrow. I was embracing today. And that was because of Ford. Seeing myself through his eyes had given me this new confidence.

"Well, he's done the same for me," I said, looking away when I felt my face burning red.

He pulled me in for a hug. "No shame in that, Harls. You both deserve it."

"Why is it that every time you and Jack are around, one of you has my girl wrapped in your arms," Ford said, trying to hide his smile as he walked in.

Harrison pulled away and Ford came around the counter and wrapped his arms around me. My back to his chest. "I missed you today."

I laughed. It had been a few hours. But the truth was—I missed him too. It wasn't normal. "I missed you too."

"I've heard it all now," Harrison bellowed.

"What's going on?" Jack asked.

"Apparently, these two can't go a whole workday without seeing one another." Harrison snatched a cookie from Jack's bag.

"I love it," Molly shouted.

"Me too, Molls," Jack said, shaking his head with a ridiculous smile spread across his face.

"Goodbye. I hear the helicopter from here. Time to go," Ford said, resting his chin on my head, while his arms held me close.

"No shame in being crazy about your girl, dude. We're leaving." Harrison kissed my cheek.

Molly grabbed her purse. "Oooh, let's give them some privacy. Word's out that the sexiest bachelor is off the market."

"Hey, I take offense to that. I'm the sexiest bachelor around," Jack said, wrapping his arms around Ford and me and shaking us for unknown reasons. I couldn't help but laugh. Ford slapped him away.

"You two can fight it out for hottest bachelor now that I'm off the market."

They both flipped him the bird and agreed to walk Molly to her car.

"You ready to get out of here?" he asked once they were gone.

"Yeah, I'm exhausted. Let me just put this away."

"Helena left us dinner. I asked her to make ramen," he said as he helped me clean up and put everything away.

"Look at you, Montgomery. You're a regular carb addict now. You're welcome." When I flipped the lights off, he reached for my bicep and stopped me.

"You ever do it in a bakery?" he whispered against my ear, sending chill bumps across my skin.

"Well seeing as I barely *did it* much before meeting you, I think it's safe to say no." I laughed, but when I turned and my gaze locked with his in the dim lighting, I didn't miss the heat in his eyes.

Before I knew what was happening, he lifted me off my feet. My legs wrapped around his waist instinctively. He walked me into the storage closet off the kitchen and shut and locked the door. He pressed me up against the wall and his hands were on my ass.

"Never been so thankful for these little skirts you wear," he said, his voice gruff.

I tangled my hands in his hair and pulled his mouth to mine. He undid his pants and pulled back to use his teeth to tear open the condom. I couldn't help but laugh at his eagerness.

"You're quite the multitasker, Montgomery."

"You think it's funny, do you?" He reached down and tugged my panties to the side before thrusting forward and covering my mouth with his at the same time. I moaned when he started to move—he had one hand on each hip and shifted us together in perfect rhythm. We were in sync. And nothing had ever felt better. He took his time, and I dug my nails into his back. Wanting more. He picked up the pace— both of us panting and ready.

I screamed out his name with my release and he groaned as he followed me right over the edge.

We cleaned ourselves up and met Jerome out front to head to Ford's place. I was so tired, I dozed off on his shoulder during the short ride home. We made our way up to his penthouse and Ford told me he'd started a bath for me, and he'd be right back. The man kept surprising me with his thoughtfulness.

"This was sweet of you," I said from the tub as he walked in holding two glasses of wine.

"Don't give me too much credit. It's as much a gift for me as it is for you. I get to watch." He wriggled his brows and handed me a glass.

I laughed and took a sip before setting it beside the tub. "So, you're off the market, huh?"

"I told you that weeks ago. Are you surprised that I'm not afraid to say it when I'm asked?" He'd taken off his suit coat and tie, and his dress shirt was unbuttoned some, and he looked sexy as hell. His hair was disheveled, and his sapphire blues locked with mine.

"No, I mean, not really. I'm just surprised people ask or care."

"It's outside noise. I'm used to it. But if they ask, I'm going to answer honestly," he said, holding up a towel when I pushed to my feet.

He wrapped me up and tossed me over his shoulder. "Oh my god. What are you doing? Montgomery, put me down."

He settled my feet on the floor and thrust a thumb at the bed. The prettiest pink, lacy bra and panty set was there along with a pair of pink Chucks. My favorite tennis shoes. And I knew he hated them, yet he'd gotten them for me because he knew I loved them.

"Surprised?"

I bit the inside of my cheek and fought back the tears threatening to escape. He watched me with concern, and I pushed up on my tiptoes and held a finger to his lips so he would let me speak.

"I love you, Ford Montgomery," I said, my voice shook as two tears ran down my cheek.

He placed a hand on each side of my face and used his thumbs to swipe the tears away. "I love you too, baby."

He pulled me close and wrapped me in his arms.

I'd said it.

And he'd said it back.

But most importantly… I felt it.

I felt it everywhere.

seventeen

. . .

Ford

EDWARD STOPPED by my office as I'd asked for an update on Harley's mother and Damon. I'd been watching them closely ever since they'd tried to meet her at her grandfather's house. I knew Damon was a dangerous dude, and guys like him didn't go away easily. I hadn't figured out yet how to play it. I'd considered giving him money to keep him the fuck away from Harley, but I knew I'd just be starting something that would have no ending. So, for now, I'd make sure that Harley and her grandfather had security round the clock, and I'd just keep an eye out for Damon. Hell, Harley was either at work or with me, so they weren't going to get to her without a fight. Maybe they knew that. But my gut told me they were still waiting in the wings.

Sick fuckers.

"What's up?" I asked as he dropped to sit in the chair across from me.

"No movement from either of them. I mean, she's out on the streets doing her thing, but neither has made a move to come near Harley or her grandfather. But that doesn't mean they won't. So, we just stay the course."

"Fuck. I need eyes on her at all times. They want her, because they think there's money there. Her grandfather is just a pawn to get to her."

"It's done. I've got Calvin outside the bakery, seeing who comes and goes at all times. And then we've got our security team on both of you when you're home."

"Good work. Keep me posted if there's any change."

"Always," he said, knocking on my desk with his knuckles before leaving.

I was returning a few emails when someone knocked on the door.

"It's open," I said.

Harrison and Jack walked in and they were both dripping wet.

"Hey, we're heading to Napa. You need anything before we leave?" Jack asked with a bag of cookies in his hand.

"Dude, do you ever stay out of that bakery?"

"What can I say? I'm a sucker for her treats." He wriggled his brows and I rolled my eyes.

"Why are you soaking wet?"

"Because it's raining fucking cats and dogs right now, and Harrison insisted on going for a walk, and I followed him."

"He's leaving out the fact that I told him I wanted to go by myself." Harrison shrugged and crossed his arms over his chest.

"What's with you?" I asked, lifting my chin in Harrison's direction. The guy looked like someone ran over his puppy.

Jack leaned forward, dripping water from his hair onto my desk, and whispered louder than most people spoke, "He's upset. Did you see the paper today?"

I shook my head, and Jack handed me his phone. Shit. I didn't pay much attention to the engagement announcements in the paper, but I shouldn't have missed this one.

Laney Mae Landers and Charles Oliver Cunningham announce their engagement.

"Fuck, Harrison, I'm sorry. Is this how you found out? In the paper?" I asked, knowing how much this news would hurt him.

"Yeah. It's fine. I'm happy for her."

"No, you're not," I said, rolling my eyes.

Our middle brother rarely got pissed off. He'd always been in control of his anger. I admired it most of the time, but other times I worried for him. It wasn't healthy to tamp everything down. The dude was bound to explode at some point. And if anyone could bring that out of him, it was Laney Mae.

"I'd have thought she'd call you herself," Jack said with a shrug.

"She doesn't owe me anything. I broke her heart, and she moved on. Like I asked her to. Can't fault her for that."

I studied him. He was as even-keeled as our father had been, but even Dad had his breaking point. Laney Mae was Harrison's. The Landers had lived down the street from us since we were young, and he and Laney Mae had been the best of friends since they were in kindergarten. She'd been a permanent fixture at our house throughout the years and ended up being the love of his life—but he'd walked away from her after Dad died. And I knew it had been his biggest regret, but he was too stubborn to admit it. Instead, he put on a brave face, acting like everything was fine. I always thought they'd find their way back to one another, but my brother had been going through the motions these past few years, sort of like the rest of us had. He'd thrown himself into work.

"Fuck that. She should have told you," I said. I didn't have a bad word to say about Laney Mae. She was one of the best people I knew, and she'd always adored my brother. But I still thought she should have told him herself. They had a history.

"It's fine. Stop making this a big deal. We need to get out of here." Harrison pushed to his feet.

"Is no one going to mention the elephant in the room?" Jack popped a cookie in his mouth as he spoke.

"What the hell are you talking about?" Harrison said, not hiding his irritation.

"*Charles Oliver Cunningham*… come on," Jack said with a smirk. "The dude's initials spell out cock. What does that tell you? He's a fucking cock."

I tried to cover my mouth before all three of us burst out in laughter. Jack had a gift for lightening the moment. And Harrison needed to laugh right now. He might be saying he was fine, but Jack and I knew better.

"That's rich. But I like it," Harrison said, pulling the door open. "Seriously. I'm done talking about it. It is what it is."

"Okay," I said, knowing this was not the last time we'd be discussing it. But we could be done with it for today.

"Later." My youngest brother paused at the door. "Give that girl of yours a big hug from me."

I rolled my eyes. "Hey, Jack."

"Yeah," he said, pausing in the doorway as Harrison had already turned to leave.

"Call me later and let me know how he is. I think this is a bigger deal than he's letting on."

"Agreed. Call you tonight."

I sat back in my chair as my phone rang.

"Yeah," I said to my assistant on the other end.

"Your three o'clock is here. Shall I bring them to the conference room?"

"Yep. I'll be right there."

I shot a quick text to my mom to let her know about Laney Mae. Harrison had a home in Napa, as he spent more time there. Jack had an apartment in the city right up the street from me, but he stayed with Mom at the house in Napa often too. I wanted her to be aware. Keep an eye on him.

A text came through as I pushed to my feet.

Harley ~ Hey. Just saw your brothers. I think something's off with Harrison. I can't put my finger on it, but he seemed distracted. Just wanted to give you a heads-up. Sorry I couldn't come up today. I've been swamped.

Damn. She knew my brothers well. I fucking loved it. Loved how she fit into my family so well.

Me ~ Yeah. I'm heading into a meeting. Good instincts, baby. I'll fill you in at dinner. Ramen sound good? Love you.

Harley ~ Yes. Your carb game is strong, Montgomery. Love you.

I laughed before slipping my phone in my suit coat and stepping in the conference room.

———

When I finished my meeting, Sam stood outside the door. She whispered so only I could hear, "Um, we have a little situation."

"What?" I kept my voice low as our clients waved and made their way to the elevators.

"Blaire Wilson is at the reception desk and she's refusing to leave until you see her."

Jesus. I'd ignored a few of her texts. I'd meant to give her a call and let her know that things had changed, but I just hadn't felt like dealing with it. I figured she'd get the message and would stop trying.

"Fuck. Send her back."

"Got it."

I settled behind my desk and tried to figure out what I'd say. She'd never come to my office before, so this was new. We didn't have enough of a relationship to justify an actual breakup speech. We fucked every couple weeks. And now we didn't. What more is there to really say?

The door swung open and Sam stood behind Blaire with wide eyes, before pulling the door closed. Blaire was an attractive woman by most standards. Tall. Lean. Blonde. With an oversized rack and an ass that matched. But I wasn't interested. And all we'd ever shared was sex— so there wasn't much I could say.

"What the fuck, Ford. You just don't respond to my texts anymore?" she hissed, tightening the belt on her trench coat. Her hair managed to stay dry, but that didn't surprise me. The woman would never actually walk in the rain, nor have a hair out of place. She probably had her driver pull up and shield her with an umbrella for the two steps she took into the building.

"Listen, Blaire, I'm sorry I didn't respond. I've been meaning to call you." I used my hands to form a teepee on my desk. "I'm seeing someone."

Her brows cinched, yet her forehead remained completely still. "I've seen some talk of that on social media, but I'm not really sure what it has to do with anything?"

She wasn't going to make this easy. "What am I not making clear? I'm seeing someone. Whatever you and I had going is—done."

Her smile appeared forced. "So, you think you're the first one to meet someone else? I've had boyfriends over the years, Ford. That didn't change what we shared."

Shit. I had no idea she'd been in relationships, as I'd assumed we were both in the same place. "Okay. I didn't realize that. But the relationship that I'm in, well, it's monogamous."

She chuckled. It was condescending and bitchy, but I'd let her pitch a fit if that meant we could be done with this. "And how's that working for you?"

"Really well, actually." I pushed to my feet. I was done with this conversation.

She remained seated. "So, what does this mean? You're in love with her? You actually expect me to believe that?"

"I don't give a shit what you believe if I'm being honest. But yes, I love her."

She pushed to her feet in a huff and yanked at the belt on her jacket, opening up to show me her red lace panties and bra, which matched her sky-high red heels.

"Christ. Close that up. This isn't happening. Don't embarrass yourself. It's over. I don't know how to make this any more clear for you. You need to leave." I moved toward the door, just as it flew open.

"Surprise," Harley said, holding a box in her hand. Her face hardened as she looked past me and dropped the box to the floor. I turned to see Blaire standing there, jacket wide open with an evil smile spread across her face.

"Yeah. Surprise." Blaire said, cocking her head to the side.

"This is not what it looks like," I said, but before the words were even out of my mouth Harley took off.

"Call me if things change, Ford," Blaire said, but I was already halfway out the door. I took the stairs down as the elevator doors had already closed.

I was panting when I got to the lobby, and the thunder from outside startled me. I hurried to the bakery and Molly stood there shrugging and pointing at the door leading out to the street. Jesus. It was dumping, and she'd taken off on foot.

"Harley," I shouted, shielding my eyes to see her up ahead. The sky was gray, and the rain came down hard and fast. Calvin was already trailing her, and I told him to head back to the bakery.

I caught up to her and wrapped my fingers around her bicep. "Baby, you need to stop. Let me explain."

"Explain what, Montgomery? Why some chick was practically naked in your office," she hissed.

Her long, wet ponytail swung back and forth, and her white T-shirt stuck to her body like a second skin. Her perky tits were on full display and I adjusted myself beneath my zipper so I could focus. Hell, I'd just had a woman throw herself at me half naked, and it did nothing to me. But a pissed off, soaked, Harley DeLuca made me hard on the spot.

"She just showed up. I haven't seen her in months. Not since you and I started dating. I told her about you, and that what she and I had was done because I'm in love with you. That's when she jumped up and opened her coat. Did you happen to notice I was at the door when you burst through. I had just asked her to leave."

She swiped at the hair that had broken free of her elastic and was sticking to her face. Her dark eyes searing through the rain as they studied me.

"How do I know you're telling me the truth?" She crossed her arms over her chest.

"Because I don't lie. I also spend every fucking free minute I have with you. If I didn't want this," I motioned my hand between us. "I wouldn't be chasing your ass out in the rain. I love you."

She sighed. "I love you too. I just—I don't know. I saw red when I walked in. Literally and figuratively, of course, because she was wearing those little scraps of red."

I pulled her up against my body and wrapped a hand around her waist with a chuckle. "I only want you. And you did once tell me that I should walk in the rain. I guess we've checked that off the list now."

She shielded her eyes with her hand. "Sorry for storming out of there."

"I wouldn't tolerate any man trying to pursue you, so I get it."

She pushed up on her tiptoes and kissed me. I pulled her closer, tangling my hand in her hair. Angling her so I could take the kiss deeper. She jumped up and wrapped her legs around my waist. And we stood out in the pouring rain and kissed in the middle of the busiest street in the city.

And it was fucking perfect.

eighteen

. . .

Harley

WE WERE HAVING our busiest day since I'd opened the bakery. Maybe it was because fall was here, and everyone wanted a warm drink and a treat now. I checked my phone quickly as it was the first break we'd had all day.

Ford ~ Baby, come up and see me. I miss you. Have you ever done it in an office?

Me ~ Miss you too. Can't get away, we're swamped today. And no… but let's rectify that.

Ford ~ The sooner the better. Love you.

Me ~ So sappy, Montgomery. Love you, too.

Ford ~ Only sappy for you.

Me ~ Get back to work. I'll see you tonight. xo

"Holy crap, that was a crazy lunch rush," Molly said as she dropped down in the chair while I wiped down the tables.

"I know. I can't wait to see how we did when we close out the register. It was nonstop today. So, we may get a late afternoon crowd in here like we did the last few days, but I have that meeting for the wedding cake in five minutes. Can you cover the counter while I meet with her? It shouldn't be too crazy. If it gets bad, I'll just tell her I need to help you."

"No worries at all. I can handle a small crowd. And this is your first wedding cake order. Are you excited?" she asked, pushing to her feet to move behind the counter.

"Yeah, I think so. A little nervous. But I've been on Pinterest looking at designs and I have a book of photos to show her to get an idea of what she wants." I moved to the back to get my binder as a group of women stepped inside. The wind whipped around until they pulled the door closed.

"Wow. It's getting nasty out there," the tall, blonde woman said, patting her hair back in place.

Molly waited on them as another lady stepped inside. She looked at me for a moment before speaking. "Harley?"

"Yes, are you Sadie?" I asked.

Her black hair was pulled back in a short ponytail and she looked a bit disheveled, which I figured was due to the wind. She tucked her hair behind her ears. "Yes. Nice to meet you."

I walked her over to the table in the back of the bakery so we would have some privacy. "Okay, well I have a ton of pictures to show you, and if you don't like any of these designs, I thought maybe you could tell me what you have in mind and I can try to sketch it."

She looked around, taking in the crowd. A few more people walked in, but Molly had it handled.

"You guys are busy, huh?" she said, glancing out the window at the street.

"Yeah. I think the cooler weather has people craving something sweet," I teased, opening my binder to show her the pictures.

She leaned forward, coming a little closer than expected. "Harley, I need you to remain very calm. The way you react will make or break if your grandfather lives or dies."

Her tone was calm, but her gray eyes were wild. I tried to control my breathing as my pulse spiked. "What? Who are you?"

I kept my expression even, but I was anything but.

She plastered a fake smile on her face, obviously aware that people might notice if she were threatening me. She held up her phone, and there on her screen was a photo of my grandfather with my mother. He was tied to a chair. He had a cut across his forehead, and he was wearing pajamas. When had they taken him? How long had he been there?

"Your mother was able to get him out of the house unnoticed during the night. But we had to wait until we knew we could get you out of here. So, you need to listen carefully, or things will go very bad for him." A smile remained plastered on her face, as if we were discussing wedding cakes and baked goods, not the kidnapping of Gramps.

I wiped my sweaty palms on my skirt, and my legs shook beneath the table. The thought of anyone hurting him destroyed me.

A weird croak left my mouth when I spoke. "Please don't hurt him."

She glanced around the bakery and smiled. "No. No tears. Not here. Listen and listen carefully. They're timing us. There is a short window to get you out of here. Your security has a shift change at four o'clock. That's in three minutes. There's going to be a diversion right then, and we're going to slip right out the door in a car that will pull up at the curb."

"Okay," I said, wiping my nose with the back of my hand.

"You're going to need to put on a brave face, Harley. Because if we get caught, he's done. Damon will have no problem hurting your grandfather, do you hear me?"

"Yes."

"Okay. Put a smile on your face and tell your friend that you have to go meet your boyfriend real quick. She'll buy that. There are enough people in here that she won't pay attention. And then we'll walk right out the door. Don't look at anyone or speak to anyone, you got it?"

"Hey," Molly approached the table and I nearly fell out of my seat.

"Oh my gosh, sorry, you scared me." I tried to force a laugh.

"Just dropping off some cookies and wanted to see if you guys chose a design yet." She set the plate down between us.

"Yes. Um, we've got it narrowed down to a few. I'll show you a little bit later. I need to run something up to Ford after we finish up here, okay?"

Someone called out to her, and she waved. "No problem. I've got this. Can't wait to see what you choose, Sadie."

"Thank you. I'm excited." The devil sitting across from me flashed a big smile.

"Well done. It's time." She typed something into her phone and pushed to her feet. As someone walked into the bakery, we stepped out. "Keep your head down."

And just like that, I was in the back of a car. The door shut behind me and we pulled away from the curb. Sadie sat beside me in the back seat. A large man sat on the other side of me, making me feel claustrophobic. I was sandwiched between them and I had no idea where they were taking me. I knew better than to get in the car. It was never going to end well if you agreed to do what your captor was asking. This was Abduction 101. But I had no choice in this situation. They had Gramps. They knew I'd come. Because I'd always come if he needed me.

"Give me your phone," Sadie said, handing it to the man beside me.

Ford and Molly could both track my location from my phone. It was my only hope that they'd be able to find me. Dead or alive, they'd at least know where I was. He put the window down and tossed it from the moving car. I looked over at him, and his hard stare sent a chill down my spine.

"You're doing well, Harley. We're almost there," the woman said.

"Where are you taking me?"

"No speaking," the man said, and he held up a roll of duct tape in warning. I needed to keep my wits about me. The goal was to get Gramps and me out in one piece.

I studied the streets in case I'd need to escape. I wanted to know where I was. Why wouldn't they have blindfolded me? My only thought was that they didn't intend on letting me go. This was a one-way trip. I pushed the thought away and continued to look out at the road, when we turned down a side street I'd never been on. We drove to the end and pulled off onto a dirt lot. A small house sat in the distance. It looked like something you'd see in a creepy movie, but this was real. This was actually happening. I didn't have my baseball bat to fight anyone off. I didn't have my phone to tell anyone where I was. I was in deep shit.

Remain calm.

Think.

They wanted something, so they'd have to keep me alive long enough to get it. I needed to remember that. Leverage it.

We pulled up close to the house, and the man yanked me from the car by the arm, causing me to lose my footing as he dragged me toward the porch. He pushed the door open, and I gasped. Gramps was tied to a chair, dried blood across his forehead, and his tear-streaked face nearly broke me. I shook free from the goon and rushed to Gramps.

"You shouldn't have come, my girl," he whimpered.

"I knew she'd come," my mother said. She and Damon were sitting in two chairs across the room, smoking cigarettes. She looked as battered as Gramps, so she'd obviously taken a beating herself. But if you choose to run with these people, that's to be expected. She'd dragged Gramps and me into her shit. Per usual. But the stakes were higher now. These people weren't messing around. They weren't just going to knock us around a little and take our money. Ford would have everyone in the city looking for me in a few hours. Damon knew that. And he'd put a lot of thought into this, so I didn't see us just walking away. And how long would it take before Ford and Molly realized I was actually missing? We could be dead by then.

"How could you sink this low?" I asked my mother. My lip betrayed me when it quivered as I tried to get the words out. I hunched on the floor beside Gramps, covering his bound hands with mine.

"Shut the fuck up," Damon said, moving to his feet and charging me. He kicked me in the gut hard. I doubled over and vomited as I fell forward.

I heard Gramps cry out. I stayed down, trying to think of any way to get out of here. Sadie and the man that had been in the car with me both took a seat on the filthy couch. I tried to make out where I was, and the best I could come up with was that this was some sort of drug den. There was an old ratty orange and yellow couch and a card table with folding chairs. A man that I'd never seen before, paced the room. He was gaunt and missing teeth.

"So, what the fuck's the plan, Damon?" he asked.

"Shut up, Stick. I know what I'm doing."

"Then let's get on with it," my mother said, and I looked up and locked my gaze with hers. Her eyes were dead. All the life gone. And she wouldn't do anything to stop Damon from hurting Gramps or me. We were completely on our own. I pushed to sit up and wiped the vomit from my face.

"So, Harley, how much cash is in that business account of yours?" Damon asked, squatting down to face me.

"A hundred and fourteen thousand dollars."

"And you made this really fucking difficult, didn't you? With your rich boyfriend trying to keep you from us. This is your fucking fault that it had to get this ugly." He was so close to me, his spit splattered in my face and I squeezed my eyes and mouth closed. His fist hit my cheek and I tumbled back down to the floor. My hand resting in a pool of my own vomit. The brown cement floors were cold and filthy.

"You're not gonna get nothin' from her if you keep beating her ass," my mother said from across the room.

Gramps whimpered in the chair above me. "Please. Please stop."

"What's that, old man?" Damon shouted, and I forced myself to sit up again. If anyone was going to take a beating, it was going to be me. They'd kill Gramps if they did this to him. Damon walked across the room and lit a smoke.

"Ah, you back for more, little girl?" He bent down and blew a puff of smoke in my face, and I didn't react at all. I kept my expression perfectly still. I wasn't going to give him any ammo.

"Tell me what you want," I said, forcing myself to look up at him. His green eyes were cold. Lifeless like my mother's.

"Give me your bank card. We're going to empty that account."

"I don't have a bank card. We ran out of the bakery, and I didn't take my purse," I said, trying to hide the tremble in my voice. I didn't want him to know I was terrified. I reached up and put my hand back on Gramp's hand and squeezed it.

"You dumb bitch," Damon wailed as he charged Sadie. He yanked her by the hair and threw her to the floor.

"You didn't tell me to get her purse," she cried, covering her head with her hands.

"Just have her transfer it," the big guy from the car said. Obviously, he was the brains of the operation, because no one else had a clue what they were doing.

"Get the laptop open, Val," Damon instructed my mother. She took another drag and blew it in his direction.

"What kind of genius plan is this? You got her the fuck away from the rich guy, and then you dropped the ball, just like always," my mother spewed. Damon walked toward her, and they argued some more.

I looked back at Gramps and it nearly broke me. Tears streaked down his sweet face, and I wanted to wrap my arms around him and tell him everything would be okay. But everything wouldn't be okay. We had no way out of here. We were outnumbered. No one knew where we were, and they'd disposed of my phone.

Damon grabbed me by the ponytail and yanked me to my feet. He dragged me over to the table and shoved me in the chair beside my mother. She turned the laptop my way.

"Pull up your account," she said. Her voice lacked any emotion.

I turned to the screen and pulled up my business account. I knew that if I emptied my entire account it would set off red flags. I also assumed this would be an easy thing for the bank to trace, as we were depositing it into Damon's account. But I wanted to give them time to investigate it. Put the pieces together. Time was not on my side. As soon as they got what they wanted, they'd dispose of me and Gramps. I needed to buy time for Ford to find us.

"Do you want me to deposit all of it? I think that will cause some red flags. Maybe you should do half of the money today and the other half tomorrow." I kept my fingers on the keyboard and waited for a response. My face throbbed from where he'd punched me, and I struggled to focus as my eye was swelling with each passing minute.

"Don't fucking try to tell me what to do, little girl," Damon shouted, moving his face next to mine. His cheek resting against mine as he stared at the screen. He reeked of booze and smoke. I held my breath and tried to focus on the task at hand. One of his hands rested on my shoulder, and he rubbed it back and forth. Making his way down to cup my breast. "Although you are a pretty little thing."

I slapped his hand away instinctively and pushed to stand, shoving him away from me. His hand came up hard and fast as he hit me across the face. I fell back and dropped to the floor.

"You got a death wish?" my mother said from her chair with a chuckle.

The big guy from the car came over and lifted me from the floor and set me in the chair. My labored breathing filled the air around me and I swiped at my mouth with the back of my hand, which was now covered in blood. Gramps whimpered from behind me. I looked up at the man who'd just put me in the chair, and our gazes locked. Something in the way he looked at me gave me hope. Maybe he wanted to help us get out of here.

"Do it all. It's a bogus account. So even if they flag it, they won't know who it went to," Damon said.

"You sure about that?" my mother asked.

"Don't fucking question me, bitch."

"Let's just try not to fuck this one up," my mother said. I glanced over at her. Looking for anything. A sign of a human being under all that evil.

Nothing.

Damon picked up his gun and held it to my head. "Do it."

The big man stood beside me. I didn't know why, but he seemed to be staying close for a reason. "You shoot her, and we don't get any money."

"Stop telling me how to do my fucking job," Damon snarled.

I asked for his account number and typed it in. "How do I know you're going to let Gramps and me go?"

"You don't," he said.

I typed slowly. Trying to come up with a way to negotiate us out of this.

But I couldn't see a way out.

nineteen

. . .

Ford

MY DAY WAS shit and I hadn't heard back from Harley since I texted her about dinner. I knew she was swamped, but that was unlike her.

"I'll be back shortly," I said to Sam before heading downstairs.

"Bring me a treat back," she yelled out and I laughed.

"Will do."

Everyone was crazy for my girl's sweets. I was just crazy for her. I saw my brothers sitting at the table through the glass door and rolled my eyes. They should have already been on their way to Napa, but they couldn't stay out of the damn bakery. I liked that they loved Harley though, even if I acted like it annoyed me.

"Are you the reason she hasn't responded?" I said as I pushed the door open and glared at Jack and Harrison.

Molly moved to her feet. "What do you mean? She's not with you?"

Alarm bells sounded, and my pulse raced. "What are you talking about?"

"She left thirty minutes ago. She met with the lady for the wedding cake and said she needed to go meet you real quick."

I pulled out my phone and shot Edward a text and Jack ran outside to get Calvin.

"Tell me exactly what she said. What door did she leave from?" I asked Molly as I pulled up Harley's number and tracked her phone. "It shows her a block away. That doesn't make any fucking sense."

I tried dialing her and it went right to voicemail.

Calvin rushed inside. "I never saw her leave. I just came on thirty minutes ago."

"Call the guy you relieved. Could she have gotten past you during the transition?" My voice was frantic, and Harrison stood beside me and put a hand on my shoulder.

Calvin thought about it. "You know, there was a little mishap right when I came on. A young girl tripped and spilled her purse everywhere. I helped her to her feet and got her cleaned up."

"Jesus Christ. They've got her," I said, dialing Jerome to get the car here now.

My phone screen lit up with a call from Edward. His voice was calm. "I was able to track her through her shoes. I've got the address. Looks like an abandoned old house about ten minutes away. I sent the info to Jerome. I'll meet you there. Have Calvin follow. I've got a group of guys on the way already and I've called my contact at the police station. He's sending out a bunch of cars as well. Don't go in without us, Ford."

I ended the call and ran for the door just as Jerome pulled up. My brothers and Molly all jumped in the car with me and I didn't have time to argue with them.

"What did Edward say?" Jack asked, covering his mouth with his hand.

"They've got her at some old house. And they've got a thirty-minute lead on us. How the fuck did this happen?" I shouted.

"I'm so sorry, Ford." Molly's words broke on a sob.

"It's not your fault. They must have said something to get her to tell you she was going to see me and then willingly leave with them," I hissed.

Harrison's gaze locked with mine. "It's got to be her grandfather."

"How the fuck could they get to both of them that easily?" I punched the back of the passenger seat hard.

"We'll find her, brother. What's the plan? Should we call the police?" Harrison asked.

"Edward already did. You guys stay in the car when we get there. I'm going in."

"The fuck you are. You go—we go." Jack pushed forward in his seat, and I'd never seen my brother so serious in my life.

"Okay, we're here," Jerome said. "Should I pull around back?"

"Just get me close to the house. I don't give a fuck if they see us. We're going in."

He pulled up beside the house and I was pushing out the door before the car came to a stop. In my peripheral, I saw several cars moving in beside us. I didn't wait. I charged the door, my brothers in tow. I heard shouting behind me as I kicked through the door and took in the scene.

Harley was on the floor beside a table and Damon looked up just as he kicked her hard. I attacked. Caught him right as he reached for the gun on the table. I dove on top of him and tackled him to the ground. I didn't know what was happening around me as everything blurred. I punched the bastard repeatedly as adrenaline surged. I'd fucking kill him. Someone pulled me off of him, and I fought to break free.

"Ford, stop." It was Harrison's voice calling me, and I turned to see Harley in a ball on the floor.

The room was filled with people now. Where the hell had they all come from? I raced over to Harley and dropped down on the floor, pulling her onto my lap.

She whimpered, and I held her against my chest. It was hard to see over the tears that were blurring my vision. Jesus Christ. She'd been held here and beaten by this piece of shit. "You're okay, baby."

"Gramps," she said through her sobs.

"I've got him," Jack shouted, and his voice cracked. "He's okay, Harls."

I looked up at Harrison, and tears streamed down his face. It was like a scene out of a movie. People didn't do this shit in real life. I looked up to see Harley's mother as she was being cuffed. She smirked, and it took everything in me not to charge her. She'd done this. She'd allowed this. Damon was dragged out of the house screaming and shouting, and I was pissed that he was able to speak. I should have beaten him harder. Longer.

A group of paramedics entered the room. One of the men directed two of the others to tend to Harley's grandfather, while the guy in charge and a female paramedic bent down to look at Harley. "We need to evaluate her injuries," he said, his gaze locked with mine.

"If you hurt her, I'll kick your fucking ass," I snarled at the paramedics.

"Montgomery," Edward said, pressing down hard on my shoulders. "Relax. They're here to help."

"It's okay. I get it," the one dude said as he placed a brace around her neck before he shifted her from my arms and onto the gurney.

The woman helped to get her to come out of the ball she was curled in, and for the first time I saw her face. Her eye was swollen shut, her mouth bruised and bloody, and her cheek twice the normal size with shades of blue and purple covering one side of her face.

Motherfucker.

He'd beaten the living shit out of her. My hands fisted beside me as I moved to my feet and hovered over her. She whimpered as they lifted her shirt to find bruises covering her stomach.

Another paramedic was hunched over Harley's grandfather insisting he drink the water he was offering. He had a gash across his forehead and bruising on his wrists where they'd bound his hands. He hadn't taken the same beating that Harley did—but watching the girl he loved so much take it was probably worse for him. They were both taken out to two separate ambulances and I jumped in with my girl. Molly rode over with Gramps. She'd been pretty quiet as she'd stood over her best friend, crying as she watched the scene in horror.

Jack and Harrison followed us to the hospital. I sat beside her holding her hand, not knowing if I should even touch her for fear of hurting her more.

"I'm okay," she said, one tear running down her swollen, bruised cheek as she looked up at me.

"I'm so fucking sorry I didn't get there sooner, baby."

"You came for me. That's all that matters. You got us out of there alive."

We pulled up to the hospital and they rushed Harley inside. They insisted I stay in the hospital waiting room, which didn't sit well with me. Jack and Harrison were there, forcing me to calm down and take a seat. Harley's grandfather was taken back as well, and Molly sat beside me and buried her face in her hands.

"How is she?" she croaked.

"She's going to be okay," I said, wrapping her in a hug. I knew she was hurting seeing her best friend like that. Hell, we were all shaken to the core by the scene we'd walked into.

"Let me bring you up to speed," Edward said from behind me.

"Tell me we've got enough to put them away for a long time?" I asked, turning to face him.

"So, not sure if you took in all the people in that room, but there was a large man off to the side. He was undercover. The Feds had been tracking Damon and Valentina for some time. That's why there were so many cops there."

"A cop let him beat the shit out of her and just stood there watching?" I seethed.

"Ford. They wanted to put them away for a long time. Once she transferred the money, they had him for enough to put them behind bars for a long, long time. They have a shit ton of charges against both of them. Kidnapping, wire fraud, selling drugs, prostitution. They won't see the light of day for a very long time."

I pushed to my feet and paced. "He should have stepped in sooner."

"He knew if he called them in too soon, Damon would weasel out of the charges. He needed to let her transfer the funds. And they were following a drug transaction set up by him and Valentina a mile away with their carrier at the same time. It was a large delivery that went to an agent. So, they've got them now."

I ran my hands through my hair and continued to pace. My mother came running into the waiting room and wrapped her arms around me.

"What are you doing here?" I asked, pulling back to look at her.

"The boys called when you were in the ambulance. How is she? How's her grandfather?"

"They've been back there for over a fucking hour. They aren't telling us shit," I shouted. The lady at the reception desk gave me an apologetic smile.

"Let me go back and see if there are any updates," she said.

"You need to calm down, son. She's a strong girl. She's going to be okay." Mom led me to take the chair beside her.

"You didn't see her. He beat the shit out of her."

"And you got to her before it was worse," she said, shaking her head in disbelief. "That her own mother could take part in something so brutal. She's going to need your support more than ever now."

"And she'll have it. But I'm fucking pissed, and I don't know what to do with that."

"You need to let it go, Ford. Anger won't help her heal."

"Mr. Montgomery," a nurse called out.

"Yes." I jumped to my feet and moved toward her.

"They are both resting now. Mr. DeLuca has been cleaned up and given some pain meds. He is severely dehydrated, so the doctor has admitted him for observation overnight. Miss DeLuca's injuries are more extensive, but remarkably, she doesn't have any broken bones. A lot of bruising and a lot of healing to do, so we'd like to admit her and just keep an eye on her for the next twenty-four hours. We are getting their rooms ready now and they will be moved upstairs in a little bit." She smiled.

"Okay. Thank you. Can I see her?"

"Of course. Come on back," she said.

"Harrison, can you call Helena and let her know to get the guest suite ready for Harley's grandfather? Explain the situation and tell her to plan for extra staff as they will both be coming home with me to recover," I shouted across the waiting room.

"Doing it now."

"I can cover the bakery for as long as needed," Molly said, and I nodded.

"Thanks. That'll make her feel better."

When they brought me to the curtained-off area in the ER, she was propped up on a pillow and her eyes were closed, one severely swollen and bruised. I walked over and stroked her hair. She looked up at me, her cheeks swollen and streaked with tears.

"Hi," she said just above a whisper as she tried to push to sit forward. "Can you make sure my shoes are in the bag with my clothes? The nurse helped me get undressed, and I want to make sure they don't get misplaced."

"Hey, lie back down. You need to take it easy," I said, kissing her forehead before reaching in the bag that sat on the chair beside her bed. "Yes. The shoes are in here."

"Good. Those are my favorites." She smiled, her head settling back on the pillow.

"You know those are what led me to you," I said.

She startled a bit, her gaze landing on mine. "My shoes?"

"Yes. I had a tracker put in them. In all of your shoes, actually. It was Edward's suggestion, but I'm sure as shit glad I listened now."

"I want to be mad." She winced as she tried to turn on her side. "But I'm glad you found me and Gramps, so I can't complain."

"Good." I ran the pad of my thumb over her bottom lip. "Jesus, baby. You scared the shit out of me."

"I was scared too," she whispered. I knew it was hard for her to admit when she was vulnerable or afraid. I understood it, but I needed her to know she could tell me everything. Anything.

"Of course, you were. That was one creepy-ass house. Straight out of a fucking horror movie." I chuckled, trying to lighten the mood. "You don't always need to be so brave."

She shook her head, and a few tears sprung from her eyes. "I wasn't brave. I was terrified. I thought they were going to kill Gramps. I didn't think you'd be able to find me once they tossed my phone out the window."

"I'd have found you no matter what." I kissed the back of her hand.

"How ugly do I look?"

"You're beautiful. You look even more badass now." I laughed and she forced a smile. Her face was swollen, discolored, and battered.

"Well, at least I don't have any broken bones, so I'm hoping to get back to work soon."

My head whipped up to look at her. "Are you fucking serious? You're not going to work for a while. Molly said she's got it covered.

Jack will step in and help during the busy hours. You know how much he likes it there."

"Yeah, but it's my business."

"And you can have someone take over while you recover. Once you're released, we'll set your grandfather up at my place. I have Helena getting the guest suite ready for him. She'll bring in extra staff to help out. You're both going to need time to heal once you're home."

Her gaze searched mine. "I can't believe you did that for Gramps. Thank you."

"I love you so fucking much, Harley. I'd do anything for you."

"I love you too," she said, reaching for my hand.

The nurse came in and informed us that Harley's grandfather had been moved, and they were taking her to the room next door to his now. They allowed me to walk beside her as they pushed her into the elevator, and she got settled in her room. The nurse went to inform the rest of the group in the lobby that they could come up and see both Harley and her grandfather. I walked over to check on him as well, per my girlfriend's insistence, before returning to sit beside her.

"Hi sweetheart," my mother said as she walked into the room. "How are you feeling?"

"I'm okay. That was so nice of you to come," Harley said, her gaze locking with mine over my mother's shoulder. She didn't know how to handle all of this. The love. The care. She wasn't used to it. She'd been through a traumatic experience, and it would take time to recover. Hopefully she'd allow herself the time to heal. I had a hunch I was in for a battle on that front, but I'd cross that bridge when I got there.

"Harls," Jack said, his voice cracking as he kissed the back of her hand, like he was afraid to touch her.

"Don't be a baby," she teased, and he burst out in laughter. I noticed her wince as she tried to shift in the bed, and I helped her to sit forward a bit and propped a pillow behind her head.

"There's my girl," he said.

"You okay?" Harrison asked, kissing the top of her head.

"Yeah. A little sore, but I'll be okay. Thanks for coming, really. That was so nice of you."

My brothers joined my mother next door to check on Harley's

grandfather. Molly stepped in the room, tears streaming down her face. "Harls, I'm so sorry."

"Stop. This wasn't your fault. Don't do that to yourself."

Molly reached for Harley's hand. "I was so scared for you."

"Hey, I'll be fine." She looked up at her best friend. "And you know how I feel about crying."

"I know. But I need to ugly cry right now. It was that bitch that came in for the wedding cake, right? She was there at the house."

"Yep. She wasn't there for a cake," Harley said, shaking her head.

I didn't miss the way my girlfriend flinched every time she moved. She was in more pain than she was letting on.

"Okay. You need to rest, baby," I said, pulling the blanket up and helping her get comfortable. Her movements were slow and strained.

"I've got the bakery, Harls. You can call as much as you want," Molly said as she blew her friend a kiss.

My brothers came back in the room to say goodbye.

"I've already let Mom and Harrison know I won't be at the winery the rest of the week. I'm going to be back up at the bakery. I may even invent a new cupcake in your honor."

Harley smiled, but her eyes were closed now. "Oh boy. I can't wait to see this."

"I'll do it with black and purple icing, and name it the badass." Jack walked backward toward the door.

"I like the sound of that," Harley said just above a whisper.

I rolled my eyes. "Call me later."

"Get some rest, Harls. We'll check on you tomorrow," Harrison said, keeping his voice low, and leaning in to give me a half-dude-hug.

My mother came around and kissed the top of Harley's head. "Feel better, sweetheart."

Mom gave me a hug before heading out the door.

I sat beside my girlfriend until she dozed off and I stepped outside her room to place a few calls to Edward to follow up on Damon and Valentina. They were being held in the county jail, and our legal team was all over it. I asked him to beef up our security for now until we knew everyone involved was no longer a threat.

They were never going to come near her again.

———

After one night at the hospital, I was able to take Harley and her grandfather home. They ran a bunch of tests and scans which had come back without concern, and they'd cleared them to leave. I helped Helena get Gramps settled in the guest room at my apartment and he'd agreed to spend the next week recovering here where we could keep an eye on him.

I made my way to the bedroom and found Harley in the bathroom staring at herself in the mirror. I rubbed her arms. "You okay?"

"I look terrible."

"Battle wounds, baby. You're always beautiful. But these bruises are reminders of how brave you are. You did what you needed to do to save your grandfather. Damon and your mother are both going away for a very long time."

She blinked a few times and her hands gripped the counter hard. "I still can't believe my mother would do it. I mean, she's never given me any reason to think she wouldn't, but deep down I guess I hoped she would have some feelings for me and for Gramps."

A lump formed in my throat. I hurt for this beautiful girl who deserved the world but was dealt a shit hand when it came to her parents.

"She's an addict and an evil human being. She never deserved you."

She turned in my arms and rested her cheek against my shirt. "Yeah. But this journey led me here. To you."

"It did. And I'm grateful for that. But I'll never forgive her for what she did to you."

"Me either," she said.

"How does a hot bath sound? Do you think it will hurt or help?"

"I think it would help. But only if you get in with me. I don't want to be away from you right now." She gripped the back of my shirt, and her body trembled.

"Let's do it." I walked her over to sit on the side of the tub while I ran the water and dimmed the lighting.

I carefully lifted her shirt over her head. There was blood on the sleeves and the neckline. I tried to hide my anger when I took in the bruises covering her midsection. I pushed her skirt and panties down her legs and unsnapped her bra. I unbuttoned my shirt, and pushed my pants and boxers down, kicking them to the side. I stepped in the scalding water, just the way I knew she liked it and offered her a hand. She tensed as she dropped down to sit between my legs, as the ibuprofen hadn't kicked in just yet. She leaned back against my chest, and I wrapped my arms around her.

"This is nice," she said, and I leaned forward to see her eyes were closed.

"Relax, baby. You're safe now."

"Safe with you," she said, her hand coming over mine, and I felt her entire body relax against mine. I felt her body quake as she started to sob, and I stroked her hair and held her tight.

"I've got you," I whispered.

And I always would.

twenty

. . .

Harley

IT HAD BEEN ten days and I was biting at the bit to go back to work. Ford was a militant caretaker. He worked from home and never left my side. Harrison had stepped up at Montgomery Media in his absence, and I think it was good for my boyfriend to see that he could rely on his brothers more than he realized. Hell, even I had learned that I could rely on others through all of this as well.

Molly and Jack kept things running at DeLiciously Yours, but I was looking forward to taking the reins back today. My bruises had faded and could now be covered with makeup. I certainly didn't want to scare my customers away.

Gramps had gone back home a few days ago, per his insistence. Ford urged him to stay, but Gramps wanted to be in his house—where he felt close to Gram. I understood it. So, they'd agreed that he would return home, as long as he accepted the security that came with it. There was no reason for it now, as Damon and my mother were both in custody. But Ford wasn't taking any chances, and I loved him for it. Gramps had a whole team keeping an eye on him for now, and we found an at-home nurse that checked in on him daily and ran errands for him. He'd been traumatized by what happened, and we'd spent hours talking and crying together the first few days after everything went down. He was grieving the loss of his child as well. My mother. Because she was dead to him at this point. There was no returning from what she'd done.

"You sure you feel up to this today?" Ford asked when he strolled into the bedroom.

"I'm so ready. I can't wait. How's my face? I don't want to scare any customers away."

He laughed as he pulled me close and wrapped his arms around me. I'd never felt this close to another person before. Like I'd found my other half. Ford Montgomery made me whole.

"You look beautiful. Battle wounds and all. But yes, you've covered what's left of them well. So, I have a lady coming by tonight with a few different gowns for you to try on for the fundraiser this weekend, if you're sure you feel up to it. I don't mind missing it if you'd rather stay home. I don't want you to overdo it."

"No way. I'm excited to go. It's a big deal for your mother, and I feel fine. I promise."

"All right. So, you'll take a look at the dresses tonight?"

I laughed. I'd come to learn a few valuable lessons from my kidnapping and ass kicking.

Choose your battles.

Ford wanted to help me and Gramps because he loved me. And that was okay. He wasn't doing it because I owed him anything, or because I was weak. Loving someone meant that you'd walk through fire for them. I had no doubt that this man would walk through fire for me. And I wouldn't hesitate to do the same.

"It's a little over the top to have someone come here with gowns, but at this point, I have no time to shop, so sure."

"Good. You ready?" he asked.

"Yes. Let's go."

Ford placed a call to his attorney on the way to work to get an update on my mother and Damon. He'd gone to great lengths to make sure this story stayed out of the press. I studied his profile as he spoke. The man was so intense and serious. Unwavering and intimidating. Yet he showed me another side—that was so much more. Loving and kind. Protective and loyal.

He ended the call. "Yeah. They aren't going to fight the charges. They're dead in the water. So, there won't be a trial. Damon's going to name a few dealers to lighten his sentence, but he's looking at thirty to forty years with the best-case scenario. Your mother is going to get twenty to twenty-five years."

My gaze locked with his. Those sapphire blues penetrating my soul.

"I'm not going to lie, it'll be strange not worrying about my mother popping up in my life. I've been looking over my shoulder for a long time, and the realization that I won't have to is still setting in."

He pulled me closer and wrapped his arm around me, hugging me to his chest. "She's never coming near you again. Not if I have a say. Do you have any idea how much better my life is with you in it? I love you so much, baby."

"I was thinking the same thing. I don't want to remember my life before you, Montgomery. Because everything is so much better with you."

He tipped my chin up and kissed me hard. My fingers tangled in his hair as I urged him closer. My need for this man was overwhelming.

We pulled in front of the Montgomery Media building and made our way inside. I put on the coffee and assessed the baked goods in the freezer. Molly and Jack had done a good job keeping things afloat. Apparently, we had a new group of young twenty-something women who were all coming in to see the hot dude behind the counter. Jack ate it up, and Molly said it only helped business. They'd be disappointed today to see me behind the counter, I'm sure, but Jack was needed back at the family business. I think he enjoyed the little break.

"My brother's going to have withdrawals from this place, I'm sure." Ford rolled his eyes and poured his coffee to go.

"Yeah, I'm sure he will. But I'm glad he's at the winery the next few days to help your mom get ready for the event. Molly said she sent him with several boxes of pastries. I just wish I'd been able to make them fresh for your mom, you know?"

"You've been through so much. Don't worry about that at all. I want you to call me if it's too much. Hell, I'll put Calvin or Edward behind the counter if I have to."

He tugged me close and tucked the hair that slipped from my bun behind my ear. He lightly traced the bruise beneath my eye that I'd covered with makeup with his finger, sending Goose bumps down my arm. Ford had a way of making me forget. Erasing my wounds.

"Love you," I said, pressing a chaste kiss to his lips, and smacking his ass as he walked away.

"Text me in an hour and let me know how you're doing. I'll bring you some lunch this afternoon."

I rolled my eyes. "You worry too much."

"Only about you." He winked and walked out the door.

I blew out a long breath and got to work. As I rolled out the dough to cut the butter cookies, I thought about my mother. She'd be going to prison for a very long time. I was still processing it and all I felt was relief. Relief that I wouldn't have to worry about her hurting Gramps or coming after me anymore. But there was still a sadness that settled in the middle of my chest. A sadness for the mother I'd always wished she could be. Aside from Gramps, I didn't have any family. I'd only known Ford for a few months, but he'd somehow filled a void in my life that had always been there.

"Hey, girl. So happy you're here." Molly ran around the island and wrapped me in a hug.

"Me too. Thanks for covering for me. You did such a good job."

"Yeah? Well, I learned from the best in the business." She bumped her hip into mine before walking over to pour herself a cup of coffee. "And it didn't hurt that you froze enough pastries for a lifetime. I just had to pull them out and frost them."

I laughed. "Well, we can start freezing a few batches a day again. Thanks for getting all the pastries together for Monica, too."

"Of course. So, are you excited for the event? Have you found a dress yet?"

"Ford has someone bringing over a few tonight for me to look at," I said, sliding two cookie sheets in the oven.

"Look at you—it's a modern-day fairy tale. I'm coming over so I can have a vote."

I laughed. "I was hoping you would."

She was right. Even with all the drama that had happened—life had become a fairy tale.

And for the first time in my life, I was hoping for a happily ever after.

———

"Damn, woman, you're killing me tonight with this dress," Ford said, helping me from the helicopter and into the car.

"Thank you. You're looking pretty dapper there yourself, Montgomery." I turned to face him and straightened his tie.

I'd never worn a dress like this before, and it felt good to get dressed up tonight. My gown was a long black sheath dress, hugging my curves just a little, and exposing one shoulder, while the other was a full sleeve. It was elegant and classic. Molly had come over and helped with my hair. I wore it down in long waves, one side clipped back with a few sparkly bobby pins. I had on more makeup than I was used to wearing and according to Molly, the smoky eye was the look we were going for. When we pulled up to the winery, Ford leaned forward to speak to Jerome who had flown here with us.

"We'll drive home. I told Paul he could call it a night and leave the helicopter here. So, feel free to come in if you'd like and enjoy the food, and I'll let you know when we're ready to go."

"I'll be fine out here but thank you."

"Jerome, there's some DeLicously Yours pastries at this shindig, and I know how much you love them," I said with a laugh because the man always came in the bakery for a pastry.

He chuckled. "Don't tempt me. I just may take you up on it."

Ford helped me out, and I wrapped my hand around his bicep. Walking in heels was a struggle for me, so I took it slow.

The lobby was turned into a large banquet space with cocktail tables covered in white linens. There were flowers and candles every which way you turned. The doors were open to the dining area which led out to the garden. Monica had arranged a large tent with heaters making the outdoor area more intimate. People filled the space, and chatter and laughter surrounded us. My gaze moved around the room taking it all in. There were twinkle lights covering the trees in the distance. It was stunning. Servers walked around with trays offering wine, champagne, and appetizers.

"Are you hungry?" Ford asked, leaning down to speak against my ear, taking a nibble while he lingered.

My head fell back in laughter. "I think you must be hungry."

"Yeah, I'm hungry for you in this dress."

"The night's young, Montgomery. You just might get lucky," I said with a wink.

"Oh, I'm counting on it."

"You two look lovely," Chanel said as she approached with a man on her arm. "Harley, Ford, this is Christopher."

We said our hellos and Chanel leaned over to hug me. She looked amazing in her lavender fitted gown. Her hair was slicked into a fancy chignon, and her neck and wrists shimmered with jewels.

"You look gorgeous," I said as Jack and Harrison flanked our sides.

"You look amazing, Harley." She held my hands and stepped back to take in my gown.

"How did things run the rest of the week without me?" Jack asked with a smirk.

"She saved a ton of money because her employee wasn't eating everything." Ford laughed.

"You were missed. There were some very disappointed female patrons the last few days," I said, giving him a hug. "Thanks for doing that for me."

"Anything for you, Harls."

"Find your own woman." Ford glared at his brother before breaking out in laughter.

"You look gorgeous." Harrison pulled me in.

"Thank you," I said giving him a peck on the cheek. "Where's your mom? I can't wait to see her."

"She's buzzing around here somewhere." Harrison smiled and waved over a server. He handed Chanel and me each a glass of champagne before offering some to the others.

"All right, we're going to socialize." Ford intertwined his fingers with mine and we agreed to meet up with everyone for dinner.

We made our way through the elegant space and I'd never been introduced to so many people at one time in my entire life. I tried to remember their names and find little things to categorize them in my head. Dinner was announced, and Ford and I moved to find our table.

"You feeling okay?" he asked, pulling me into his arms as we scanned the room for our seats.

"I feel great."

I spotted Jack and Harrison in a group and pointed them out to Ford.

"Oh good. There's Hanky and Marie standing with Chanel. They must be sitting with us. I can't wait for you to meet them," he said as I looked up to see where we were heading.

Classical music played in the background, and the smell of fresh bread and honey filled my senses. When we approached the group, someone tapped Ford on the shoulder to say hello. I looked up to see Chanel waving me over. As my gaze moved beside her all the air left my lungs. My legs wouldn't move. Ford turned toward me and studied me.

"Are you okay?"

Fight or flight.

"I need to go." I turned on my heels and hurried through the lobby. I rushed around groups huddled together and ignored my boyfriend calling my name. I needed air.

This wasn't happening.

It couldn't be.

I pushed the large double doors open, leaned down to take off my heels, and started to run down the driveway. I didn't know where I was going, but I knew I couldn't stay here.

"Good Christ, Harley. What are you doing?" Ford shouted, his breaths labored as his fingers wrapped around my forearm.

"I need to go."

"You need to go where? Are you sick?"

"No."

"Baby, what's going on? What happened?"

I leaned forward, resting my hands on my knees. I couldn't catch my breath. I couldn't breathe.

Ford squatted down to meet my gaze. "Jesus. I think you're having a panic attack. Just stop and breathe."

He moved behind me and wrapped his arms around me, rubbing my arms and whispering in my ear. "Everything's fine. You're okay. I've got you."

This man.

He was everything good in my life.

Tears streamed down my face, and I didn't try to stop them. I turned in his arms and looked up to see him. The concern in his eyes nearly broke me. I shook my head, wanting to tell him without saying the words.

"Baby, you need to tell me what's going on."

"What's Chanel's last name?"

"What? Reynolds, why?"

I took a few steps back, away from him. Away from here.

I covered my face as I broke down in sobs.

"Harley. You're scaring me. What the fuck is going on?" Ford moved in front of me, holding my shoulders in place, and forcing me to look up at him.

"What's Hanky's name?"

"Jesus. What the fuck is going on? His name is Bryce."

I shook my head with disbelief. "My biological father is Bryce Reynolds."

He barked out a laugh. "Baby, no. Maybe they have the same name. Hanky cannot be your father. He's a good man. This is a mistake."

"Ford, that man inside there, standing with Chanel. He's my father. That's the man I met at the restaurant." Memories flooded from that night, as my boyfriend took a step back and everything came together. His father's car accident. That night in the alley. That Ford's father had looked so familiar to me. "What was the date of your father's accident?"

He shook his head. "June seventh. Why the fuck are you asking me that?"

"Oh my god." I bent down and rested my hands against the cool pavers beneath my feet to stabilize myself. "Your father was there that night, Ford. He was one of the men at the table with Bryce."

He stared at me. Studied me. Waiting to see what I'd say next. I swiped at the falling tears as sobs wracked my body.

"You saw my father the night of his accident?"

"Yes. He came out the back door with Bryce. They left together. They were arguing, but it wasn't about you. Your dad was furious with him—*about me*. They were arguing about me. About him hiding me and not acknowledging my existence."

Ford bent over, resting his hands on his knees for support. This tall, beautiful man clad in a black tux—could no longer bear what I was saying. "That's impossible."

"It's the truth. And Ford," I said, my mouth trembling so severely I could barely get the words out. "Your father did not get in the driver's seat. Bryce did. I was there, hiding beside the dumpster. Your father demanded that they go to Bryce's house to tell his family what he'd done. Your dad was angry. I remember being happy that at least one person acknowledged what he'd done. They were shouting as they got in the car, and they sped off. Your father was in the passenger seat when they left the restaurant."

Ford dropped his head before pushing to stand and pulling his phone from his coat pocket.

"I need you to come pick up Harley. We're on the east drive. Take her home. I won't be leaving tonight, so I won't need a ride." His tone was icy. Distant. Jerome pulled up within seconds and Ford helped me to my feet and led me to the car. He opened the door and assisted me inside, leaning over to kiss my forehead. He didn't speak a word. He turned on his heels and walked away. Just like that. He waltzed right out of my life.

The lump in my throat made it difficult to swallow. Tears continued to stream down my face, and I covered my mouth with my hands to keep my sobs at bay. Sadness coursed through my veins. An overwhelming feeling of loss enveloped me. The realization that everything had just changed was sinking in.

Because fairy tales didn't exist.

At least not in my world.

twenty-one

· · ·

Harley

I WALKED into my apartment and slipped out of my party gown and into my pajamas. I couldn't wrap my head around the events that had transpired tonight. It was like a bad nightmare playing out before me. I made myself a hot tea and settled on the couch. The lump in my throat threatened to suffocate me. I could still remember that day like it was yesterday. The one that I now knew changed both of our lives.

My mom had cornered me outside Gramps' house.

"You missed my graduation and now you're asking for a favor?"

"I'm your mother. Just do this for me. I'm in trouble."

"You're always in trouble. It's the only time I see you," I said, pushing past her and walking toward my car.

"You can meet your dad. I know you've always wanted to. And I think he'll actually do whatever you want. You are his child, after all. Rich fucking asshole. He owes you."

I froze. I'd asked for years about him, but she'd never given me anything. "So, you want me to meet my father? Today. After all these years?"

"We had a deal that you'd stay away. But things change. I need the money, and he's not responding to me. So... why not give him a glimpse of what he missed? Abandoned. Left me to deal with you all on my own."

I reached for my mug and took a sip. The ring it left on the coffee table reminded me of my mother's discolored teeth. I used my napkin to clean it up. The woman was so far gone. The fact that she actually believed she'd raised me by herself was ludicrous. *All on my own*, my ass. She'd been a shit mom from day one. We'd barely gotten by during those years when I'd lived with her, and most of the time she'd put me in dangerous situations. I'd lived with my grandparents since middle school. And there she was trying to take credit for a job well done. But I'd pressed her that day because I was curious. Why did I care about a man who'd never claimed me as his own?

"I thought you said he wasn't reachable. Now you're willing to give me his name. Why now? Because I'm eighteen and an adult in my own right? It's bullshit, Valentina. You're using me, just like you always have."

"I'll split the money with you," she whined.

I turned around to look at the gaunt junkie following behind me. Like I'd ever want anything from this woman. Nope. We were long past that. I was leaving for Europe tomorrow. I'd been saving for three years for this trip. I didn't need her help, or anyone's help for that matter. This woman had made it so that I'd learned at a very young age how to fend for myself. But, the idea of meeting my father—the man who'd knocked up my so-called mother—and then walked away from both of us. It was tempting. I wouldn't mind showing him I was fine. I was more than fine. I was the salutatorian of my high school. I had a full ride to Berkley in the fall. I'd saved up enough cash to travel to Europe for two weeks. It would feel good to let that asshole know I'd done just fine without him.

"Tell me his name and how to find him."

"Really, baby girl? You'll do this for me?"

I nodded. I wasn't doing it for her. I was doing it for me.

"Yep. Tell me what to do." I leaned against my VW Bug, the sun shining down on my mother's gaunt frame and greasy hair. She was a beautiful woman once. But she'd snorted enough powder to waste away. Alcohol slowly deteriorating her physical appearance. And trading sex for drugs—well, that had taken a toll of epic proportion. She was beyond help. I'd spent a decade being this woman's crusader, but after she'd allowed her creepers to come anywhere near me enough times—I'd thrown in the towel.

You can't save someone who doesn't want to be saved, right?

I'd had a lifetime of that lesson.

"Okay. So, tell him that he needs to transfer double the norm for the next few months. Just say I'm in trouble and I'll keep up our bargain."

"He has your bank account information? He's been giving you money over the years?" I asked, studying her. The woman would never tell me the truth. I don't know why I bothered asking.

"Just a few times. When you and me were in trouble."

"You and me? As if you ever took care of me." I shook my head and opened the car door. Why was I even engaging with her? You can't fix this kind of crazy.

She handed me a folded scrap of paper. "His name is Bryce Reynolds. This is his work address. I was escorted out of his building, and he has security outside watching for me. But they won't be expecting you. Just wait outside this address and follow him. He goes to dinner on Thursday nights in the city."

I didn't know whether to be more shocked at the fact that I finally knew his name, or that my mother had some pretty impressive investigative skills. When Valentina DeLuca wanted something, she was full of surprises. Unfortunately, she only wanted booze and blow most of the time.

"How will I know what he looks like?" I crossed my arms in front of my chest. She seemed to have this all figured out.

"This is a recent picture of him. I got it off his website." She held up her phone and I took it from her. Studying the face of the man who'd been nothing more than a sperm donor. He was attractive. Older than I would have guessed.

I handed her the phone back. "I'll see what I can do."

I recall purposely not telling her that I was leaving the following day, because the woman would probably have come by Gramps' house and robbed us for the money I'd saved for my trip. I'd learned very creative ways to hide money from her over the years. I'd had plenty of experience with her showing up three shades of drugged-up and rummaging through the house like a crazy ass. I'd made a conscious decision a long time ago not to tell her much.

"Okay. You can do this, kid. Do it for your mama."

My thoughts kept coming, playing on repeat in my head. I closed my eyes and tried to push them away. It wasn't a memory I wanted to revisit. I moved to my feet and paced around the room, wanting to forget every detail from that day. I'd left for the city right then because

I wanted to avoid traffic. I'd done some window shopping to pass the time, and I'd tried to come up with a plan about how to approach the man.

Hey, asshole, thanks for leaving me with a crackhead.

Congrats, Mr. Reynolds. It's a girl.

Nice to meet you, big guy. I'm here to give you the award for deadbeat father of the year.

I remember rehearsing what I was going to say, playing every scenario out in my head. But once I got there and stood beside the building like some sort of creeper—butterflies swarmed my belly. He was my father, after all. At the very least, he'd donated his sperm to make me. He'd been a willing participant at some point in the process, and I wanted to meet him.

I remember the moment I spotted him, and he moved toward the parking lot across the street. Holy hell. I could still feel the panic that coursed through my veins when I realized we were parked in the same lot. I hadn't thought that one out. In my defense, it had all happened in a matter of hours. A lifetime of wondering had played out in a short period of time. I'd assumed I'd follow him on foot, so I had to adapt quickly. I vividly remember keeping my head down and waiting until he got inside his swanky BMW and that's when I'd hopped in my Bug. I'd stayed a few feet back. My heart raced today as I thought about it. I'd wiped my sweaty palms on my jeans several times as I drove. I dropped back down on the couch and picked up my tea and took another sip, wondering why I'd willingly put myself in that situation. Curiosity was the best I could come up with. My sperm donor had pulled over beside the curb, and I'd followed, remaining a few cars back in the red zone. I knew he wouldn't stay there long, as it had been the corner of a busy intersection. I could still hear the cars honking around us, as a tall guy hopped in his car.

When they pulled away from the curb, I'd trailed behind. He turned into the valet at a restaurant, and I'd followed.

I walked around to the front of the restaurant and took a few deep breaths. That feeling of panic, of pure adrenaline surged through my body even now. Nervous energy surrounded me as I thought back to that moment. And for whatever reason, I didn't back down.

Bryce Reynolds.

Bryce Reynolds.

Bryce Reynolds.

I'd said my father's name in my head on silent repeat over and over. The man had an expensive car and a swanky suit and a tall friend. That's literally all I knew about him at the time. Oh, and I assumed he had kickass sperm, because, well—me.

I can still feel the cool handle on the door as I gripped it and pulled it open. I remember smiling at the hostess as I'd waltzed past her like I owned the place. But inside I'd been dying. Terrified of what would happen.

I'd spotted him and turned in the other direction, huddling near the bathroom because I'd realized there were other men at the table. Four total. It was going to be even more awkward than I'd anticipated, but it still didn't stop me. I was like a dog with a bone that night. I'd stood there gathering my thoughts, reminding myself that I didn't owe him anything. He'd turned his back on me a long time ago. I recall the moment I took that step toward where he and his friends were sitting. My heart raced.

Fuck Bryce Reynolds.

I marched up to the table. All four sets of eyes paused when they saw me.

"Hello, gentlemen, I'm Harley DeLuca. I'm really sorry to interrupt your little happy hour. But I need to have a word with Bryce Reynolds." I crossed my arms and plastered a fake smile on my face.

The tall man that had hopped in the car with my sperm donor studied me. The other two chuckled. And Bryce Reynolds, aka my father—well, his face went white.

"What is this regarding?" the tall man asked.

"It's regarding the fact that jackass here is my father. Or my sperm donor, I guess. And his cracked-out baby mama, who he left me with to fend for myself, wants more money. Shocker." I raised a brow, begging any of them to say one fucking word.

"This is a misunderstanding. Gentlemen, please give us a minute," my sperm donor said.

They all pushed to their feet and walked to the bar, with the exception of the tall dude. He stood off to the side, watching us. Like I was going to rob his friend or something. I wanted to flip him off, but I had bigger fish to fry right now.

"Listen to me," Bryce said, keeping his voice down. "I have a deal with your mother. What is it that you want? Money? Tell me how much, and I'll wire it to you. But you can't come into a public place and call me out. That's not the deal."

"Not the deal? I don't recall making a deal. And I don't want your money, you asshole. I want nothing from you. My mother, on the other hand, well, she's your problem. And she wants money. But that's not what I'm here for." My bottom lip betrayed me. The man was looking everywhere but at me. He was worried about anyone knowing I was his daughter. Shame covered his face. He was embarrassed by me.

"I'll transfer the money to her. You need to go, Hadley."

"It's Harley." My voice shook. "And I'm doing just fine without you, by the way. Just fine. I'm going to college on a scholarship. And I've worked really hard to get where I am. I am not my mother."

Nothing came out as planned. My big, cocky speech fell apart as it left my lips. I fought back the tears. I would not cry in front of this man. At least not in public. I'd learned how to contain my emotions over the years.

"Um, I'm sure you're not, Harley. I'm sorry, but I can't do this right now. I can transfer you some money though." He pulled out his phone and opened his notes. "Tell me your bank info and I'll take care of it. You tell me how much. But you really need to go. Now."

My mug almost slipped from my grasp when I replayed those words in my head. I got up to put it in the sink. Heading to the bathroom, I could still recall the way that fucker glanced over his shoulder to see who was watching. He didn't care about me. He didn't want to know me. He didn't care what kind of student I was or who I was as a person. He wanted nothing to do with me the day I was born, and nothing had changed that day either. I placed my hands on the counter and stared at my reflection in the mirror. The man had hurt me to my core and I still felt it today.

"I don't want your fucking money, you asshole."

I'd stormed away, and for whatever reason I'd walked through the kitchen and out the back door. I didn't think I could hold it together if I had to walk through the restaurant. But I knew there was no way in hell I was going to cry in front of that man.

I'd found myself in the alley near the valet, and I'd crouched down beside the dumpster. He'd treated me like trash, and there I was sitting beside a big, stinky garbage bin. I could vividly remember trying to calm my breathing and sliding down the wall to sit on the ground. That's when I let the tears fall.

Only once I was alone.

Always when I was alone.

And I'd let them. I'd rested my head on my knees and muffled my sobs with my hand. A sick feeling settled in my stomach when I thought about that moment. I'd never cried over my father before that day. But being there, seeing him face-to-face. The way he'd looked at me, like I was the shit beneath his shoes. It hurt.

It hurt a lot.

I knew I was more than that. I'd worked hard to be different from my mother. Hell, I'd made it a mission to be the opposite of her. I had never even tasted alcohol back then. I didn't smoke. I didn't have boyfriends and I hadn't had sex yet either. How many girls heading off to college could say the same? I'd tried so hard to be different. I'd studied. And I'd worked damn hard. And it had all been intentional. But in that moment, I felt like I'd never be free of her shadow. I'd always just be Valentina DeLuca's daughter.

It was something that I never wanted to feel again.

And fuck her for putting me in that situation. For asking me to do that for her. She was a selfish asshole back then just like she was now.

I think what crushed me most was that I'd gone there for myself. A part of me thought maybe he'd be interested in knowing me. Surprised that I'd turned out well in spite of where I'd come from. Maybe he'd even be impressed with me.

But he'd offered me money and begged me to leave. I shouldn't have been surprised. He'd never wanted me, why would that have suddenly changed?

I washed my face and patted it with a towel before making my way back to the couch, staring at the muted TV as the news flashed a graph of tomorrow's weather. I closed my eyes and I could still hear the can rolling down the alley, and the smell of sour milk and cigarettes that wafted from the trash bin.

I pushed to my feet and used the sleeve of my shirt to wipe away the tears. Shouting came from the other side of the dumpster and I peeked out. Bryce Reynolds was arguing with the tall guy as he handed the valet his ticket. They were already leaving? And the tall man was pissed.

"You're going to fucking tell your wife, Bryce. Do you hear me? This is unacceptable. She's a kid. She's your fucking kid. Jesus Christ. How could you do this?"

Thanks, tall dude. At least someone else realizes how fucked up this is.

"Let me fucking handle it," Evil Daddy Dearest said.

The car pulled up, and they continued to shout before they got inside.

"You've done a shitty job of handling it so far. This ends now."

I heard a muffled response from Bryce as the car sped off.

There was a little satisfaction in the fact that his friend seemed appalled by him.

I swiped at my face when I realized a single tear was rolling down my cheek. Even today, it still stung. And even more so now that I'd learned that he was someone important to Ford and his friend had been Ford's father. I flipped the television off, trying hard to forget how I felt when I stepped out from behind that garbage can. I'd handed my ticket to the valet attendant, and I couldn't wait to get on the plane the following day. I wanted to get away from everyone and everything.

I wanted to forget about the rejection.

Leaving on my trip to Europe would be a fresh start.

One I'd desperately needed at the time.

I laid my head down on the throw pillow on my couch and stretched out my legs. The memories were almost too much. And the truth about who Bryce Reynolds was to me, to Ford—I didn't know how this would play out. I held my phone in my hand, silently willing Ford to call me.

To tell me we were going to be okay.

twenty-two

• • •

Ford

I WALKED up the driveway as I processed all that she'd just told me. My head spun. Vision blurred. There was a ringing in my ears as I pushed open the doors and entered the gala. I couldn't think straight, as anger coursed through my veins. Had it all been a fucking lie? This man who'd been like a father to me—had not only lied to me about my own father, but he'd abandoned the woman I loved. Was it true?

Things fell into place in my mind as I scanned the dining room. Why would my father have been driving Bryce's car? I'd never asked him about it, because well, I didn't think I needed to. But it never added up. My dad being so angry that he'd driven off the road. It hadn't sat well with me. But it sure as shit had fueled the guilt I felt about my father's death—the thought that he'd been that angry. Hanky had been conscious at the scene. He told us and the police what happened, and no one ever questioned it. Including me. Because I'd been busy drowning in grief. And Hanky, well, he was family.

My father's best friend.

Had it been guilt that caused him to step up after my father passed away?

Show me the truth, Dad.

My brothers walked toward where I stood at the entrance to the dining room, and right behind them was Hanky.

"Where'd you go? Thought you were going to introduce me to this new, amazing lady of yours?" Hanky said, and my brothers' faces hardened as they took me in.

"What's wrong?" Jack asked, both of them moving beside me.

I stared at my godfather. My confidante. "Her name is Harley. *Harley DeLuca."*

His reaction was all I needed. His face turned stark white, and his gaze filled with fear as it met mine. My fist flew before I could stop it. Jack caught Hanky before he fell to the ground, and Harrison hustled me out into the lobby.

"What the fuck are you doing?" he snapped, and Jack assisted Hanky out to the lobby as well, closing the doors to the dining room.

"Tell them," I said.

He shook his head as his wet gaze met mine.

"Fucking tell them, you coward," I shouted.

"It was a mistake. A one-time thing. I was young. Should I ruin everyone's life over that? I protected my family," he said, wiping at his mouth and smearing the blood coming from his lip.

"She was your fucking family, you piece of shit. You left her with a monster. And you turned her away the night of the accident. Dad wasn't okay with it, was he? Admit it. All these fucking years you let me believe he drove that car off the road arguing with you about *me.* But you were the one driving that car. You were the one that killed him." I shoved him back as my brothers watched with disbelief.

"Ford Robert," my mother hollered as she came through the double doors from the dining room and asked security to keep people out of the lobby.

"Tell her, Hanky. Tell her what you did. How you left your daughter, Harley, to fend for herself with that drug-abusing lunatic. How you abandoned your own child. How you turned her away when she came to you when she was grown—offering her money to keep your little secret like she was worthless. Tell her that Dad found out, and that's what you were arguing about the night of the accident. Tell her that you were driving the goddamn car when he was ejected and killed. It was all you, Hanky."

My mother moved to stand beside me. Her face morphed in pain as she stared at him in horror. Hanky didn't speak. He avoided her gaze like a fucking coward.

She took a step forward and slapped him hard across the face. "I think enough has been said. The fact that he wasn't denying it was enough. I need to speak to my boys. Go home, Hanky."

Mom took my hand while Harrison and Jack followed behind us. She led us into her office, and we all dropped to sit on the couch and chairs.

"How do you know this?" she whispered.

"Harley recognized him tonight. She wanted to meet her father after she graduated from high school. She followed him to a restaurant. It was the night of Dad's accident. She said Dad was furious with Hanky and they were shouting. She was out in the alley after Hanky rejected her and made her feel worthless. She said Dad was in the passenger seat of the car, Mom. She never knew what happened after because she left for Europe the following day. She put it all together tonight. Do you think Hanky lied because he was drunk?"

Tears ran down my mother's face, and I glanced at my brothers. Jack's face was beet red, and his hands fisted at his side. Harrison sat completely quiet and shook his head as a tear ran down his face.

"I don't know, son. But we're going to find out, I can tell you that. Where is Harley now?"

"I was in shock when she told me. I had Jerome take her home. Everything was a lie, Mom. All the anger and the guilt over what I did —it wasn't even what they were fighting about. And he let me think that. He let me drown in it. I want to destroy him for what he did to her. For what he did to us."

"He killed Dad, and he'll be held accountable," Harrison said, coming over to sit beside me.

"I'll kill him with my bare hands. Hanky is Harl's dad? How is that possible?" Jack pushed to his feet and paced the room.

"He called it a mistake," Harrison snapped. "A one-time thing. But he had a daughter, and he turned his back on her."

"Harley is four years younger than Chanel, which means Hanky and Marie were married with both kids when he got Harley's mother pregnant." I shook my head, trying to wrap my head around all of this. It was too much to process.

"Chanel and Baron are her siblings," Harrison said.

"And obviously Dad wasn't okay with what he'd found out that night. He must have been fucking furious," Jack said, yanking at his overgrown hair. He tugged at his bow tie and let it fall to the ground.

"Harley said that Dad insisted they drive right to Hanky's house and he come clean. Somewhere along the way, Hanky drove that car off the road. Was it intentional? Was it because he was drunk and angry? We'll never fucking know. He holds all the answers."

"Oh, we'll know. Don't you worry about that. Secrets always come to the surface," my mother said, walking to her desk and reaching for some tissue.

"What happens to Marie, Baron, and Chanel if we take this public?" Harrison whispered.

"And what happens to Harley? We thought her mom was a piece of shit? Now her father is a bigger piece of shit? Where does that leave her?" I asked.

"Where they both left her most of her life. On her own," my mother whispered.

Harrison left the room and we all sat in silence. He returned two minutes later holding a bottle of whiskey. He took a swig and passed it to me. I passed the bottle to Jack, who handed it to Mom. We all gaped as she tipped her head back and took a long pull of whiskey.

"What are you going to do?" Harrison asked me.

"I don't have a fucking clue." I reached for the bottle and took another swig.

"Well, I think we should all go back to the house. Spend the night there. Together. You need to call Harley and make sure she made it home safely and is doing okay." Mom wiped at her face again and reached for her cell phone. "Daniel, it's Monica. We have a family emergency and the boys' and I need to leave. Can you handle the rest of the event on your own? Have Jasmine and Sabrina assist you, please. And I need you to make sure that Hanky has left the premises. Thank you."

And just like that, the four of us left the winery and headed home. To the home we'd shared our entire life with our father. The home that Hanky had visited almost daily over the years. And nothing would ever be the same. I tried to call Harley and it went to voicemail, so I hung up. What needed to be said couldn't happen over voicemail. I texted Jerome, and he informed me that she arrived home safely. He said she didn't speak at all and requested to be taken to her apartment. A sick feeling settled in my stomach.

———

We'd all been in shock last night. We helped Mom to her room, and I stood outside her door and listened to her muffled cries. It enraged me. Jack, Harrison, and I stayed up until the morning hours drinking. My head pounded and my mouth was so fucking dry, I fumbled around the nightstand to find my water bottle.

Sunlight flooded through the opening in the curtains and I sat back and guzzled my water. I reached for my phone to see if Harley had called. Where the fuck did we even stand now? The man I'd worshiped was her piece-of-shit father. She'd seen my father on the night of his accident. The irony was not lost on me. Dad died fighting for the woman I love. What were the fucking chances? I ran a hand over my face.

Would she feel the same about me? Did this change anything between us? Why the fuck should it? It had nothing to do with either of us. Yet she hadn't called me back, and we were in the midst of a fucking shitstorm. I needed to deal with this Hanky nightmare now.

I wandered out to the kitchen and heard Jack shouting. My head continued to pound, and I leaned against the doorframe and watched as my brothers argued about how to handle the situation.

"He's not going to fucking tell them on his own. Hell, he's kept Harley a secret for twenty-three years. Why come clean now?" Jack said, punching his fist on the table.

"Because we aren't giving him a fucking choice." I moved to the coffeemaker and poured a cup of coffee. It made me think of my girl. Everything did. Fuck. I dialed her number but ended the call before the first ring. What the hell would I even say right now?

Hey, I punched Hanky for abandoning you and killing my father, and now I'm trying to figure out what the hell to do next.

No. I'd need to speak to her in person. We were in the midst of this hell, and I had to figure out what to do before going to her with it. Hanky needed to be held accountable for what he'd done to her, and to my family.

I dropped down to sit at the kitchen table beside my brothers, just as Mom walked into the kitchen and took a seat beside me. Her eyes were puffy, with dark circles beneath. She looked like she hadn't slept at all.

"Chanel called. She'd like to come over and speak to us," Mom said.

"Is he coming with her?" Harrison asked, running a hand down his face.

"No. She's coming alone. I don't know what she knows. And as angry as I am with Hanky—I would never hurt Chanel by telling her something that her father should have told her. So hopefully she knows what's going on and that's what she wants to speak to us about."

"Jesus. This doesn't even seem fucking real," Jack said, pushing to his feet when the doorbell rang.

My pulse raced. I'd known Chanel my entire life. This would change everything for both of our families, and it sucked that Hanky's choices would trickle down to everyone. But this couldn't be ignored. He would have to face the consequences of his actions.

When Jack and Chanel entered the kitchen, there was no doubt in my mind that Hanky had come clean. She looked as shitty as the rest of us. Her hair was pulled back in a ponytail and she was makeup-free. Her tear-streaked cheeks let us all know she'd been crying. She wore a hoodie and leggings and it was all very… un-Chanel. The woman never left the house unless she was dressed to the nines.

She dropped in the chair across from me, and when she looked up, two tears ran down her face. Her lip trembled as she tried to speak. "I don't know what to say. I don't know how to fix this. But he's my father and I can't turn my back on him. So, I'm here first as his legal representation."

"What the fuck, Chanel," I barked.

She put her hands up to stop me from my tirade that was going to follow. She knew me well. That worked to her favor. "Ford. Stop. Let me finish. I'm not here to defend his actions. They are not defendable. But I need you to know a few things before we move forward. I called in a favor and had the police report sent over from the night of the accident. I was also able to access the hospital records through the firm. I've read through everything over the last several hours. Dad was not at the legal limit. His blood-alcohol level was .5. He wasn't drunk. Why did he lie about who was driving that car? Well, according to him, he panicked. He was scared. He had been drinking, but not much, which is clear from his blood alcohol level. But he said he feared you all would blame him for killing your father. He said he's blamed himself for the last five years. It doesn't make it excusable, but it's a fact that matters. I want you to know that if my father's blood alcohol level had been above the legal limit, I would have advised him to turn himself in. That's the truth."

We all sat quietly.

Listening.

Processing.

"Well, for what it's worth. I'm glad he wasn't drunk. That would change things for me, as far as the way we proceeded." My mother stood and poured a cup of coffee for Chanel and handed it to her. "And, please know that we don't hold this against you. We love you. This has nothing to do with you or Baron or your mother. But my issues with Hanky, well, I don't know how to move forward."

"I understand that." Chanel swiped at her face, and her gaze locked with mine. "I know there is a lot more here than his blood alcohol level, but I thought it was an important detail to clear up first. I brought a copy of all of the records so that you could see them as well." She handed me the stack of papers, which I would be going through later today.

"How about the fact that he let Ford believe Dad was upset about their argument? He let my brother carry that fuckin guilt for the last five years." Jack's words cracked as he spoke. My brother never cried. He was a fighter. He liked to attack and bark at people when he was angry. But this was Chanel. And he was struggling.

She covered her face with her hands and spoke through her sobs. "It's inexcusable. He was a coward."

Mom moved over to sit beside her and placed a hand over hers on the table. "He had a secret he'd been covering up for a long time. I'm guessing he just panicked."

"Yes. Let's talk about that. The fact that he hid his daughter for twenty-three years. He left her with a fucking monster, Chanel," I said as my fists came down on the table.

Her gaze locked with mine. Tears streamed down her cheeks, and she squared her shoulders. "It's not excusable, Ford. What he did to her is—"

"It's what? He left her with a drug addict," I shouted, pushing to my feet and pacing around the kitchen. "And the one time she actually went to him five years ago, he offered her money to go away."

"He told us about meeting her. He doesn't have a defense for what he did. But there is more to the story than you know. It doesn't make what he did okay, not by any stretch."

"Tell us," my mother said.

"Dad said that around twenty-four years ago he was at a bar, being stupid, obviously. Baron and I were young, and he and Mom were fighting a lot, I guess," Chanel said, pausing to take a sip of her coffee. "He said he just wanted to have some fun. He had no intention of cheating. He was out with a group of guys from the office. One of them had a friend that invited him to this underground poker tournament."

"This sounds like a lot of bullshit, Chanel. And then what, he got a woman pregnant? At a card game," Jack said, rolling his eyes.

"Let her finish." Harrison held his hand up to Jack and motioned her to keep going.

"He said that there weren't even women there. Someone gave him a drink, and he doesn't remember what happened next. He woke up in bed with some woman in a basement the next morning. He believes he was drugged. I know it doesn't make what he did okay, but this is what he says happened. The woman then called him a year later and said she had a baby with him. She asked for a chunk of money and Dad insisted on taking a paternity test. They agreed to keep the results quiet as long as he paid up. The results came back positive and he was scared. It was a cowardly reaction. He should have come clean. Told the truth. He transferred money into her account every month for the last twenty-three years, and he assumed it was going to Harley. He was afraid to tell Mom what happened. He messed up, I know he did. But this is where we are right now."

"Jesus Christ," I hissed. I didn't know what to believe. Knowing what I knew of Valentina, did I believe this story possible? Yes. But Hanky should have stepped up and taken Harley from her. He just turned his back on her.

"He's made a lot of mistakes. But all we can do is move forward," Chanel said.

"I don't know how to do that," I said honestly, and looked over at my family. They would do whatever I wanted them to do. If supporting Harley meant cutting Hanky off, then that's what they would do. Hell, just the fact that he'd lied about my father's death was enough to cut ties with the asshole. The Montgomerys would always stand together.

"I don't either. There's no playbook for this mess. Dad is moving out of the house right now. He's going to a hotel. Mom needs time to sort all of this out. I mean—it's a lot to swallow. The fact that he lied about the accident—that we have a sister we didn't know about." Chanel shook her head and reached for her coffee mug.

I moved back to my seat and faced her. "Listen. I know this is tearing you apart. And I'm sorry for that. We think of you as family. I don't hold this against you, Baron, or your mother. But I don't see how I can ever forgive your father."

Fresh tears broke free and ran down her face. "I know that, Ford. And I'm really sorry for what he did. If there was a way to fix this or right his wrongs. I'd do it. I think we all would."

"I know you would," my mother said, squeezing Chanel's hand.

"Um, well, Ford, how do you think we should proceed with Harley?"

"Meaning?"

"She's my sister. She's Baron's sister. We were also robbed of knowing her." Her voice wobbled.

"I don't know. I don't have a fucking clue how any of this is going to work. I haven't spoken to her. I don't know how she feels about everything. I need to talk to her in person. But I do know this... Harley doesn't want anything from your father. The one time she went to him, he was cold. He offered her money to go away. He made her feel small." I pushed to my feet again. How the fuck do you take away twenty-three years of damage?

She nodded. "I get it. She probably hates us. But I'd be grateful if you could tell her that we didn't know anything, and we'd like to get to know her."

"I think that's fair. It's all very new and raw, so maybe you can reach out when things settle," Harrison, the endless peacekeeper said.

"Yeah. For sure. I love you guys. I truly do. And I'm really sorry that this happened. I'm sorry that my father lied about your father's accident. I'm sorry that their last conversation was a fight about something that my father should have shared a long time ago. Harley never should have been kept from us. Your dad knew the difference between right and wrong. Apparently, mine does not." Chanel pushed to her feet and set her mug on the kitchen counter.

"I'll walk you out," I said. I needed to remember that Chanel was innocent in this. She'd been a friend for as long as I could remember, and she was also Harley's sister. She was hurting too.

"Thanks for hearing me out."

"Thanks for clearing the air." I shoved my hands in my pockets, because for the first time in all the years I'd known this woman, it was awkward. Things would be different now. Maybe forever.

"It's a start." She waved before walking out the door.

I made my way back in the kitchen to find my brothers pouring bourbon in their coffee.

"It's not even noon," I said.

"Hey, we can deal with this reality tomorrow when we go back to our regular lives. But for today, can we not just do whatever the fuck we need to do to cope with this?" Jack said.

"I liked you better when you were eating donuts," I said, reaching for the bourbon and taking a swig right from the bottle.

My mother shook her head and moved to her feet and reached to take the bottle from my hands. She tipped her head back and took a swig. We all three laughed at her.

"Hey, if you can't beat 'em, join 'em." Mom shrugged.

We sat around the table talking the rest of the day. We drank too much. We shed some more tears. And we came to a decision.

We wouldn't press charges against Hanky or reopen the investigation into my father's death, as we had considered doing when we thought he'd been driving under the influence. We'd sifted through the police report and the hospital records, and we felt confident that his blood alcohol proved that alcohol was not the cause of the accident. Dredging this up would not bring Dad back. It would be hurtful to us, and the innocent members of the Reynolds family. Mom felt strongly that Hanky had probably been punishing himself for a long time, but she didn't think there would ever be a way she could forgive him. And what he'd done to Harley, there was no moving past it. He knew he had a daughter, and he left her to fend for herself.

It was inexcusable.

Unforgivable.

I tried Harley once more. She sent me to voicemail again. Maybe this just wasn't a talk we could have over the phone. I needed to talk to her in person.

I numbed myself late into the night, knowing that Monday morning would be waiting for me. And I would need to face reality.

twenty-three

. . .

Harley

TO SAY that the last day and a half had been the longest of my life, would be an understatement. I hadn't spoken to Ford since I left the party Saturday night, and now here it was, Monday morning. He'd called me late Saturday but I'd fallen asleep on the couch with my phone in my hand, and of course it had died at some point. He hadn't left a message. I didn't reach out to him because I didn't know what to say or even how he felt about everything that happened. He phoned me again last night and I stared at the phone. Too afraid to pick it up. And he didn't leave a message this time either. I mean, the truth is—he'd spent the last five years blaming himself for an accident that he thought he caused. Now he finds out that his father and Bryce were actually arguing over me? Maybe he'd blame me for his father's death. Maybe this was too much for him. I mean, he loves Bryce, *or Hanky*, like a second father. He's known me for, what five months? He's known Hanky his entire life. Who's he going to believe?

I made my way toward the bakery, and the sun had yet to come up. I had zero energy. I hardly ate yesterday, as I never got out of bed. I gave myself one day to sulk. My life had never been easy, and just when I was feeling a shift, like my luck had changed after meeting Ford, I got knocked back on my ass. I'm still fatigued from the ass-kicking I took from Damon and the kidnapping orchestrated by my mother a few weeks ago.

Fuck my life.

Haven't I had my share of hard knocks? I just survived that horrific event, after a lifetime of the shit that came along with being Valentina DeLuca's daughter, and now, now—my deadbeat father happens to be the godfather of the man I love? I mean, come on. You can't make this shit up.

I blew out a long breath as I continued my trek. I'd survived a lot in my twenty-three years. More darkness than most people faced in one lifetime. And I'd go through it all again if it meant it would lead me to Ford. To the man who saved me. The man who made me want things that I never dreamed of.

A normal life.

A happy life.

A family.

People that care.

Fuck you, universe.

You gave me shit parents, and no matter how hard I tried, I couldn't escape them. Neither had ever been there for me—yet, somehow, they'd become my cross to bear.

I flipped the lights on in the bakery and headed in back to put on the coffee. I wondered if Ford would come to work today. Would he stop in for coffee like he did every other day, or just completely ignore me. Would he officially break up with me, or was this it?

Adios, Amigos. He's done.

"Hey, Harls." Molly strolled into the kitchen, took off her coat and reached for her apron.

"What in the world are you doing here this early?"

"I figured you'd need the moral support. Just in case he no-shows this morning, or if he does come and it's awkward—I'm here for you, girl. I've got your back. Always."

I pushed back the wetness that threatened to escape my eyes. I'd never cried more in my life than I had in the last forty-eight hours. And I hated it. It made me feel weak. Hell, maybe I was weak now.

Maybe my cold, jaded heart had softened for this man. Because it ached. A dull pain had set up permanent residence in my chest.

"Thank you," I said, and my voice wobbled.

Damn you, Ford Montgomery.

He made me soft, and then he left me alone.

She put an arm around my shoulder. "No. No more of that. You've done nothing wrong. You were dealt a shit hand, and it's not your fault."

"I was dealt a shit hand at birth. Can a girl not catch a break?" I asked. She laughed, and I swiped at the falling tears. "Sometimes I just feel so tired."

"I know you do," my best friend said, squeezing me tighter.

Molly had spent the day with me yesterday. She just sat on the bed beside me, trying to cheer me up. I'd pretended to be asleep when she finally left, because the thought of breaking down in front of her, in front of anyone—it was too much. I didn't want her to feel sorry for me. I didn't want anyone's pity.

No. I'd given myself the one day, and now it was time to pull up my big girl panties and get it together.

"You going to beat the crap out of that dough?" Molly asked with a laugh as I pounded it a few more times.

"Maybe."

"Tell me again why you didn't pick up his call last night so we would at least know what happened?" she asked, peeking up at me with one eye.

I shook my head. "I don't know. I was afraid to answer. If he's going to dump me, he's going to have to do it face-to-face. I mean, I'm sure Bryce lied. Made up an excuse. Damn Molly, why does *he* have to be the man that walked out on me? Couldn't I just get a random deadbeat father?"

"I get it. But I don't think Ford would believe him over you. After all, you have the truth on your side. Have you thought any more about the fact that you actually have siblings? I know you haven't met Baron yet, but you like Chanel. Maybe you'll gain a brother and sister out of this mess."

Always the optimist.

"Um, I'm guessing they'll hate me and blame me for all of this. And if Ford confronted Bryce, or told his brothers, then their families are involved. They might all hate me," I said, cutting out the little circles and placing them on the cookie sheet.

Thank you, butter cookies for being a dependable joy in my life.

"Why would they hate you?" she asked, crossing her arms in front of her chest and shaking her head.

"Why is my mom a drug addict? Why did my father want nothing to do with me my entire life? The hell if I know. The universe hates me. I'm a lone ship. A stray dog. It's easy to blame me, Molls. And I'd be the simplest solution. They can make me the scapegoat. I mean, you've seen gangster movies. The bad guy is usually the last man standing. It's the side act, the one-man shows—they take the fall. Think of *The Godfather.*"

"So, who are you in this scenario? Fredo?"

I laughed. I actually laughed. But tears followed, because god-for-freaking-bid I get a reprieve for a moment to not feel sad. "Probably, and Bryce is Al Pacino—of course he gets to be the godfather. Literally and figuratively. He's got all the power. All the money. And everyone's respect. Even though he's a complete asshole."

"Give me that dough. You're either going to shred it to bits or hurt yourself."

We cleaned up the kitchen, and the door chimed. We stared for a moment at one another before I made my way to the dining room.

Please be him.

Please be him.

"Hope I'm not too early, Toots. But I want to bring those pumpkin donuts to my bridge club today. Thought I'd catch you before the doors opened," June said. She was one of my favorite customers, but I wasn't in the mood for small talk. She was in her seventies, and funny as hell. On a normal day.

Today was not a normal day.

"No problem at all. How many would you like?" I asked, reaching for the large box.

"Two dozen ought to do it. Where's that hunky man of yours?"

June was always the first customer here on Monday mornings. And Ford was usually on his way up to his office when she'd show up.

"He's running late today," I said, pushing the lump back in my throat.

"Well, he sure is one good-looking man, huh? Mmm… mmm. You're a lucky lady."

Thanks for the reminder, June. Let's get a little more salt and throw it right in that wound.

"Yep. Very lucky," I said, tying the twine around the box as the door chimed again.

And again.

None of the people who came through the door were Ford.

The next few hours went by, and I still hadn't heard from him. Definitely not a good sign. Molly and I were swamped and worked right through our lunch break. When things finally started to slow down, I restocked the display case as my best friend sat up on the counter beside me and ate her sandwich.

"You okay?" she whispered.

"No," I said. It was the truth. "But I'll survive. I always do."

The door chimed and I let out a breath. Could I not have a minute to just pull myself together?

I pushed out of the display case to greet my unwanted customer and froze when I saw Ford. Jack and Harrison stood on each side of him.

"Hey," he said.

I couldn't speak. I didn't know what he was going to say, and I honestly couldn't take any more heartache today. I liked it better when my heart didn't feel so much. I wanted to go back to not caring. To the days before I met Ford Montgomery. I knew my heart couldn't handle one more ding. Not today. Not from him.

"We need to talk," he said, shoving his hands in his pockets.

"Pfft." Molly hopped off the counter, making all sorts of irritated noises and crossed her arms over her chest as she moved beside me. "Really? You need to talk?"

His sapphire blues shifted from her to me. He appeared completely puzzled by her coolness.

"I tried you twice, and you sent me to voicemail. I figured it was best to speak in person." His gaze locked with mine.

"In the bakery, with an audience? Is that the easiest way for you to do this?" I hissed, squaring my shoulders.

"What? No? We just, well, it's been a rough couple of days, and we drank too much, for starters. So, we're severely hungover, and I wanted to come straight here to see you. And these two, well, I don't know why they're here."

"Moral support," Harrison whispered.

"I actually came for the cupcakes." Jack shrugged. "And of course, for you, Harls."

I tried to slip my armor in place as I had no idea what Ford was going to say, but I could feel myself unraveling with his nearness.

"Did you honestly think I was upset with *you*?" he asked.

"I don't know what to think, Montgomery. You helped me into the car and told me to leave. And then…crickets. Nada. Zilch. I mean, yeah, you called, but you didn't leave a message. I don't know if you blame me for your father's death. If you blame me for telling you the truth about Hanky. I don't know anything." My voice wobbled, and I did my best to keep it together. Molly placed a hand on my shoulder in comfort, and I bit down hard on the inside of my cheek to fight back the tears.

He ran a hand through his hair, which was more disheveled than I'd ever seen it. He wore a white T-shirt and jeans. I'd never seen him so—casual.

And, of course it worked for him. He looked sexy as hell. Even if he was in the midst of dumping me in front of everyone.

"Baby, no. I was never upset with you. I didn't want to leave a voicemail about something so—fucked up. You didn't pick up my calls, so I thought you were upset with me. How could I ever blame you? I'm fucking pissed *for you*. I love you. And what Hanky, er, Bryce did to you… it's unforgivable. Of course, it sucks to learn that he lied to us about the accident, but that has nothing to do with you, and everything to do with him. His character. Who he is. I think my father brought you to me. Brought us the truth. And for whatever fucked up reason, I'm proud of Dad for fighting for you. That's who he was. He would never have been okay with the way you were treated. He brought us together in his own way. And he'd be happy the truth was out. I know it in my gut. And, at the end of the day, Hanky has to live with what he's done to Dad and to you. But you and me—I love you. Nothing could change that."

I covered my mouth with my hand and shook my head. No words came. Tears started to fall, and a sob left my throat.

He came around the counter and put a hand on each of my shoulders, bending down to meet my gaze. "I love you so much."

"I thought you changed your mind. I thought you'd choose him over me," I said through my sobs. "I thought you'd blame me."

"Never. Never, baby. I love you. And I'm sorry for what he did to you. But know this—I will always choose you. You're it for me, Harley DeLuca."

I wrapped my arms around his middle and rested my cheek on his chest as I tried to get my breathing under control. "I'll always choose you, too."

"He came clean with his family. They know everything. He was driving the car that night. You were right. You were right about everything. He lied about it because he feared we'd blame him."

I pushed back to look up at him. "But he let you blame yourself."

"He did. But this is a man who turned his back on his own child, so I can't be too surprised."

"So, what happens with his family? I mean, I know how close you all are with them. How are they taking the news?"

"I think it's safe to say they're in shock right now. But as far as you're concerned, no one thinks that you are to blame. Everyone is appalled at what he did to you. I've only spoken to Chanel, and I know she wants to reach out to you. We told her to give you some time."

I shook my head with disbelief. I was surprised that they didn't blame me. I know it didn't make sense for them to hold his actions against me, but in my world, injustice was not uncommon. I was the daughter of an addict. The lines between right and wrong were always blurred. And disappointment was something I was prepared for. Before Ford Montgomery came into my life, I wasn't used to anyone standing up for me. Sure, Gram and Gramps tried, they took me from my mother in the end, but they'd always feared her. Feared she'd stop loving them maybe. Feared they'd lose her to that world completely if they ever drew a line in the sand. But Ford, well, he'd drawn a line in the sand, and he stood on my side.

And it felt good.

Scary at the same time. I wasn't used to feeling joy or happiness.

But I was going to try. Because this man made me feel things I never thought possible. And I wanted to keep feeling them. With him.

"I don't blame Chanel or her brother. I can't believe I actually have siblings," I said.

"Chanel and Baron are good people, baby. They'll be nothing but kind to you. And I don't know where Marie will fall. I know that Hanky has moved out of the house for now."

I nodded. "Wow. He kept the secret for so long. He almost got away with it."

"He did. But I think he's been drowning in all this guilt, I really do. It's good that it all came out."

"Yeah. We'll see what he does with it."

"Hey, any chance you can cover her the rest of the day?" Ford asked, turning to look at Molly.

Her eyes were glossy with emotion, which made me laugh. My best friend was loyal to the core. She'd been afraid he'd hurt me, too. "Yes, the afternoons are easy, aside from the drug dealing kidnappers, that is." Molly laughed.

"I can stay and help for a few hours, as long as I can taste whatever I want. Sugar helps me when I'm hungover." Jack waltzed behind the counter and helped himself to a cupcake.

"I'll head upstairs and make sure everything's running smoothly," Harrison said, pulling me in for a hug and lifting me off the ground. He whispered in my ear, "I'm sorry about Hanky. But you've got a family now, and we'll never leave you."

"Thanks," I said when he set me back on my feet.

"Bring it in, Harls," Jack said, arms wide open and icing on his top lip.

I laughed and moved toward him as he enveloped me in a warm hug.

"Love you, girl."

"Love you, too," I said, swiping at my cheek.

"Enough. Back off." Ford pushed his brother away and took my hand to lead me around the counter.

It was overwhelming to be loved like this. Because when Ford Montgomery loved you, so did his family. They lived large and loved hard. And I was happy that I'd found my way to this man.

And I was never going to let him go.

twenty-four

. . .

Harley

IT HAD BEEN two weeks since everything had unraveled, and Ford and I were finding our new normal. We'd both been through a lot over the last few weeks, and it was nice to just enjoy one another without any drama. We worked long hours, but in our off time—it was just the two of us. I relished it.

"That was a crazy morning, huh?" Molly said as she wiped down the tables and restocked the display case.

"Yeah. I'm glad it finally died down. I can't believe how busy we were."

The door chimed and my inner grump cringed. I needed a little time to get this place back in order.

"Oh, hey," Molly said.

I looked up to see Chanel. Chanel Reynolds. She was what? The daughter of my sperm donor, which technically made her my sister. Butterflies swarmed my belly, and I wiped my hands on my apron and came around the counter to greet her. I knew she wasn't coming here in anger, Ford had spoken to her a few times, and she was very upset by what her father had done.

"Hi, Chanel. What can I do for you?" I asked. Molly scooched past me, tossing me a look, before she went in the back to the kitchen.

"Can we sit?"

Chanel wore a winter-white sweater dress and knee-high black heeled boots. She always looked so chic and elegant. Her hair was pulled back in a long blonde ponytail. I studied her features, and for the first time since I'd met her, I recognized some similarities, when her dark gaze that mirrored my own locked with mine.

"Of course," I said as we dropped to sit at the back table.

"So, I didn't know if it was okay for me to come by? I mean, if I ask Ford, he just keeps saying to give you time. And I get it, Harley, I really do. But the truth is, we've already lost so much time. What my father did to you," she said, pausing to pinch the bridge of her nose. Her eyes watered, and I saw genuine pain there. "It's inexcusable. But, my mom and my brother and me... we didn't know about you. And I want to know you. I want to make up for lost time. And I understand if you hate me, I really do. But I can't *not try*."

A tear ran down my cheek, catching me off guard. I swiped it away fast and let out a long breath. "I could never hate you. This isn't your fault, Chanel. Or your mother's or Baron's. And Ford told me about what your father said. That he believes my mother, or the people she was with, drugged him. I want you to know—that is *very possible*. They aren't good people. So, he's probably telling the truth there. And believe it or not, I do understand why he was afraid to tell you all what happened. He just handled it really poorly, and I don't know that I could ever forgive him, but that doesn't mean you shouldn't. He's been a good dad to you and Baron from what Ford has told me, and I don't want to cause a rift in your family. So just know that if you and I, or your mom and brother and I form a relationship, that isn't contingent upon you not speaking to your father. You can have us both in your life."

Tears streamed down her face. "Well, I didn't expect that. Thank you for saying it though. I don't know what will happen with my father. I don't know how to feel about him. There's a lot of lying and deceit there, you know? But what I do know is that I have a sister, and I've always wanted one. And you're also dating one of my best friends. And he hates everyone, so the mere fact that he's crazy in love with you tells me how special you are. So, I just want a chance to get to know you, if you're open to it."

I reached my hand across the table and squeezed hers. "I'm open to it."

"That makes me really happy, Harley. So where do we start? We have a lot of years to make up for," she said with a smile.

"Well, we can just start now. I wouldn't mind getting some fashion tips from you." I laughed.

She clapped her hands together. "Ah, you're singing my tune. You know one of the perks of being sisters, right?"

"What's that?"

"We get to raid one another's closets." A wide grin spread across her face.

"Well, not sure how much you'll want to borrow from me."

"Hey, don't knock the hipster-boho-chic look you rock. I envy it. I just dress up because my work requires it. But you own your own business. That takes a lot of hard work and discipline."

I chuckled. She was trying. Giving me a little more credit than I really deserved, I mean she was a partner at a law firm. I'd been beyond impressed with her long before I knew she was my sister. "Right back at you. Harvard Law. A partner at a firm."

"Did I just hear Harvard Law?" Molly peeked her head over the counter, and I couldn't help but laugh.

"Come here. You've met before, but we didn't know we were related." I laughed.

"Yep, I'm the big sister."

Molly smiled and looked between us. "So, I take it the talk went well."

"It did. And she said I could raid her closet," I said with a smirk.

"Oh, thank god. I love our girl here, but she could use some serious fashion help."

We talked for a while longer and agreed to meet for lunch this weekend. She asked if Baron could join us so she could make introductions. I agreed. It would be awkward, you know, meeting your brother twenty-three years later. But I would follow their lead. If they wanted to give this a shot, I was open to it. Molly went back behind the counter when a customer walked in.

Chanel stood, and I leaned over and gave her a hug. She held me there for longer than normal, and I soaked it in.

"Keep reaching out to Ford. He'll come around," I whispered. He'd mentioned to me that she'd called him several times, but he hadn't found the time to return her call.

"I get it. He's hurt. And it sure makes this an uncomfortable situation because I know it would be easier for Ford if he just cut us all off, so he didn't need to deal with Dad." Her gaze locked with mine, and I saw the hurt. The disappointment.

"Listen. I've lived in the shadow of my mother my entire life. More like a dark cloud. And I'm the first one to say that I am not my mother. I don't want to be held accountable for all her wrongs. And you shouldn't be either."

"Hey, I'm the older one, shouldn't I be the wiser one?" she said with a chuckle. "Thank you. I'll keep working on Ford. He's a good man. And, I've known him since we were little kids, and I can honestly tell you that I've never seen him happier."

I smiled and bit down on my bottom lip. "I'm really happy too."

"I can tell. It suits you, you know? Happiness. You both wear it well. I'll see you Saturday, Harley. Thanks for the talk."

She made her way out of the bakery and I watched as she walked down the street a bit. My sister. She also fit in my life in an unexplainable way. All of the voids in my life, things that had been missing for so long I'd given up hope, were now being filled.

And I liked it.

———

The last month had blown by in a blur. Ford and I were together and enjoying the quiet. We talked, we ate, we laughed, and we had lots of amazing sex. We had Netflix marathons and watched documentaries—and had more sex. This man. He was like finding a missing piece to a puzzle that I'd been searching for my entire life. Everything was good when he was beside me.

For the first time in my life—I was really happy.

Complete.

Whole.

I never thought another person could provide that for me, in fact I despised when women put too much stock in a man. But now—I totally got it. I wasn't giving away my power by being with this man, I was strengthening it. I was stronger with him by my side. Seeing myself through Ford's eyes had empowered me in so many ways.

He made me feel like—*more*. More than just a baker. More than just a good student or a pretty girl. More than the daughter of Valentina DeLuca. More than the daughter of a man who didn't want to claim her.

Just more.

"So, did you tell them you're moving out?" Ford said when he walked in the bathroom. He leaned against the wall behind me, so I could see him in the mirror as I put on some mascara.

"Not yet. I want to make sure you're sure about it before I go packing up all my stuff."

"Baby, it's time to say goodbye to the youth hostel." He chuckled. "Come with me for a minute. I want to show you something," he said, taking my hand and leading me down the hallway of his enormous apartment.

I waved at Helena as she smiled at me from the kitchen.

"Where are you taking me, Montgomery?" I groaned as the smell of bacon lingered as we passed. Yeah, Helena made us breakfast every morning. This was not a normal life, but somehow it had become mine.

Ford pulled me into the library and shut the door. He flipped on the light and stood behind me, angling me toward a wall of empty shelves. "I had these built-ins added for your collection. I want this to be *our* place. Mine and yours. Together."

I studied the shelves before turning around to face him. "You're just making all sorts of room for me, aren't you?"

"I've only known a few things for certain in my life," he said, pushing my hair back from my face.

"Yeah? What's that?"

"I knew I loved my family, from a very young age. I knew I wanted to work at Montgomery Media someday and follow in my father's footsteps." He grazed his lips over mine, teasing and taunting me.

I moaned. "Yeah. What else?"

"I knew I was a leader before I could speak in full sentences. I knew I enjoyed reading the first time I read a book on my own."

"Yes, go on," I said as I tangled my fingers in his hair and urged him closer.

"I knew I was going to love you forever that morning when I woke up in your shitty apartment and you'd taken care of my drunk ass the night before. I knew we had an unspeakable connection and I'd never felt it before. And I knew I'd die without it. Without you."

"Was that the morning after you puked on my Chucks?" I laughed against his mouth.

"Yes, ma'am. That very morning."

"I love you," I whispered.

"Move in with me, baby. Make it official."

"Okay." I wasn't going to fight him. He'd asked a few times, and I just wanted to be sure we weren't rushing. But being here with him… it was right. It's where I belonged. I'd never belonged anywhere before I met Ford. And now, I belonged with him. He was mine and I was his.

He spun me around and pressed my back up against the wall. "Good. Let's celebrate by christening every room in the penthouse."

I laughed as his mouth crashed into mine. His hands tangling into my hair and angling my head so he could take the kiss deeper. Taking and claiming me in every way.

"What if Helena comes in?" I said through my labored breaths.

"The only one *coming* in this library is you."

I laughed against his mouth. "Is that so?"

"That is so. Fuck. I love these skirts you wear. They're so—accommodating." He reached for a condom in his wallet before lifting my skirt and pushing my panties to the side.

"What can I say, I'm an accommodating girl," I said as he lifted me up and my legs wrapped around his waist.

"You're my girl," he said before he moved his hips, filling me little by little.

"Always." My breaths came hard and fast as we moved together. Always in sync.

I cried out my release, just as he tumbled over the edge right along with me.

He smiled and helped me to my feet. "Not a bad way to start the day. Now let's go get some bacon, and maybe I'll take you again at the bakery after work."

"Don't get cocky, Montgomery. I'm not that easy."

We laughed as we righted our clothing and I stopped in the bathroom to clean myself up. He stood behind me, and I glanced up in the mirror and caught him staring at me.

"What?" I asked with a laugh. "Don't get any ideas. I need to get to work. You already made me late."

"I'm just glad you agreed to move in. I love you. You make me so happy, baby." He wrapped his arms around me and rested his chin on my shoulder, and I pushed the lump in the back of my throat away.

"You make me really happy, too. I never thought I'd say that to anyone. Never thought I'd feel it."

He turned me around to face him and lifted my hand to his lips, kissing my palm.

It was a damn good start to the day.

A damn good start to the rest of my life.

epilogue

. . .

Ford

HARLEY and I had been living together for six months, and I fucking loved it. I wanted more. Hell, I wanted everything. It was her twenty-fourth birthday, and when Molly told me Harley had never had a birthday party, I knew I needed to rectify that.

"That was nice of your mom to have us out for lunch today," Harley said when we stepped off the helicopter and made our way to the car.

"Baby, it's your birthday. She wants to celebrate you. But I'd prefer to keep you all to myself," I said, pulling her closer once we were in the car. I wanted her to think it was just lunch with my mother. But I'd been working on a surprise for her for several weeks.

"Oh, we're going to the winery. Not the house?" she asked as I held her hand and led her up the walkway.

"Yep. She wanted to have lunch outside."

"Nice. Well, it's a perfect day to eat outside," Harley said. She wore a long flowy skirt and a white T-shirt. She had on her light-blue Chucks, as I'd stocked the girl's closet with every color tennis shoes I could find. And yes. They all had trackers in the soles. I wouldn't even try to deny it. I was a wealthy man, and there were evil people in this world who would go after the ones I loved to get to me. And I loved

Harley more than anyone in the world. So, keeping her safe would always be my priority.

We entered the lobby and the hostess greeted us there. "Ford, Harley, nice to see you. Your mother is at the table waiting for you." She led us through the door and then moved to the side.

"Surprise." The room erupted with cheers and laughter.

Harley nearly jumped in my arms when she startled. I pulled her close, wrapping my arms around her middle as her back rested against my chest and she took in the scene before us. She tipped her head back and looked up at me. Her cheeks flushed pink and her dark browns were wet with emotion, and my chest squeezed.

I wanted to give her new memories. Happy memories.

Hell, I wanted to give her everything.

"Happy Birthday, sweetheart." My mother pulled my girlfriend into her embrace.

"I can't believe you did this," Harley said, her hands covering her mouth as her eyes scanned the room.

"Guess who helped Molly make your birthday cake," Jack said, scooping my girl off the ground and spinning her around. "Happy Birthday, Harls."

"Thanks, Jack. You're quite the baker extraordinaire these days." She laughed before glancing over her shoulder at me as Harrison reached for her. My gaze locked with hers and I saw it there. The joy. The peace. The love. Everything she deserved.

After Harrison set her back down, Molly charged forward and hugged her best friend. She'd helped me with the guest list, and we'd invited a few of her friends from college, as well as a few of her favorite customers from the bakery. Her grandfather waited patiently to give her a hug. When Harley realized he was there, tears streamed down her beautiful face.

"Gramps. I can't believe you're here," she said, swiping at her cheeks.

"I had my first helicopter ride this morning. I don't think I mind traveling in style one bit. Happy Birthday, darlin'." He hugged his granddaughter tight.

After a lot of negotiation, Harley had helped him pack up his home and we'd moved him into a one-bedroom apartment I'd used as a rental in my building. Having him near gave my girl peace. She wanted to look after him. She'd stop by to see him every day after work, often taking him baked goods and dinner.

We moved through the room, greeting friends and family as they wished her well. She stopped when she saw Chanel. Harley, Chanel, and Baron had been going to lunch once a month. But she and Chanel spent a lot of time together outside of their lunches. They'd grown very close. Like sisters should be. Chanel would come over and help Harley choose outfits when we had events to attend, and she and I had gotten our friendship back on track. Baron and Harley were still getting to know one another, and he'd just invited her to go to dinner this week, just the two of them. She was happy to be forming relationships with her siblings. They were making up for lost time, and there was no rule book on how to go about it, but they all really liked one another, so that was a start.

"Happy Birthday, Harley. I hope this is the first of many birthdays that we celebrate together," Chanel said, wrapping her arms around her.

"Quit hogging her." Baron shoved Chanel out of the way and reached for Harley. "Happy Birthday, Sis."

My girlfriend bit down on her bottom lip and I knew she was fighting back all the emotion that was building.

"Thanks for coming. It means so much to me." She hugged him, and they held the embrace for longer than usual. So much spoken without needing to say a word.

Marie squeezed Harley's hand. She'd joined them at their lunch this last month, and of course my girl had won her over. It was impossible not to love Harley. She'd just been given parents who weren't capable of giving her what she deserved.

"Happy Birthday, dear," Marie said with a genuine smile.

Marie and Hanky had separated. In the end, it wasn't that he'd made a stupid mistake and put himself in a situation that allowed him to be taken advantage of. She said she thought she would have forgiven him for the indiscretion, if he'd told her what happened. Her issue was that he'd found out he had a daughter all those years ago and didn't step up and protect her. Marie didn't feel like she knew who he was anymore. The lies ran too deep. She and my mother remained close and they both cried and grieved over the details surrounding my father's death many times since the whole story had come to light. All at the hands of Hanky. He would wallow in his own misery, and that was justice enough for us. Bits and pieces of the story had gone public as someone at the fundraiser had filmed me punching Hanky. He'd been hounded by the press and people were making all sorts of assumptions about it. Of course, Valentina found a way to let the world know that he was her daughter's father from prison. She'd found her two minutes of fame, even if it was from behind bars. But Harley took it all in stride. She never made a public statement, and she stayed away from the gossip.

I didn't know where Chanel and Baron stood with their father at this point, but I knew my girlfriend had encouraged them to forgive him. Harley's heart was large, and even though she didn't want a relationship with him, she didn't want him to lose everyone and everything.

My girl had seen the dark side of life, and she'd found her way out. She didn't want anyone to live that way—including the man who'd abandoned her. She hadn't forgiven her mother or her father for what they'd done to her, but she'd made peace with it. She didn't wish them any ill will.

Me, on the other hand. That's not how I operate. I wanted Valentina DeLuca to rot in her cell for what she'd done to her daughter. And Hanky, he'd turned his back on the woman I love most in the world. He'd allowed her to suffer all those years. It was unforgivable. He'd also lied about my father's death, and I didn't see myself ever moving past it.

But a weight had lifted from my shoulders after the truth had surfaced. And for that I was grateful. All of these injustices, all of the lies—they'd brought Harley and me together in a roundabout way. She'd been what was missing in my life. There was a peace in knowing that my father had met her. Even under the oddest of circumstances, he had died fighting for a girl he barely knew. A girl who would become the love of my life.

She'd found her tribe. Her people. And this is exactly where she belonged. With me. Forever.

We stayed much later than I anticipated, but it was nice to see my girl enjoying herself. We'd made it back to the apartment by dinner and we stopped to pick up her favorite ramen. We dropped Gramps at his place on our way home.

Harley went to change her clothes, and I grabbed a few plates and told her to meet me in the library. I'd had Helena set some things up for me while we were gone, and I wanted to give her birthday present to her there.

"What's this?" she gasped as she took in the candles lining all the bookshelves. "It looks like a fairy garden."

I laughed. "What the hell is a fairy garden?"

She walked over to me and reached for my hand. "I don't know, but if fairies had gardens, I think it would be all twinkly like this."

"Good to know. So, I wanted to add to your book collection for your birthday. I had the engraved plates made for your shelves, and bought you a few, um, dozen new books to fill up some of the space."

She turned to read the plates. "Historical romance, contemporary romance, new adult romance. Look at you, Montgomery. You even know my genres."

I wrapped my arms around her shoulders, her back rested against my chest, and we stood in front of the shelves. "I added your classics to mine, but I wanted to make sure your books had their own special place."

"I love that. Very thoughtful." She stepped forward, running her fingers over some of the spines, taking in the new titles. She walked over to our merged section of classics.

She paused and turned to look at me. "What's this?"

A black velvet box sat on the shelf there. "I don't know. Why don't you open it and see?"

She reached for the box as I dropped down on one knee. When she swiveled back around and saw me, tears streamed down her gorgeous face. "Montgomery, what did you do?"

"I love you, Harley DeLuca. I love you and your silly tennis shoes. I especially love your flowy, easy-access skirts. I love you with icing on your face. And I even love all the white flour and sugar you've brought into my life." I chuckled, and she dropped down on her knees to face me. Clutching the ring box in one hand and grasping my fingers with the other. "I love the way you fit into my family. The way you fill up all the space in my heart. I love your strength and your honesty. I promise to love you until I take my last breath. Marry me, baby."

Her whole body shook, and she flung herself at me as she broke out in sobs.

"You know patience isn't my strength," I reminded her.

She laughed, her body vibrating against mine. "Of course, I'll marry you. I love you, Montgomery."

I reached for the box and pulled out the round, brilliant diamond ring. I slipped it on her finger, and she stared down at it. Two tears landed on her hand and she looked up at me.

Dark browns overflowing with emotion.

"It's beautiful," she whispered.

"You're beautiful," I said, pressing my lips to the back of her hand.

"Thank you for today. For the party. The proposal. It doesn't even seem real."

"This is just the start. I plan on loving you every single day for the rest of our lives," I said, pushing to stand and pulling her to her feet and into my arms.

She jumped up and wrapped her legs around my waist. "I love you, Ford Montgomery. And I'm going to hold you to it."

"I would expect nothing less. Are you hungry?" I turned her to see the blanket with the noodles set up as a picnic in the corner of the library.

She shook her head. "Only for you." She tangled her fingers in my hair. "Always for you."

I dropped her down on the leather couch and settled above her. "Love you, baby."

My mouth covered hers.

She was all I'd ever need.

My everything.

The End

Do you want to see Harrison Montgomery fall hard…read Peacekeeper FREE in Kindle Unlimited!

https://geni.us/Peacekeeper

acknowledgments

Greg, Chase & Hannah, thank you for being my biggest supporters and always believing in me.

Willow, honestly, I don't think this book would have been written without you. The daily sprints, the endless encouragement, the patience, the friendship, the support, the laughter, the snapchats, the kindness…you are one in a million. I am so thankful for you!

Pathi, Natalie, Annette, Abi, and Doo, thank you for being the BEST beta readers EVER! Your feedback means the world to me. I would be lost without you!

Thank you, Sarah Hansen (Okay Creations) for working your magic once again!

Sue Grimshaw (Edits by Sue), Thank you for your encouragement, your guidance and your support. It means the world to me. I am endlessly thankful for your feedback!! xo

Ellie McLove (My Brother's Editor), thank you for being YOU!! I appreciate you more than you know!

Rosa Sharon (My Brother's Editor) thank you for making my words shine!!

Tamara Cribley (The Deliberate Page), so thankful to get to work with you again. Thank you for your patience and for always remaining calm when I'm having a panic attack!! I love all the little details and special touches that you add to each series!

Jo and Kylie (Give Me Books Promotions), you know how much I adore you, and cannot wait to finally meet you at the Four Brits Book Fest!! You keep me calm, and handle every hurdle with absolute grace! So thankful for you!!

Ashlee (Ashes & Vellichor), what would I do without you? Thank you for bringing my characters to life with your amazing trailers and teasers!! You amaze me each and every time you send me something!! So grateful that I found you, and now you're stuck with me for life!

Shauna (Wildfire Marketing Solutions), I am so happy to have found you!! Thank you for all of your encouragement and support with this release!!

Mom, thank you for your love and support. Love you!

Dad, you really are the reason that I keep chasing my dreams!! Thank you for teaching me to never give up. Love you!

Sandy, thank you for reading and supporting me throughout this journey. Love you!

Eric, there is no one that listens and supports me more than you!! Love you, E$!

Sissy, thank you for making me laugh when I need it most. Do you have to let it linger??? Love you!

Pathi, having you in my corner makes all the difference. I love when you call with feedback…your positivity keeps me going most days! Thank you for your endless support!

Natalie (Head in the Clouds, Nose in a Book), from the newsletters to the book meetings…you complete me! I'd be lost without you!

Krista Thompson, seeing as this book releases on your special day…HAPPY BIRTHDAY, TOOTS!

Steph, you are the best book event coordinator around! Thank you for always supporting me! Peas & Carrots!

Nicole, the daily snaps keep me going!! Even if I constantly lose our streak!! So thankful for YOU!

To all the bloggers and bookstagrammers who have posted, shared and supported me—I can't begin to tell you how much it means to me. I love seeing the graphics that you make, and the gorgeous posts that you share. I am forever grateful for your support!

Lisa, Julie, Eric, Jen and Jim, I am very thankful to have such supportive and encouraging siblings in my life. Thank you for sharing my posts and helping me get my books out there! Love you!

To the Badass Author Babes IG group, thank you so much for making me laugh daily and for all of the support and guidance! I am so thankful for you!

Nicole, Sue, Thompson, Pathi, Bell, Natalie, Annette, Carol, Margy, Steph, Mindy, Kristin, Laura, Anne, Jess, Danielle, Brooke, Claudia, Abi, Kelly, Maggie, Leigh Anne, Julie, Nancy, Bev, Leslie, Florence, Tina, Renae, Cindy, Kelly & Kate, Darleen, Althea, Jess, Ariel, Heather, Shannon, Brandon, Logan, Brock, Caroline, Liva, Kennedy, all the amazing ladies at d'annata boutique and Bloom boutique, and all of my friends who have supported me along this journey...thank you so much!!

keep up on new releases

Linktree Laurapavlovauthor

Newsletter laurapavlov.com

other books by laura pavlov

Magnolia Falls Series
Loving Romeo
Wild River
Forbidden King
Beating Heart
Finding Hayes

Cottonwood Cove Series
Into the Tide
Under the Stars
On the Shore
Before the Sunset
After the Storm

Honey Mountain Series
Always Mine
Ever Mine
Make You Mine
Simply Mine
Only Mine

The Willow Springs Series
Frayed
Tangled
Charmed
Sealed
Claimed

Montgomery Brothers Series
Legacy
Peacekeeper
Rebel

A Love You More Rock Star Romance
More Jade
More of You
More of Us

The Shine Design Series
Beautifully Damaged
Beautifully Flawed

The G.D. Taylors Series with Willow Aster
Wanted Wed or Alive
The Bold and the Bullheaded
Another Motherfaker
Don't Cry Spilled MILF
Friends with Benefactors

follow me...

Website laurapavlov.com
Goodreads @laurapavlov
Instagram @laurapavlovauthor
Facebook @laurapavlovauthor
Pav-Love's Readers @pav-love's readers
Amazon @laurapavlov
BookBub @laurapavlov
TikTok @laurapavlovauthor